TYRANNY OF INDULGENCE

The Basilica Diaries
Book Five

Richard Kurti

Also in the Basilica Diaries series

Omens of Death

Palette of Blood

Demon of Truth

Carnival of Chaos

TYRANNY OF INDULGENCE

Published by Sapere Books.

24 Trafalgar Road, Ilkley, LS29 8HH

saperebooks.com

ISBN: 978-0-85495-844-3

"The hardest victory, is the victory over self."

Aristotle

1: TREASURE

Rome, 1517

It appeared in the middle of the night, and once it had arrived, it seemed to drain all life from the palatial entrance hall.

Cut flowers drooped in their jade vases. The prowling house cat diverted via the music rooms. Even the small sparrow which had been fluttering around the ribs of the vaulted ceiling for three days, escaped into the humid air that blanketed Rome.

Clearly, this was no ordinary trunk.

Marissa wiped the sleep from her eyes as she padded up the steps from the scullery. Throughout the long winter months she had been the first to rise, lighting the fires in all six drawing rooms, the lower banqueting chambers, as well as the master's two studies. She had longed for summer and the chance to enjoy another hour in her bed next to the laundry, but August had smothered Rome with such an oppressive heat that the *maggiordomo* who organised the servants had ordered Marissa to open the windows on the upper floors of Agostino Chigi's mansion as soon as the bells of Chiesa di Santa Dorotea tolled five. So there was no lie-in for Marissa after all.

No wonder she was confused when she stumbled across the large wooden trunk sitting at the bottom of the sweeping marble staircase. Marissa rubbed her face, blinked, then took another look.

It was the same size as the trunks used to store linen below stairs, but this one had been reinforced with thick iron straps which wrapped around its sides. Marissa approached cautiously. The trunk was heavily marked — the metal was scratched, the wood scuffed and dented. On the front of the chest, she saw two protruding metal loops where heavy padlocks had been fitted; strangely, these had been left open. She walked further round and saw another lock in the trunk's side, holding a large iron key.

Marissa was puzzled. If this was a treasure chest, why had it been left unlocked?

She crouched down and noticed a series of official crests embossed on the lid — they were identical: crossed keys framing a conical taira. Even Marissa knew what it meant, for it was impossible to avoid that crest in this city. It was the symbol of the Holy See.

Marissa edged backwards. If this was a Vatican trunk, she didn't dare touch it, so she hurried away to rouse the *maggiordomo*, whose irritation at being woken so early was quickly replaced by unease when he set eyes on the trunk. "How did it get here?" he demanded.

"I don't know sir."

"It wasn't here last night when I locked up." The *maggiordomo* glared at Marissa. "Did you let someone in?"

"No sir!"

"But you were the first up."

"I swear, sir, it was here already."

"That doesn't make any sense." The *maggiordomo* had seen many strange things in his long years of service, but there was something sinister about this.

He sniffed the air and frowned. "Do you smell that?"

Marissa shook her head.

The *maggiordomo* leant over the trunk and drew a deep breath. Then his face creased in disgust.

"What is it, sir?"

"Don't let anyone near this," he ordered, and bolted up the marble staircase, two steps at a time, straightening his hair as he went.

A few minutes later he reappeared, leading the *consigliere* down the stairs, obsequiously explaining what had happened.

Instinctively, Marissa withdrew into the shadows, for she was now out of her depth. The *consigliere* was Master Chigi's most trusted advisor, on the inner circle of all his influential business dealings. If this mysterious trunk had the power to raise the *consigliere* from his bed, it really was something to be feared.

Marissa watched as the two men paced around the trunk, trying to hide their bewilderment. Thanks to his seniority in rank, the *consigliere* dared to get closer … which is when he noticed the leak.

"What is *that*?" he demanded, pointing at a dark liquid that was oozing from the bottom of the trunk onto the hard marble floor.

The *maggiordomo* hurried forward to take a look. "That wasn't here earlier, sir."

"But what is it?"

The *maggiordomo* dropped to his knees to investigate. Gingerly, he reached out a hand and dipped the tip of his forefinger into the ooze. He rubbed it between his fingers, assessing the viscosity, then brought it closer to his nose. One sniff and the *maggiordomo* retched. Quickly he wiped his finger on his nightgown. "We should open it, sir. Whatever is in there will only get worse in this heat."

But the *consigliere* shook his head. "Summon the master."

"At this hour?"

"Tell him I requested it."

*

It must have been a shock for Agostino Chigi to see his own palazzo at this time of day, for his normal routine was to lounge in his private chambers until eleven o'clock, indulging himself with Rome's finest courtesans. A long lunch was usually followed by confidential meetings with his advisors, then in the evening Chigi would set out across the city to conduct his real business. It was an unorthodox routine, but when you were Italy's most influential financier and the Pope's personal banker, you could do whatever you wanted.

Unlike everyone else, Chigi wasn't frightened to see the trunk. Instead, he was annoyed. Even at the best of times, Agostino Chigi looked unhappy. His rheumy eyes and pointed red beard exuded an air of gloom, but this morning his face was further creased with a scowl as he descended the staircase. "You know perfectly well what that is," he snapped at the *consigliere*. "Don't be an imbecile."

"But what is it doing here, my lord?" the *consigliere* replied.

"I don't do details! That is your job."

"Indeed, my lord. And what should happen is that these chests are returned under armed guard, directly to the Vatican. They should not appear in the middle of the night, in your palazzo, exuding a foul liquid."

Chigi descended a few more steps, then halted as the smell reached him. "Open it."

The *consigliere* turned to repeat the order to the servants, only to find they had all melted away. "*Figlio di puttana*," he muttered.

"Come on!" Chigi snapped. "Open the damned thing."

The *consigliere* held his breath and approached the trunk. He stretched out a hand and slipped his fingers through the brass loop on the lid, then hauled it open. He staggered backwards as the air filled with a terrible stench.

Chigi covered his nose with his arm. "*Testa di cazzo!*"

With his hands clamped over his mouth and nose, the *consigliere* craned his neck to peer inside the trunk … and saw the severed heads of eight men neatly stacked, and crawling with maggots. The *consigliere* groaned and desperately tried not to vomit.

But Chigi had noticed something else. "What does *that* say?"

He pointed to a folded sheet of paper nailed to the inside of the lid. The *consigliere* reached out to retrieve the sheet, then withdrew to the safety of the stairs. He unfolded it, and suddenly looked pale.

"Well?" Chigi demanded.

"It's in German, my lord." He read the beautiful Gothic script aloud. "*Ich scheiß auf den Petersdom.*"

"Meaning?"

The *consigliere* gulped. "Forgive me, my German is a little rusty —"

"*Meaning?*"

"I shit on St Peter's."

2: PROGNOSIS

Cristina Falchoni walked down the steps of the *Ospedale per Incurabili* in a daze. Even though she had been to the hospital countless times over the years, either conducting investigations or visiting friends who were having treatment, suddenly everything seemed unfamiliar.

An hour earlier, she had breezed up these steps with her confident stride; now it felt as if reality was dissolving around her. Cristina reached out to cling onto the stone balustrade, concentrating on the rough texture under her fingers, trying to draw strength from its solidity.

Walk. Just walk.

That was the answer.

And keep walking until it felt as though the world had finally settled back on its correct axle.

One foot in front of the other … one street at a time … Cristina concentrated on simply moving and nothing else.

As she drifted through Rome, her breathing began to steady until finally she was able to look up again. She glanced at the faces of people walking past but found she couldn't pull them into focus; she couldn't even understand what they were saying — their voices were muffled and their words somehow jumbled.

She must have slipped into some kind of trance, because without knowing how she had got there, Cristina found herself standing in a side chapel of Santa Maria Maggiore, gazing at Michelangelo's *Pietà.*

She had always loved this sculpture of Mary holding the body of Christ moments after he had been taken down from the cross. Genius had transformed a single block of white marble into the most poignant expression of grief. You could almost feel the final vestiges of warmth escaping from Christ's body as he lay cradled in his mother's arms. But it wasn't the technical brilliance that moved Cristina now. Gazing at the sculpture, she started to realise that God might not have abandoned her after all. Faced with the worse loss a mother could endure, the Virgin Mary had found the courage to move beyond rage and sorrow, and discover serenity in the midst of suffering. Cristina closed her eyes and prayed, hoping that she could be touched by the Madonna's healing spirit.

And as she calmed, she tried to make sense of what had just occurred.

The surgeon positioned a chair by the open window and invited Cristina to sit. "When did you first notice something was wrong?"

"I didn't think anything was wrong," she replied. "I spend most of my days writing, and just put it down to fatigue."

Gently the surgeon took her right hand and started to examine it. "Go on."

"By the end of the day, there would be a swelling around my wrist."

"Was it painful?"

"A little. It made my fingers stiff, so that it was hard to hold a quill. But in the morning, after a good night's sleep, it felt better."

"The swelling disappeared?"

"No. But it eased."

The surgeon nodded. "You should have come to see me straight away."

"My housekeeper Isra applied poultices and bandages. I thought it just needed time to heal."

"But it's got worse?"

Cristina nodded.

"Can you still hold a quill?"

"It's difficult. Painful."

"Have you lost weight?"

"A little."

"Any fevers?"

"No."

"Are you sleeping well?"

Cristina's brows rose. "Is anyone in this heat?"

"What about the fatigue — are you tired during the day?"

"I work hard in my library. Of course I get tired."

The surgeon squeezed Cristina's thumb. "Can you feel the pressure?"

"Yes."

He moved to the index finger. "And this?"

"Yes."

The surgeon tested each finger in turn, checking there was no loss of sensation.

"That's a good sign, isn't it?" Cristina asked.

The surgeon focused on the examination. He moved his attention to the lump on her wrist. "What about this? Is it tender?" He pressed the swelling and Cristina winced.

"Sorry." He took a magnifying glass from the desk and examined the lump closely. "May I see your left hand?"

"There's nothing wrong with that."

The surgeon took her hand and examined it anyway, testing each digit, then checking for any swelling. He seemed to spend a long time pressing her palm, feeling for abnormalities.

Finally, he looked up. "I'm afraid there is a problem."

"Rest? Bandages? No writing for a month?" Cristina offered pre-emptively.

"Actually it's … more serious than that."

"But you have a cure?"

"I've treated this before. The symptoms are identical." The surgeon glanced down momentarily. "There are medications to alleviate the pain. And we can ease the swelling in the fingers, so that you can still use a quill."

"Alleviating symptoms isn't a cure though, is it?"

The surgeon folded his hands together as he tried to compose his thoughts.

"*Is* there a cure?" Cristina pressed.

"I'm afraid not."

"So … what is it?"

"It has all the signs of a cancer."

Shock pulsed through Cristina's body. She could feel sweat break out on her skin. Her throat tightened. She glared at her right hand as if it had betrayed her. "Cut it out," she whispered.

The surgeon shook his head. "Where it is … you would lose the whole hand."

"Better to live with one hand than die with two."

"I'm afraid there is a further complication," the surgeon explained. "There are signs the disease has already spread to your other hand. And that suggests it might be … elsewhere."

It was a death sentence. Delivered with calm professionalism, but a death sentence nonetheless.

The surgeon reached across the desk and gently touched her arm. "We must try to be positive."

A wave of emotion washed over Cristina, bringing tears to her eyes. "Positive about what?" she asked. "What exactly is there to be positive about?"

*

"*Mi scusi.*"

An elderly woman wrapped in a black shawl shuffled past Cristina and lit one of the votive candles in front of the *Pietà*. She offered a short prayer then dropped a coin in the box. "For my grandson. He's teething." She glanced at the marble Madonna. "But Our Lady helps."

Cristina watched the old woman walk away, confident in the belief that her family had divine protection. Was that the best way to cope? To silence your questioning mind and abandon yourself entirely to faith?

She looked at the swelling in her right hand. Death came to everyone, but she was only forty-five and had hoped for another ten years before having to wrangle any serious illness. Cristina knew many women who were fit and healthy well into their sixties; why could that not be her?

Her eyes wandered over the sweeping lines of the *Pietà*. She looked at Christ's right hand, his fingers caught either side of a fold in his mother's robe, as if he was clasping onto her for the last time. Then she looked at the Madonna, one hand open, waiting to receive Divine comfort, while the other held the weight of her son with all the protective power of a parent.

And then Cristina realised — this was the answer. It was directly in front of her.

In her most desperate hour, the Virgin Mary had remained resolute. She did not crumble or crack. She did not fail her son. Instead, she became as strong as marble.

How would Cristina overcome the illness that was trying to consume her? The same way she had conquered all the other obstacles she had encountered in her life. By not crumbling.

Cristina lit a candle, bowed her head to offer a prayer, then strode out into the Roman heat.

*

"Unacceptable! Disgraceful! And an insult to me!" Agostino Chigi's face flushed as red as his beard as he thundered across the entrance hall.

"We are just trying to do our jobs, my lord," Capitano Domenico Falchoni replied.

"This is precisely why peasants are kept below stairs! They do not know how to behave in civilised surroundings."

"Deputato Tomasso and I are from the Guardia Apostolica del Vaticano, and we are investigating the appalling murders that were discovered *there*." Domenico pointed to the trunk that was still sitting at the bottom of the sweeping marble staircase … and still oozing blood.

"I don't care what badges are embroidered on your tunics," Chigi scoffed. "You have no business interfering in the smooth running of my palazzo. This is not just my home, it is a place of business which plays a vital role in the prosperity of the Holy See and the stability of the entire Church. Yet you have the arrogance to barge in here, close off rooms, direct my servants, and instruct me where I can and cannot walk!"

Domenico took a deep breath as Chigi talked to him like a child rather than the most senior officer in the Apostolic Guard. It was infuriating. All they had done was throw a security cordon around the palazzo's ground floor so that the trunk would remain undisturbed until evidence had been gathered and the severed heads identified. But Chigi was having none of it. No doubt he thought he was above the protocols of a murder investigation.

Ten years ago, Domenico would have answered back and got into trouble, but the moment he turned fifty, he had discovered an inner calm that was both personally liberating and professionally effective. The trick was to think of silence as a strength rather than a weakness. You could submit with silence, but you could also use it to control, and the difference was all about technique.

For example, while listening to Chigi's tirade, Domenico never broke eye contact with the man and never lowered his head. And when the banker had finished, Domenico slowly counted to three before responding. Three was the perfect number. Any less and you appeared too eager to please, any more and you gave the impression of being too scared to speak.

One. Two. Three.

"Lord Chigi, we must identify the heads and search for any clues that may have been inadvertently left by the killer," Domenico said.

"I will not have my palazzo turned into a morgue!"

"Then where can we work?"

"Ask him!" Chigi pointed to the *consigliere*, then turned his back on them and strode into the music rooms.

"Well?" Domenico stared at the *consigliere*.

"It can't be here. Not in the entrance hall."

"Then where?"

"Perhaps the cellars. In the ice room, where the poultry and beef are stored."

"You really want us to examine human remains where they keep the food?"

The *consigliere* shrugged. "It's all meat."

Domenico and Tomasso decided to move the trunk themselves to ensure minimal disturbance of the evidence. They gritted their teeth and tried to breathe as little as possible as they manoeuvred it down the stone steps and into the cellars. Two servants from the household followed in their wake, mopping up the trail of blood dripping from the trunk.

The *consigliere* directed them into the largest of the ice rooms, where three huge sides of beef were hanging from ceiling hooks. "Here will do."

They put the trunk down, and Tomasso tied a scarf around the lower half of his face to stop himself from retching. He then started plucking the severed heads out one by one and lining them up on the stone floor.

"How long have they been dead?" Domenico asked his deputy.

Tomasso brushed the maggots off the flesh with his glove. "Over twenty-four hours — that's how long it takes for the maggots to appear. And less than three days — as the heads are still seeping blood."

Domenico turned to the *consigliere.* "Do you know who they are?"

The *consigliere* looked at the heads with distaste. "Not specifically. But I know *what* they were." He pointed at the two parallel lines shaved into their cropped hair. "This pattern is part of the guards' uniform."

"Chigi has a mercenary army?"

"Not exactly. We have forty-two of these trunks. All identical. They're sent north across the Alps into the German states. Every priest selling Indulgences is allocated a trunk. When the trunk is full of gold, they are brought back to Rome under armed guard and delivered straight to the Vatican."

Domenico looked sceptical. "I thought that practice died out centuries ago?"

"Giving money to the Church will always be fashionable."

"But selling salvation to the faithful to reduce their punishment in the afterlife belongs in the Dark Ages."

"Far from it. We are living in the golden age of the Indulgence." The *consigliere* perched himself on a heavily scored butcher's block. "Only confession and contrition can bring about the forgiveness of sins. That is the doctrine of the Church. And to prove his contrition, a sinner must make reparations. Buying an Indulgence for *la fabbrica di San Pietro* is just such a form of reparation. It shortens the time the sinner must spend in Purgatory, and it provides the Vatican with much-needed cash to finance the building of St Peter's Basilica. Everyone wins."

"And Lord Chigi receives a generous commission on each shipment, no doubt?"

The *consigliere* nodded. "Financial expertise should always be generously rewarded. It's why he is affectionately known as *Il Magnifico*."

Domenico frowned. "If everybody wins, why I am staring at the rotting heads of eight guards?"

It was a good question and the *consigliere* pondered it for a moment. "It could simply be theft. A chest stuffed with gold would tempt a saint."

"But it's not that simple, is it?" Deputato Tomasso looked up from his grisly task. "A thief would have taken the money and fled. Not gone to the trouble of filling the trunk with the victims' heads and smuggling it into your palazzo. This was a message."

"And for anyone who can't read the symbolism, they spelled it out." Domenico brandished the note that had been nailed inside the lid. "'*Ich scheiß auf den Petersdom*.'"

The *consigliere* sighed. "Sounds like the obscene rant of a lunatic."

Domenico pointed to the line of severed heads gaping up at them from the floor. "This is not the work of a lunatic. Think of the organisation needed to position that trunk in the heart of Lorg Chigi's palazzo without anyone witnessing it."

"How did they get past all the locked doors without leaving a trace?" Tomasso added. "That takes planning and skill."

"And inside information," Domenico suggested.

"Isn't it your job to provide the answers?" the *consigliere* replied sourly.

"I'm afraid this is the one thing that every pope fears: rebellion against the Church." Domenico handed the neatly written note to the *consigliere*. "You and *Il Magnifico* need to explain to the Holy Father the full implications of this."

"Us?" The *consigliere* recoiled. "Why do *we* have to tell him?"

"Didn't you just say this entire scheme of selling Indulgences to finance St Peter's was Lord Chigi's idea?"

"Yes, but this is a legal matter. Which is your jurisdiction."

"The trunk was planted in Lord Chigi's palazzo. He was intended to be the messenger."

"No, no," the *consigliere* gave a shrewd smile. "Any rebellion against the Church is a matter for the authorities of the Holy See. Which means you."

"In other words," Tomasso stood up and pulled down his scarf. "You don't want to be in the room when the Pope flies into a rage."

"Can you blame me?" the *consigliere* replied. "The Holy Father relies on gold from the German states. It is the only thing standing between the Vatican and bankruptcy. Without the Indulgence money, the Church crumbles."

3: WILLPOWER

The builder frowned. "It seems very complicated."

"Just follow the plans and all will be well," Isra Sahin replied sweetly, pointing to the large schematic the builder was holding.

"Who drew these up?"

"The mistress of the house."

"Ah. That explains it."

Isra managed to refrain from making an acerbic comment. She had been dealing with the surly reluctance of builders for two years, and she knew they could be as touchy as old women. The slightest criticism and they would down tools and stomp off the job. She suspected that a lot of it was down to a distrust of the 'foreign' design.

Inspired by the geometric urban parks they had seen on their expedition to Tunis, Cristina and Isra had decided to turn the courtyard of their townhouse in Piazza Navona into an Islamic-themed garden.

They had started by dividing the space into four sections using pathways that symbolised the four Rivers of Paradise: milk, honey, water, wine. They wanted the paths to be decorated in mosaics, but convincing the builders to create geometric designs rather than images of sailing ships or classical gods had been one of the early battles.

Then there was the planting. Isra had designed a plan that alternated orange and lemon trees with pleasing symmetry, but that upset the horticulturalists, who insisted that palm trees would grow better in the shade of the courtyard. There were more conflicts over the pergola and the trellises, but Cristina and Isra held their ground. And it was worth it. All their battles had been fought in the name of peace, for they had ended up with a garden of beauty, harmony and tranquillity; a space inspired by the wisdom of the Levant and which captured the spirit of the Maghreb.

Now they were working on the final element: a central water feature to add the calming sound of splashing water and enhance the cooling atmosphere of the space.

"Be simpler to put a bench there," the builder said. "Got a cousin who makes 'em."

"But that's not what we want." Isra took the schematic from the builder and turned it ninety degrees so that it was the right way up. "Just stick to the pipework plan and have faith."

The builder frowned again. "How will the water circulate? As soon as the cistern empties, the fountain will stop."

"But the cistern won't empty. That's the clever part. The pipes gradually decrease in diameter, increasing the pressure. So by using syphons, three interconnected reservoir tanks and a hydraulic ram, the water will continually circulate."

"Right." The builder nodded, but it was obvious that he hadn't understood a word she had said.

"Trust in the diagrams." Isra tapped the schematic. "Don't worry — if it doesn't work, we won't blame you."

She heard the main door to the house open, then shut.

"We're in the garden!" she called out.

There was no reply.

"Cristina?" She looked over to the kitchen door, but no-one appeared. Then she heard footsteps going up the stairs, and moments later the library door slammed shut.

That was strange. Normally Cristina would come straight to the garden to check on progress. Maybe she was preoccupied.

When Cristina was following a line of thought she could often be distracted.

While the builder got to work in the garden, Isra busied herself with kitchen duties, but two hours later she still hadn't heard anything from Cristina.

Lunchtime came and went without an appearance. Cristina often forgot to eat when she was deep in her research, but Isra sensed that this time something was wrong. She went up to the first floor and put her ear to the library doors. Silence.

Isra knocked on the door. "Cristina?" she called.

No reply.

Isra knocked again, then entered.

An explosion of inquiry had erupted in the library. Dozens of books had been taken from the shelves and laid across the floor, papers with scribbled notes were strewn over the desks, and a small carafe of wine still lay where it had been knocked over.

Sitting on the floor in the middle of all the chaos was Cristina. But she wasn't reading — her head was in her hands, and she was weeping.

"What on earth's happened?" Isra rushed over and put her arms around her. Cristina turned and clung to the housekeeper like a small child.

It was rare to see Cristina weep. Everyone thought she wasn't emotional, but that wasn't true. She felt things deeply but kept her feelings to herself. That was how she dealt with the world: contain it, analyse it, master it.

"It's all right, I'm here," Isra soothed. "Let me help."

Cristina held up her hands. "There is no cure," she stuttered through her tears.

"Then we'll find better dressings to ease the discomfort. You can live with this."

Cristina shook her head. "There is no cure. It's a cancer. And it's going to kill me."

Isra gasped. She pressed her face into Cristina's hair, and they sat huddled on the library floor, cradling each other in silence, trying to find the words to wrestle back control of their lives.

Finally, Isra stood up. "Come." She guided Cristina to one of the library chairs and poured a small glass of wine. "Drink."

Cristina did as she was told. When she had finished, Isra cupped her face so that she was looking into her eyes.

"Nothing is impossible, Cristina."

"This is different."

"Why? Why is it different to any of the other problems you have conquered?"

"Because death cannot be defeated."

"Then we will find another surgeon. Get a second opinion."

"It's no use!" Cristina gestured to the books scattered across the floor. "These were my second opinion. I've searched. There is no cure."

Isra's voice was firm. "Listen to me. Remember all the times people told you something was impossible, that it couldn't be done? But you never gave up. You always proved them wrong. You need to do that again, for yourself."

"But this is not just another problem," Cristina whispered. "This is the end of everything."

"I don't accept that." Isra bent forward so that their foreheads were touching. "And I am here for you. Whatever it takes, wherever we have to travel, we will find a way to cure this."

Cristina pulled back and stared at her books in exasperation. "You think those writers didn't try everything? You think they weren't all gripped with the same fear? Eventually, illness defeats us all."

"Strength doesn't come from the body, Cristina. It comes from the mind. From an indomitable will. And you are the most stubborn, strong-willed person I know. That will be our salvation. I swear."

The moment Domenico entered the Vatican gardens, he could smell the animals. It was even worse than usual thanks to the oppressive heat which smothered Rome, but there was no point complaining because he knew nothing would be done to ease the stench.

Shortly after his inauguration, Pope Leo X had ordered the Vatican menagerie to be moved into the huge Belvedere Courtyard behind the Sistine Chapel, so that he could more easily show off his snow-white elephant, Hanno. The Indian elephant had been a gift from King Manuel of Portugal, and he delighted everyone with his playful antics, especially his ability to suck up water with his trunk and spray the cardinals. When Hanno died, Pope Leo decided to enlarge the menagerie to include civet cats, chameleons, apes, parrots and lions, as well as more familiar animals like deer and gazelles.

Although it was true that anything exotic tickled Leo's fancy (he was a Medici, after all) the menagerie was not just a folly, it also served a political purpose. King Manuel had gifted Hanno to the Pope in order to win his backing against Egyptian rivals in the spice trade, and the menagerie provided supplicants with the means to woo Pope Leo by presenting him with ever more obscure beasts.

As he walked under the portico which led to the Belvedere Courtyard, Domenico saw that Pope Leo and Cardinal Riario were waiting next to a cage of monkeys. Even from a distance,

Domenico could sense the tension between the men — the Pope was stroking a marmoset, intrigued by the tufts of white hair growing from the side of its head, while Riario looked on unmoved. Seeing the cardinal's reticence, Leo thrust the monkey at him to hold, but Riario recoiled and dropped the animal.

"Shame on you!" the Pope chided as he scooped up the marmoset from the ground. "He is God's creature too."

"Apologies, Holy Father," Riario mumbled. "You caught me unawares."

In truth, everyone in the Vatican knew the real source of the tension between the two men, and it was nothing to do with monkeys. Cardinal Riario had spent his entire life as a Vatican apparatchik, mastering the mechanics of power and acting as a fixer for three successive popes; when he wasn't on manoeuvres he could be found in the papal library immersed in theological study. Everything in the man's life had been directed towards one goal: becoming Pope. Yet in the last election, conclave had overlooked him and favoured the Medici buffoon instead. It was a bitter blow for Riario. He was now fifty-six years old, while Pope Leo was just forty-two, which meant he would occupy the papal throne for many years, effectively robbing the cardinal of any chance of realising his ambition. Having devoted his life to the Church, spiritual and temporal, Cardinal Riario now had to kiss the ring of a man he regarded as trivial.

"I don't think he likes you," the Pope cooed into the marmoset's ear. "No, no, no. He only likes his books, doesn't he? Horrible man."

Keen to move the conversation onto a less infantile footing, the cardinal beckoned to Domenico to join them. "What are your instincts on these brutal killings, Capitano?"

"We've identified the victims. All eight men were private guards in the pay of Agostino Chigi."

"Bodyguards?"

"No, Your Eminence. Their only job was to protect Indulgence gold which was being transported to Rome from the German states."

"Has Chigi put up a reward for information?" Pope Leo asked. "Because he should."

"As far as I know, Lord Chigi has not offered a reward, but…" Domenico's voice trailed off.

"But what? Speak freely," Riario prompted.

"There was something odd about his reaction."

"He is an odd man," Pope Leo observed.

"Most people would be appalled to discover something like that in their home," Domenico continued. "Severed heads. A blood-soaked trunk. The security of your palazzo violated. You'd think he would be desperate to help solve such a barbaric crime and catch the perpetrators. Yet Lord Chigi was more irritated than afraid."

"Irritated?" Riario was intrigued. "You think he may be involved somehow?"

"Why would a man steal from himself, Your Eminence?"

"Perhaps because he is no longer happy with his commission?" Riario suggested.

Domenico frowned. "But to go to such extraordinary lengths…"

"What are you driving at?" Pope Leo demanded. "You cast aspersions on the man simply because he is irritable? Remember the vital importance of the Indulgences to the construction of St Peter's Basilica." He put the marmoset back in its cage and fastened the door.

"Forgive my vagueness, Holy Father. But if I were pressed for an explanation, well, Lord Chigi's reaction made me wonder if something like this might have happened before and been hushed up."

Pope Leo stared at Domenico. "Who would dare conceal the theft of papal gold?"

"Perhaps you can ask him yourself, Holy Father." Cardinal Riario looked to the far side of the courtyard, where Agostino Chigi was making his way towards them, weaving between the tiger cage and the peacocks.

The financier was sweating profusely by the time he reached them, but tried to defuse the tension with small talk. "How is the toucan I gifted you, Holy Father? He was fresh off the latest expedition from the New World, so it may take him a while to acclimatise."

Leo cut him dead. "Is it the first, Chigi?"

"Holy Father?"

"Is this the first shipment of gold to be stolen?"

The financier shuffled uneasily.

"Remember to whom you speak," Cardinal Riario warned, sensing weakness.

"It is the first theft to have occurred with such violence, Holy Father."

"So you withheld critical information from the Pope?" Riario pressed.

"I did not want to burden the Holy Father with unnecessary—"

"Tell me everything!" Pope Leo demanded.

Chigi took a handkerchief from his sleeve and mopped his face. "It is the ninth shipment to have been stolen, but the first to come back and haunt Rome with such horror."

"Nine thefts? Of my gold?" Pope Leo's face was tense with rage. "And you never thought to tell me?"

"I did not want to trouble you with details, Holy Father."

"Nine chests of gold is hardly a *detail*!"

"When compared to the hundred and eighty-four shipments that arrived safely —"

"We should have struck back with ruthless efficiency the first time this happened! The very first time!"

"Forgive me, Holy Father."

Cardinal Riario joined the attack. "Do you not see, Chigi? The power of deterrence could have made the first theft the final theft."

"Perhaps, Your Eminence."

"That is God's gold," the Pope barked. "Paid to rescue souls from Purgatory. There is only one Church. One Heaven. One Hell. I gave you privileged access to spread God's grace through the gift of Indulgences, and this is how you repay me? With dishonesty?"

Chigi sank to his knees. "I beg forgiveness, Holy Father," he sobbed. "Have mercy on me."

The Pope said nothing. He just let the financier wallow in his guilt.

Desperate to redeem himself, Chigi prostrated himself on the ground until his nose was in the dirt. "What do I have to do to repent, Holy Father?"

"Up," Pope Leo finally commanded.

Chigi clambered to his feet and wiped the dust from his velvet clothes.

"Explain how this has happened."

"The previous thefts have all taken place north of the Alps, as the shipments were returning to Rome," replied Chigi. "The German people are difficult, Holy Father. Stubborn, wilful, burdened with resentment. And the geography of the German states is harsh. Dense forests, isolated communities. It is a breeding ground for bandits and criminal gangs."

Pope Leo was less than impressed. "That is not an explanation, Chigi. It is a diatribe against the German people. The very people whose gold is funding the Vatican."

"Perhaps you would allow me to put the matter into a more strategic context?" Cardinal Riario suggested. It seemed to Domenico that the cardinal relished the chance to deepen the banker's humiliation.

"Someone needs to," Leo replied.

"I have been in regular correspondence with Albrecht von Brandenburg, Archbishop of Magdeburg. He has been a great champion of Indulgences and understands that the more money he sends to Rome, the brighter his star will shine."

"Got his eye on my crown, no doubt," the Pope muttered.

"He is certainly young and ambitious, Holy Father. But he has consistently warned against seeing the German states as a single entity. In truth, they are a fragmented collection of principalities, free states and bishoprics, each with their own power base and agendas. Theft of Vatican gold might be seen as an outrageous crime in one city, while fifty miles away it might be applauded as the act of a German patriot."

Pope Leo sniffed his disapproval. "So we need to establish which German leaders hate the Vatican?"

"A list of who *doesn't* hate the Vatican might be shorter, Holy Father."

The Pope nodded grimly. "I want swift and decisive action to restore the flow of gold."

"If I may be permitted?" Domenico said.

"Speak."

"What Cardinal Riario describes would certainly help explain the note."

"What note?"

"Did Lord Chigi not tell you? The note that was nailed inside the trunk." Domenico glanced at the banker, who studiously avoided eye contact.

"Show me."

Domenico handed Leo the note. As he read it, the Pope's faced tensed. He passed it to Riario.

"'I shit on St Peter's.'" The cardinal turned to the Pope. "This changes everything, Holy Father. It is blatant defiance."

"But is it the scrawling rage of a fanatic? Or does it reflect what the German people are thinking?"

"Albrecht has not reported widespread discontent, Your Holiness."

"Does the Archbishop really know what is going on beyond the gates of his palaces? And if he does, would he tell me the truth, or merely what I want to hear?"

Cardinal Riario nodded sombrely. "Sometimes I do wonder if Albrecht's ambition blinds him to other considerations."

"Whoever is stealing God's gold must be caught and punished with the utmost severity," the Pope declared. "We must send an unequivocal message to all the German states that we will not tolerate insurrection or disobedience." He turned to Domenico. "You are to send an armed unit of Apostolic Guards north, across the Alps, to discover the truth and arrest whoever is behind these atrocities."

"Very good, Holy Father."

"Use only your most trusted commanders. Absolute loyalty to me is paramount. The Indulgence money must keep flowing, or St Peter's will never be finished."

4: TASKFORCE

It is extraordinary what can be achieved when a pope commands it.

Hierarchies have an inertia all of their own, effortlessly generating reasons why things cannot be done, and perpetually sliding responsibility between departments; but when Pope Leo X ordered a papal taskforce to be prepared by the end of the week, all obstacles melted away.

Deputato Tomasso threw himself into the business of assembling the military unit for Operation Danube. He was delighted to have been given this command, as it confirmed he was both the most trusted and the most senior of the Apostolic Guards working under Domenico. He also knew that if he succeeded, it would virtually guarantee that he would become the next captain.

Not that he wanted Domenico to step aside; far from it. But the capitano was now fifty years old, and the long years of demanding service were starting to take their toll. Domenico was not as fast as he used to be and could often be seen quietly wincing as joints clicked and muscles grumbled. Tomasso was seven years younger, but what a difference that made — he felt as sharp and quick as he had in his twenties, and relished the prospect of difficult missions.

He handpicked fifteen of the best soldiers in the Apostolic Guard, then split them into smaller groups in charge of weapons and armour, horses, tents and survival kit, and logistics. There would be no carts; everything had to be strapped to the horses for flexibility and speed of movement. For his second in command, Tomasso selected Lieutenant

Dante, a softly spoken and efficient man with not an ounce of fat on his lean frame.

"How much ammunition should we take, sir?" Dante asked, surveying the crates of musket shot in the weapons room. "It's a trade-off between speed and security."

"I have applied for papal warrants to commandeer ammunition and weapons en route, Dante. So, as long as we're not in hostile territory, we can always resupply."

"That makes it easier." The lieutenant nodded. "I'll liaise with Cardinal Riario to get the most recent Vatican alliances marked on our maps."

This was precisely why Tomasso had chosen Dante — he brought a thoroughness to every situation that could be the difference between success and failure.

"We don't want to go knocking on the doors of a sworn enemy of Rome, sir."

"The Vatican? Enemies?" Tomasso gave a wry smile. "Hard to imagine."

As Lieutenant Dante hurried off to collate the expeditionary maps, Tomasso saw Domenico return to the barracks. He raised his hand in greeting, but Domenico ignored him. Which was strange. With Operation Danube just days away from launching, Tomasso would have expected his captain to be checking every detail of the preparations; but Domenico just strode with his head down, entered his office and closed the door behind him.

Something was wrong.

Had Pope Leo changed his mind about the mission? Had fresh information come to light? Whatever it was, the sooner Tomasso knew what was going on, the better he would be able to adapt his plans. He crossed the courtyard and knocked on the captain's door. "Sir? It's me, Tomasso. Do you have a moment?"

No reply.

"Captain?" he tried again. "Is everything all right?"

Silence from inside the office. Which was alarming because Capitano Falchoni never ignored his men.

Tomasso knocked one more time, then pushed open the heavy door and entered. Domenico sat behind his desk, head cradled in his hands.

"What's wrong?" Tomasso asked. "Has there been another murder?"

Domenico shook his head. "I've had a letter from Cristina."

"Why didn't she just come and talk to you?" Tomasso was puzzled.

"She's buried in her library, determined to find a solution."

"A solution to what?"

Domenico picked up the letter from his sister and read out some extracts. "'Don't interrupt me… Don't tell anyone… Let me deal with this in my own way.'"

Tomasso felt a knot in his stomach. "What's happened?"

Domenico handed him the letter, and Tomasso read it in silence.

Confusion hardened into denial, then his eyes flicked back to the top of the page to read the words again. Gradually, understanding crystalised into fear. The woman he had loved from a distance for all these years was … dying.

The letter dropped from his hands and fluttered to the floor. "We have to go to her."

"She has forbidden it."

"She isn't thinking straight."

"She always thinks straight!" Domenico snapped. "That's who she is."

But Tomasso knew what was right. "We must go to her. She will be terrified. And alone."

Domenico bent down to retrieve the letter. "Being alone is how she will deal with this. It's how she will focus her mind."

"No. I won't be pushed away."

"It's not about you, Tomasso. This is what Cristina wants."

"If you won't come with me, I'll go on my own."

Domenico had long known how his deputy felt about Cristina, but being men and soldiers, they had never openly discussed it. Now things were different. "If you love her, you'll do as she asks."

"It's because I love her that I won't," Tomasso replied. "When someone is in torment, we don't turn away. No matter how painful it is. We need to go to her."

"She doesn't want to see anyone," Isra repeated.

"I'm not just anyone," Domenico replied. "I'm her brother."

"Then respect her wishes." Isra moved defensively across the bottom of the staircase, then quickly realised what a futile gesture it was; if Domenico and Tomasso were determined to go upstairs to the library, there was little she could do about it. "Please, do as Cristina asks."

Domenico glanced at Tomasso. "Exactly as I predicted."

Tomasso shook his head. "No-one admires Cristina's strength and resilience more than me. But sometimes she doesn't know when she has to reach out to others." He looked at Isra. "You know it's true."

"I know what she can achieve when she focuses her mind." Isra was resolute. "If she's left alone, she can find a cure."

"And what if she can't?" Domenico asked. "What then?"

The question sat heavily in the entrance hall of the house on Piazza Navona. No-one wanted to go where that question led.

Domenico started towards the stairs. Isra reached out to stop him, but he brushed past her.

"This is a mistake," Isra whispered.

"Maybe. But if we're going to make a mistake, we should err on the side of humanity."

Isra looked warily at Tomasso. "And you agree?"

"It was my idea."

"I thought as much."

As Domenico pushed open the doors to the library, he was shocked by the sight that greeted him. The shelves were half-empty, and books were strewn across every available surface, as if Cristina was reading a hundred different volumes simultaneously; a mosaic of hastily scribbled notes had been pinned to the walls, with lengths of string connecting disparate ideas; half-finished glasses of wine were dotted across the desks. The windows were wide open to try and get some relief from the heat, and a small robin was perched on the ledge, watching over everything like a guardian angel. Cristina herself was standing beside the verge-and-foliot wall clock, winding the mechanism.

"Not today. Nothing personal. But if it's not food or drink, the door stays shut." Cristina had tied her hair into a topknot, and secured it with a feather quill, adding to the sense of disorder. Her hand turned the clock key with an obsessive energy, so that when the weight hit the top-stop, she seemed disappointed.

"Cristina, let me help you," Domenico whispered.

"No, thank you."

She put the winding key back on its hook then marched towards the desk to immerse herself in her books. But

Domenico was quicker — he strode across the library and caught his sister in his arms.

"Let me go!"

"No." He held her tightly, feeling her fast, shallow breaths.

For a few moments, Cristina allowed him to comfort her. She closed her eyes and rested her head upon his shoulder as Isra and Tomasso entered the library.

Suddenly Cristina snapped open her eyes and wriggled free from him. "Would everyone please leave!" She strode along one of the bookcases, plucking down volumes at random. "I must study."

"This is not the way to fight the illness," Domenico replied.

"How would you know?" Cristina piled the books on the long desk and went back to retrieve some more. "You are all action and no thought!" She slapped her hands on the sides of her head. "This is where I have to fight the battle — in here! Which is why no-one but me can do it. It is nothing personal, but please leave. All of you." She slid a large volume off one of the bookshelves, slammed it on the desk and waited for everyone to go.

But they didn't.

"Ignoring the doctors won't make you well," Domenico ventured.

"They have missed the cure. All of them. It's out there somewhere, but they haven't seen it. They've missed it, so it's up to me to find it. And I will." She picked up a quill and started leafing through the volume in front of her.

Domenico saw that she was turning the pages too quickly to read anything; she was just handling the book to try and find solace. "What if there is no cure?"

"Leave me alone!" Cristina clamped her hands over her ears and screwed her eyes shut.

It was the same gesture toddlers used when they were having a tantrum, and it shocked Domenico. His sister prided herself on never turning away from truth, no matter how difficult. Follow the logic, even into darkness. So for Cristina to wilfully block the world out felt … wrong.

"She's right," Isra turned to Tomasso. "You are not helping. It's best you leave."

Neither Domenico nor Tomasso moved.

Desperate to break the deadlock, Cristina paced back to the verge-and-foliot clock. She took the key from its hook, slid it into the mechanism and tried to wind the main weight. But nothing happened. She tried harder, but the cog wheels wouldn't budge. Cristina scowled.

Tomasso gently took the key from her and put it back on the hook. "You just wound it. A few moments ago."

Cristina blinked. "Oh … I must…" Her voice trailed off.

The air in the room seemed to get heavier. Everyone knew they were facing a terrifying and impossible problem, yet somehow, they had to deal with it.

Domenico knew that a daring change of strategy was the only way to survive when the battlefield turned against you. Perhaps that could work now. "St Peter's needs you, Cristina. And I have an assignment I want you to accept."

Isra was stunned. "She has given her life to that damned basilica! It's all the worry that brought this on."

"That's not true."

"She has to focus on herself."

Isra glared at Domenico, but he knew where he was going with this, and he turned his attention back to Cristina. "You've given so much of your life to St Peter's and look what you've achieved. Even half-built, it is towering over Rome. But it needs you again, or there is a risk it will never be finished." He studied her, trying to see if he had nudged her mind into a different orbit. "Come and talk to Raphael. Then you'll understand."

There was a flicker of movement on Cristina's face. "He's not interested."

"What do you mean?"

"The new chief architect isn't interested in what I think. Bramante cared, but when he died…"

"How do you know?" Domenico persisted. "Have you spoken to Raphael?"

"Only when he was appointed."

"That was three years ago. Much has changed."

Cristina shook her head. "When Bramante died, my influence over St Peter's died with him."

"Which is precisely why the build is now in such peril."

Cristina looked up, and Domenico knew that she was thinking about the enormous construction site on Vatican Hill. He could see that she was tempted by the bait … but would she take it?

In the silence, the robin fluttered into the room from the window and perched on the desk, chirruping with curiosity.

"Come and see for yourself, Cristina."

5: MISSING

Stone by stone, St Peter's Basilica was rising.

Donato Bramante completed the four giant pillars which would eventually support the cavernous dome, and had lived just long enough to see them joined with enormous, coffered vaults. When Raffaello Sanzio da Urbino took over as chief architect, he set about extending the vaulting north and south into the transepts, and west towards the apse, effectively growing the arms of the cross from the centre outwards.

"Now you can really feel the scale of the place," Cristina said, looking upwards to study the vaulting. "And Bramante was clever to start building in the centre; he knew he would be dead long before the basilica's completion, but these piers establish the scale of St Peter's, forcing all subsequent architects to follow his vision."

Suddenly Cristina turned to look at Domenico. "But where is everybody? Why is it so quiet?"

"You have correctly identified the problem." Domenico perched himself on an idle winch. "This is why you need to reengage."

The construction site should have been in full cacophony, swarming with workmen raising the walls and building shuttering for the ceilings. But the only workmen to be seen were a handful of carpenters patiently erecting some scaffolding.

"How long has this idleness been going on?" Cristina demanded.

"The schedule started slipping a year ago because everyone indulges the 'genius Raphael'. The biggest mistake you made was withdrawing to your library when Bramante died."

"This is absurd! The whole project has stalled."

"And yet the expenditure has not. The Pope is still pouring money into the construction."

"For what?" Cristina gestured to the deserted shell. "Where is it all going?"

"Good question." Domenico shrugged. "Raphael is certainly no Bramante. He behaves more like a prince than an architect. The artist is the toast of Rome, and wherever he goes, he is surrounded by an entourage of disciples, assistants and sycophants. Personally, I think he was too young to be given the job at all."

"Age is no excuse," Cristina retorted. "Michelangelo was twenty-three when he carved the *Pietà*. Raphael is thirty-four, and he needs to respect the great office he occupies. An absentee architect is no use to anyone."

"I'm afraid his reputation protects him from all criticism."

"Well, it won't protect him from me." Cristina strode out of the shell of the building, pushed aside the huge awnings that had been slung to contain the dust, and emerged into one of the construction yards, where mountains of stone were waiting to be shaped into rectangular blocks. There was enough travertine to keep a small army of masons busy, but all Cristina could see were two men sharpening their chisels. In this heat, even that minor exertion had drenched the men's faces in sweat.

"Where is everybody?" Cristina asked as she approached the stonemasons.

"You'd have to ask the foreman," the older man replied.

"And where is he?"

"Not in today."

"Why?"

"Doesn't matter. We know what we've got to do." The mason slapped a large chunk of travertine. "This'll keep us busy all day."

"It will take more than two stonemasons to build St Peter's." Cristina couldn't hide her anger. "Where is Raphael?"

"Who?"

"Raphael. The chief architect?"

A smile creased the older mason's face. "I know who he is. But we haven't seen him for weeks."

"So where is he?"

"Have you searched the brothels?"

The younger mason snorted with laughter, and added, "Or the bedrooms of the grand palazzos?"

"He's probably cuckolding some count or other."

Cristina left the workmen chuckling at their jokes; she had no intention of trawling through the dark underbelly of the city to find Raphael.

Instead, she went to see the art dealer, Ludovico Labirinto. He was not pleased to see her; he hadn't been pleased to see Cristina ever since she exposed his most prolific client as a fraud some fourteen years earlier. But Labirinto was a pragmatist, and he knew that the quickest way to get the woman out of his office was to give her the information she needed. On his recommendation, Cristina and Domenico made their way to La Rustica, a country lodge on a vineyard just north of the city walls, where Raphael was allegedly working on a portrait commission for a wealthy jeweller.

Using their papal warrants to get past the servants, they made their way into a palatial orangery at the back of the lodge, where they found a decadent party in full swing. So decadent, in fact, that it was on the verge of tipping into an orgy.

A dozen women from some of the finest aristocratic families in Rome had shed their dresses and were sprawled across the furniture in little more than their undergarments. They were laughing and drinking heavily, as a young man moved from woman to woman, painting bucolic images on their bodies. One contessa had some sheep gambolling up her thigh, while a marchesa had a serpent winding around her neck and plunging into her cleavage.

"I want a cherub on my buttocks!" a young duchessa called out.

"And I want some wings on my *farfallina*!" the contessa replied boldly, which triggered shrieks of laughter from her friends.

"Fear not!" the young man declared, wielding his palette. "I have enough paint in my brush to decorate all of you!" He made an obscene thrusting movement with his pelvis, triggering more salacious laughter.

Cristina and Domenico looked on from the side of the room; no-one had even noticed their arrival.

"Please tell me that's not him," Cristina said.

"I'm afraid it is," Domenico replied. "That is Raphael."

The man Cristina remembered being appointed chief architect was earnest and focussed, talking fervently about his longing to devote his formidable talents to the Vatican's greatest project. But three years of being adored by Rome's finest had turned Raphael into a lustful libertine. And he had the looks to match — a velvet beret was angled over long, golden curls, framing a face with delicate, almost feminine features. He had the air of a man to whom things had always come easily, and he was effortlessly comfortable with his talent, for even though he was drunk and aroused, the transitory images Raphael painted on his admirers' bodies were dazzling.

"*Ragazze*!" the painter declared. "I feel a still life coming on!"

There were salacious cries from the women, who were obviously familiar with the routine. Raphael twirled a finger in the air, and all the ladies turned around and bent over obediently, thrusting their backsides into the air.

"What a canvas!" Raphael declared. He approached the first woman and lifted her petticoats to reveal her naked buttocks. "On here, a ripe peach, I think!" He moved on to the next woman and revealed her white cheeks. "And here, a juicy apple, perhaps." The next aristocrat obligingly hoisted her own clothes. Raphael studied her buttocks for a moment, before declaring, "These could only be a pair of lovely apricots, ready for plucking!"

The women yelped and wiggled at Raphael, but before he could move further down the line, Cristina's voice cut across the jollity.

"Do you have any idea of the sacrifices people have made for you?"

Her words pricked the orgiastic bubble. The women hastily covered themselves, while Raphael turned and glared at Cristina with unconcealed irritation. "Who the hell are you?"

"I am the woman who is looking for the chief architect of St Peter's Basilica," Cristina replied as she strode towards him. "I am the woman who has sweated blood for twenty years to protect the vision of the basilica. Countless people have died to keep it alive, and I think you owe it to them to get back to work, Raffaello Sanzio da Urbino."

The air seemed to thicken with tension.

Raphael looked Cristina up and down, then with a casual shrug pronounced, "A true artist is only interested in the future, not the past."

"Not the artists I know," Cristina replied.

"What has gone is dead. My vision is what runs through St Peter's now. And my inspiration comes from all that is beautiful." He turned to his entourage of admirers. "Isn't that right, *bellezze*?"

The women cooed and tittered. Emboldened by the endorsement, one of the marchesas pointed accusingly at Cristina and declared, "Boring! Boring!"

The others immediately took up the chant. "Boring! Boring!"

The marchesa raised the stakes. "Show your arse or get out!" And she started tossing grapes at the intruders.

Cristina turned to her brother. "Can't you arrest them?"

"For what? Being puerile?" Domenico took her arm and led her out of the orangery.

But Cristina's anger didn't subside in the open air. "The entire project is stagnating because of that child!"

Domenico sighed. "The Pope loves him, and Raphael exploits that."

"He needs to spend some more time with great artists, and less time with giggling aristocrats."

"There is only one man in Rome who can call him to heel, and that is the Holy Father himself."

"Then I need an audience with Pope Leo."

"Very well, I'll put in a request. But there is something you need to see first."

"It cannot wait, Domenico. I need to see him immediately." Cristina grabbed the reins of her horse and hauled herself into the saddle.

But Domenico hesitated. "A threat has been made."

"To Raphael?"

"To the Holy Father, and to the gold that finances everything he does."

Cristina frowned. "How serious a threat?"

"Eight severed heads in a wooden trunk."

"What?"

"I'll show you." Domenico slipped his foot into the stirrup and mounted his horse. "But I hope you had a light lunch, or you might just see it all again."

6: TROUPE

"I'm too old to bother with making appointments." Cardinal Riario strode down the corridor leading to Pope Leo's audience chamber at such a pace that Cristina and Domenico struggled to keep up. "Stay close, and don't stop for anyone."

"Does the Holy Father understand how the Vatican really works?" Cristina asked.

"Honestly? He is still dazzled by the baubles of power. And he has mistaken amusement for art. We have fantastical pageants on the Capitoline, and bullfights in the Belvedere Gardens, while St Peter's languishes. Is that incompetence or inexperience? You tell me."

Cristina could hear the brittle resentment in the cardinal's voice. "It requires strength to operate the levers of power," she replied, trying to convey that she understood his disappointment. "Strength and experience."

Riario gave her a sideways glance. "Try telling that to Conclave."

Up ahead, they saw one of Pope Leo's principal secretaries sitting behind a desk that guarded the doors to the papal rooms. Hearing footsteps, he looked up from his ledger and smiled at the cardinal. "Good morning, Your Eminence. Is there anything I can help you with today?"

"Not you. The Holy Father," Riario said, without breaking his stride.

"I'm afraid his engagement diary is full —"

"Too bad."

The secretary stood up to block his path, but the cardinal brushed him aside.

"Your Eminence, you can't go in!"

Riario pushed on the doors and entered the audience chamber, sweeping Cristina and Domenico along in his wash, to reveal a trio of dwarves dancing a galliard for Pope Leo.

Domenico leant into Cristina and whispered, "The Pope's banker." He pointed to Agostino Chigi who was beaming at the performance.

"They were captured during a raid on an Ottoman fleet just off the coast of Syracuse, Your Holiness," Chigi explained. "Once they danced for the Sultan Selim the Grim, and now the dwarves are at your service."

Pope Leo's jowls quivered with delight, and when the dance ended he applauded enthusiastically. "They will make a splendid entertainment for my next banquet."

"Do with them what you will, Your Holiness. They are my gift to you."

Cristina couldn't bear to watch the spectacle a moment longer. "Is that what you want?" she asked the dancers directly. "To be nothing more than an after-dinner entertainment?"

"Forgive me, Your Holiness." The Pope's secretary shuffled nervously by the doors. "I told them you were busy, but they wouldn't listen."

Pope Leo silenced his secretary with a flick of his hand. "They're here now. They might as well stay."

But Chigi was not so indulgent; his grand generosity had been tarnished by Cristina's harsh words. "Delighting the Holy Father is a Christian duty."

"But humiliating other people is not."

"They are Ottoman infidels. They do not share our sensibilities."

When Cristina looked at the dancers, she saw that beneath the bravura of performance was an unease that came from years of abuse. She turned to the Pope. "Holy Father, I do not wish to presume, but distracting you with trifles when the Vatican is facing a moment of peril is not the behaviour of a trusted advisor."

Chigi glared at her. "You must be the interfering Falchoni sister. Your reputation precedes you."

"As does yours," Cristina responded, holding his gaze.

Leo could hear the determination in her voice, and it jolted him back to his duty. He snapped his fingers at the secretary, "Take them away. Feed them well."

"Yes, Your Holiness."

The secretary bustled the dancers out of the room, and Pope Leo gestured for Cristina and Domenico to approach. "To which particular moment of peril do you refer?"

There was a time when Cristina would have been more circumspect in addressing the Supreme Pontiff of the Universal Church, but her devastating diagnosis had pulled everything into a painfully sharp focus. Elaborate etiquette consumed time that she no longer had.

"Vast quantities of money are being spent on building St Peter's, but when you actually go to the construction site, Holy Father, it is to all intents and purposes, abandoned. Progress has stalled. Which means money is being squandered, mishandled, or more than likely stolen. Across Rome, contractors and suppliers are enriching themselves, while the basilica itself has barely progressed since last summer. And the reason for this woeful state of affairs is simple: the decadence and self-indulgence of Raphael. His puerile behaviour is threatening to destroy decades of arduous work. And now you have received a bloody warning from the German states which threatens to choke off funding for the basilica. Butchering the soldiers bringing the Indulgence gold to Rome was an appalling crime. And yet, I share the anger of whoever did it."

"Mind your tongue," Chigi warned. "Remember where your loyalties lie."

Cristina ignored the banker and focused on the Pope. "I have just returned from a hunting lodge where your chief architect is painting fruit on the backsides of some of the most privileged women in Rome. If I am appalled by such decadence, what do you believe the serious-minded Germans would think if they could see how their money was really being spent?"

"There is no excuse for the savagery of their crime," Chigi declared.

"I agree. But it is a warning that needs to be heeded."

All eyes focused on Pope Leo, who massaged his temples with his fingertips as he marshalled his thoughts. "Is it really a warning? Or is it merely a criminal act?"

Chigi jumped in with his answer. "The German states can be wild and lawless places. It is well known that bandits roam freely through the dense forests."

Leo turned to Cristina. "And you agree?"

"Holy Father, it is impossible to know what is going on while standing here in Rome. The information we receive may be compromised; ambassadors and cardinals all have their own agendas. What is clear is that someone has committed a violent and desperate act which threatens to turn St Peter's into an unfinished folly."

"Holy Father," said Domenico suddenly, "the taskforce you commissioned has been assembled and is ready to depart. You wanted only the most trusted and committed troops, and that is why I believe my sister should head north with them, across the Alps, to lead the investigation."

Cristina glared at Domenico. "I have my own battles to fight."

"What could be more important than securing your legacy, Cristina?"

"With all due respect," Chigi interrupted, "this is a ludicrous suggestion. It is inappropriate and will render Operation Danube ineffective."

Cardinal Riario drew back his shoulders, ready to engage in battle. "I have known Signora Falchoni for twenty years. We have not always seen eye to eye, but her commitment is beyond question. If it weren't for her efforts, St Peter's Basilica would never have been started. She will not be remembered by history, but the Vatican is indebted to her. She also has one of the sharpest minds in the city."

"For a woman," Chigi conceded grudgingly.

"For anyone," Riario slapped the banker down. "And if anyone can untangle the politics of the German states and root out the killers who have committed this atrocity, it is Cristina Falchoni."

Pope Leo fixed his gaze on Cristina. "And you have the strength for this?"

Cristina hesitated. Did the Pope know of her illness? Had he been informed of the personal battle she was facing? She glanced at Domenico, who gave an imperceptible nod to accept the mission. "I have the strength, Your Holiness. But I also have one stipulation."

"What stipulation?" Pope Leo asked.

"I will go north with the taskforce. We will discover the truth. Whoever is responsible for the theft of the Indulgence money and the murder of your soldiers will be captured and brought to justice. The flow of gold will be secured. But only if you give me your personal guarantee that the money will be used to restart the building work on St Peter's. It must not be squandered or frittered away by an architect who has no sense of duty."

Cristina knew that Pope Leo would not like being spoken to like this, but she also knew that St Peter's was his chance to immortalise both himself and the entire Medici dynasty. "You have my word," he replied. "Now go and fulfil your duty."

7: DREAMS

Packing should be exciting. The task of choosing which items to take on a long journey should be galvanised with anticipation as your mind races through the possibilities of what might be encountered.

Not this time; not for Isra.

As she filled Cristina's battered wooden trunk with clothes for a cooler climate and boots for all weathers, Isra was full of misgivings. Embarking on a dangerous expedition to the German states would be challenging enough if you were strong and healthy, but Cristina was also fighting an existential threat inside her own body. It made Isra feel powerless, especially as she wouldn't be there to protect her friend. She had asked to accompany Operation Danube but was refused because it had been designated a high-level military mission with 'no room for passengers'. Isra would just have to trust in Tomasso's leadership.

Perhaps that was why she rolled two pistols and a dagger inside one of the tunics, and pushed them to the bottom of the trunk.

Moments later, the bedroom door clattered open, and Cristina bowled in carrying a small pile of books. "You'll have to find room for these as well."

"Seriously?"

"Just because I'm away from my library doesn't mean the medical research has to stop."

Isra glanced at the trunk which was already full to the brim.

"You could always take out the weapons," Cristina suggested.

"There aren't any weapons. You said you didn't want any."

Cristina smiled and plunged her hands into the trunk. A short rummage later she pulled out the pistols.

"You shouldn't be defenceless," Isra warned.

"Tomasso's men will be heavily armed. They will be with me at all times, and right now I need medical encyclopaedias more than weapons."

Isra started loading the books into the trunk. She certainly had a gift for packing, utilising every inch of space. "What you really need is plenty of rest, good food and a calming routine," Isra advised. "Putting yourself in danger will not heal you."

"How dangerous can it be when I'm surrounded by fifteen heavily armed soldiers?"

"You're the one always lecturing me about looking after the body, Cristina. Respect what it's telling you now." Isra did a test closing of the trunk's lid and was satisfied. "Just enough room for the last-minute things, then you're done."

Sensing Isra's disquiet, Cristina crossed the room and stood by her side. "You're right, Isra. And I know you're only thinking about what's best for me. But there is another way of looking at all this. Sometimes it's stress that makes us strong. The more trees are battered by the wind, the stronger their trunks become. And a broken leg only fully recovers when you put weight on it. Stress is a vital part of life."

"It's not me you have to persuade," Isra replied. "It's the cancer growing inside you."

"Let's not argue. Not on my last day in Rome. How about some mint tea in the garden?"

"Finally — an idea I can get behind."

As Isra prepared the drinks, Cristina inspected the half-finished network of water pipes that would eventually feed the small fountain in the centre of their Islamic garden. "Looks like the builder is sticking to the plans."

"He really isn't happy about it." Isra handed Cristina a cup of mint tea. "I can hear him grumbling to himself as he works."

"So little faith," Cristina sighed.

"With a bit of luck, it will all be finished by the time you return."

"You've done an amazing job on this garden. It has a real sense of tranquillity." Cristina sat down on a bench under the shade of a lemon tree. "It will be the perfect place to heal."

Isra nodded and sipped her fragrant tea. No-one said it, but both women were thinking the same thing: would this garden be where Cristina was healed? Or would it be where she made her final peace with life? It was the great unknown hanging over them.

The robin which had been fluttering in and out of the library for the past few days swooped down and perched on the bench between the two women; it was as if he wanted to join in the conversation.

Isra smiled. "He always looks so curious."

"You know, it's strange … ever since the surgeon gave me the diagnosis, I look at young people in a different way," Cristina reflected.

"What do young people have to do with anything?"

"I'm ashamed to admit it, but now I look at them with envy. They're so full of life, so unworried, so unaware of what's lying in wait for them. A few days ago, I was part of that flow. Now I feel as if I've been pushed into a backwater to die."

Isra refilled Cristina's cup. "That's not going to happen. I won't let it."

"I dreamt about my baby brother last night. Even after all these years, Aldo's death still haunts me."

"How could anyone forget something like that?"

"At the time, I felt so powerless. I still wonder if there was anything more we could have done to fight his illness. Perhaps that's why my life has been devoted to knowledge. Knowledge is supposed to give you control. Yet here I am, a middle-aged woman, facing the same sense of helplessness as when I was a girl."

The robin fluttered away; maybe the conversation was too dark for such a beautiful summer day.

"Tell Pope Leo you simply are not well enough for the expedition," Isra said.

"I can't do that."

"Take the time to focus on yourself."

"No." Cristina closed her eyes to marshal her thoughts. "If this really is going to be the end, my life cannot have been for nothing. I've devoted so much to St Peter's … even if my learning cannot beat the cancer, my willpower can still save the basilica. I have one last chance to give my life meaning."

"But it already has so much meaning," Isra insisted. "The lives you've touched, the experiences we've had, the memories we share. That is meaning."

"It is. Yet in time, it will all fade. St Peter's, on the other hand, will never fade. It will stand for centuries, maybe a thousand years. But only if it is completed."

8: CONVOY

Operation Danube left Rome at dawn the following Monday.

Fifteen of the Vatican's most experienced Apostolic Guards were under the command of Deputato Tomasso, with Lieutenant Dante as his number two; Cristina was the only civilian on the taskforce. In about a week, they would arrive at the Brenner Pass, which would take them through the Alps and north into the German states.

The troops carried tents with them, but these were only to be used as a last resort, because setting up and striking camp burned up time that could be spent travelling. Instead, Lieutenant Dante rode ahead in the afternoons to secure a tavern with lodgings and stables large enough for all the horses. After a couple of days, the taskforce settled into a smooth and efficient rhythm.

Tomasso understood that routine was the secret to all good convoys, and he was surprised by how easily Cristina fitted in. She rode without complaint and always kept up the pace; when they stopped, she would pick up her books and continue studying. Every night after supper, and every morning before breakfast, Cristina would read and make notes. Hers was the first candle to be lit, and the last to be extinguished, because she had set herself two ambitious goals: first, to continue the search for a cure; second, to improve her German language skills.

Five years earlier she had decided to teach herself German in order to study the writings of the renowned physician, Johannes de Ketham. It was a much bigger task than she'd anticipated, mainly because there were over two hundred

German dialects. Now she focused her efforts on High German, reasoning that wherever they ended up, someone was sure to speak the language of officialdom.

Every night without fail, Tomasso would knock on her door to check she was all right. "Is there anything you need, Cristina?"

"More time would be nice. But failing that, more candles."

It was clear she wanted to be left to herself, and Tomasso respected that. And so it went on all week, until on Saturday afternoon they entered Trento, in the foothills of the Alps. It was a much-needed opportunity to resupply: the stirrups on Dante's saddle needed to be repaired, and one of the horses had to be swapped after developing a limp. For the rest of the troops, it was a chance to enjoy one last Italian meal before heading into the land of boiled pork and black bread.

As usual, Tomasso knocked on Cristina's door, but this time his question was different. "Would you care to join me for dinner?"

"I was going to have supper in my room."

"Why not take a break from studying, Cristina? I think you've earned it."

"You know, I wasn't planning on eating much, but actually I'm starving."

"That'll be the mountain air. Come, there are some amazing smells coming from the kitchens."

They found a table tucked away in the corner of the tavern, and ordered wild game stew, followed by *erbolata*, a cheese and herb tart.

"So, are you fluent in German yet?" Tomasso asked with a teasing smile.

"I'd forgotten just how much the Germans love long words," Cristina replied. "They do this thing where they make new words by combining lots of nouns. It produces some real tongue twisters."

"Grammar isn't my strong point, I'm afraid."

"Do you know what the German word for friendships is? *Freundschaftsbeziehungen.*"

"What?"

"They take the word friendship, *Freundschaft*, and the word relationships, *Beziehungen*, and smash them together."

"That's quite a mouthful."

"What do you think the German for 'glove' is?"

Tomasso shrugged. "Not a clue."

"*Handschuh.* Which literally means shoe for the hand. And a person who throws snowballs while wearing gloves is called a *Handschuhschneeballwerfer.*"

"That could be useful when we're up in the mountains," Tomasso laughed, then he tried to pronounce the word but failed miserably.

The next morning, the taskforce set off just after dawn and made timely progress, arriving in Bolzano by lunchtime. As they pressed on, the world changed around them.

Vast mountains loomed up on either side, making them feel powerless and insignificant; the air cooled and felt so fresh it seemed to cut their lungs; once the sun started to drop, dark shadows spread a sense of unease across the valley floor. No wonder everyone felt relieved when Castle Reifenstein finally came into view.

The building itself looked austere, like a fairy tale castle stripped of charm, but it had been offering refuge to travellers for generations because it marked the start of the Brenner Pass.

At thirty miles long, Brenner was the lowest pass in the region, so was open all year round. This was why the Roman Legions paved it, then promptly marched along it to conquer Europe. Ever since, merchants, refugees, armies and pilgrims had been crossing the Alps through the Brenner Pass. Despite this, it could still be a treacherous journey, which is why Tomasso had hired one of the trusted mountain guides to accompany them until they reached Innsbruck. He was expecting to meet a grizzled old mountain goat of a man on the castle's rampart walkway, but when he arrived the only person waiting was a pasty-faced youth in his mid-twenties with a shock of black hair. Tomasso caught his eye.

"Are you Sigmund?"

"For my sins," the youth replied with a weary sigh.

"Is something wrong?"

"Something is always wrong in the mountains. The only question is whether you're unlucky enough to be standing in the way."

"Oh. Right." Tomasso realised that Sigmund was only young on the outside; inside, his soul was already a thousand years old.

"You must be the delegation from the Vatican."

"Deputato Tomasso of the Guardia Apostolica." He extended his hand but was surprised at how damp Sigmund's handshake was.

"At least you weren't foolish enough to rely on the power of prayer to get you through the mountains," Sigmund observed.

"So far, the journey's been good. Blue skies the whole way. Should be smooth going."

Sigmund gave a cynical laugh. "Don't be fooled. The mountains are nothing like the lowlands."

Tomasso looked up at the cloudless sky where the last rays of sun were scraping over the mountain ridges. "It looks pretty calm to me."

"And that is exactly how the mountain gets you. It lures you with the promise of a blue sky, then from nowhere a squall whips in, cuts you off, and before you know it, you freeze to death."

"Is that so?"

"People are scared of the heights in the mountains, but it's not the height that kills you." Sigmund gazed up at the nearest peak as the sun slipped off its snow-capped sides. "There's ice. Avalanches. Blizzards. Howling winds. Suffocating fog. But worst of all, the mountains are fickle. I once took a lacemaker across the Gimlet Pass. Sunshine all around us. He needed to pause to catch his breath. Before he had taken three gulps of water from his flask, a storm blew in. The blizzard was so thick, the merchant vanished from sight, even though he was no further than you are from me."

"What did you do?"

"On the mountain, death is always lurking close by." Sigmund pronounced grimly. "I reached out and grabbed him. To stop him moving. I have known people get so disorientated by the snow, they walk clean off the edge of a cliff. So I grabbed him and held him. And we didn't move until the storm loosened its grip."

"But you could have frozen to death," Tomasso said.

"Those are the choices the mountain gives you: freeze or fall."

"Well, I'm glad you'll be guiding us," Tomasso said, and he meant it. "Do you think we'll make the crossing in a single day?"

"Maybe. Maybe not. Only a fool would try to second-guess the Brenner Pass."

Tomasso shuddered as the chill of the mountain evening caught up with him. "What time do we start?"

"Say your prayers. Eat a small breakfast. Be ready to leave an hour after sunrise."

After supper, Cristina went down to the castle chapel to reflect on the mission ahead, and to pray for personal strength. But she had not been meditating long when she heard the creak of the heavy oak doors. She turned and saw Tomasso standing by the font.

"I'm sorry. I didn't mean to interrupt." He looked awkward.

"No, no. I've nearly finished." Cristina crossed herself, rose from her knees and sat on the pew at the front of the chapel. "Did you find the guide? Siegfried, was it?"

"Sigmund." Tomasso gave a wry smile. "But I almost wish I hadn't."

"If you don't trust him, don't use him."

"Oh, he knows his stuff. It's just … he's such a pessimist. He enjoys seeing the worst in every situation."

Cristina laughed. "We can't all be optimists, Tomasso."

"I'll never understand people like that. Why embrace gloom?"

"I can see the logic."

"Really?"

"If you expect the worst, you will often be pleasantly surprised at how things turn out. But if you always expect the best, you'll be constantly disappointed."

"I suppose that does make sense. But it doesn't feel right." Tomasso approached the altar, crossed himself, then sat down next to Cristina. "When I think of the people I've known, it always seems that bad things happen to the merchants of doom. It's almost as if they bring it on themselves."

"And do you think the opposite could also be true?" Cristina asked. "That optimism leads to good outcomes?"

Tomasso glanced at her hands. "I hope so. I really do."

"Maybe that's what prayer is really about. Not a conversation with God, but with yourself."

For a few moments, they gazed in silence at the altar and the huge crucifix that hung above it. Tomasso got up and approached the rack of flickering votive candles. He lit one and stared at it. "I've been praying for you, Cristina. Every day."

"Thank you."

He turned to look at her. "But truth be told, I'm frightened."

"Of what we'll find in the German states?" she deflected.

"No, not that." Tomasso replied confidently. "We have the best men and we're well armed. No, I'm frightened about what will happen to you, Cristina."

How could she tell him that she too was frightened? It would help no-one. "You should have more faith in the medical textbooks. And my ability to study them."

"But what if you cannot beat this illness? I can't bear the thought of…" He couldn't finish the sentence.

"I do not accept failure easily. You should know that by now."

"But there are things we cannot control. Some things are beyond the human grasp."

Cristina didn't want to go where this was leading, and it was easier to focus on the mission than on herself. "I am more fearful of what we'll find north of the Alps. The violence of that attack … the premeditated cruelty … the decapitated heads … there was something inhuman about it."

Tomasso reached under his collar, undid a small clasp, and pulled a fine chain from inside his tunic — it carried a medallion of St Christopher. "This was given to me by my grandmother. To keep me safe in battle. I want you to have it."

"No, I couldn't possibly —"

"Please." He pressed the necklace into her hand. "It would mean a lot to me if you wore it. And I know my grandmother would approve."

"You really think it will protect me against the Germans?"

Tomasso nodded. "It also helps having fifteen heavily armed men on your side."

Cristina laughed and put the chain around her neck. "Thank you. And thank your grandmother."

"Let's make a pact," Tomasso said. "I will protect you against the German hordes, but you must promise to beat the cancer that's inside you."

"I never make a promise I cannot keep." Cristina drew a deep breath to wrestle back control of her emotions. "But I'll do my best. That I *can* promise." She leant forward, put her arms around Tomasso and hugged him tightly.

In all the time Tomasso had known her, Cristina had never hugged him like this. Only then did he realise how deeply frightened she was for her own life.

9: FOREST

The Brenner Pass was breathtaking.

It threaded its way through the forbidding mountains like a river lazily searching for the path of least resistance. Sometimes mountain walls swooped up on either side of the road at dizzying angles; at other times the valley made a gentle V-shape, affording spectacular views of the curtains of snowcapped ridges which separated Italy from the German states.

Cristina was fascinated by the variety of travellers heading in both directions. There were merchants driving heavily loaded carts hoping to make their fortunes; there were peasants with nothing but ragged bundles on their backs, hoping to find a better life in a new country; there were students, toll collectors, tinkers, official delegations, and men who looked as if they were barely one step ahead of the law. It was like one of those paintings from the Low Countries showing the 'Procession of Humanity into the Gates of Eternity'.

The long, scorched summer had made for perfect conditions in the Pass. The valley floor was dotted with patches of rich green pasture on which local herdsmen had unleashed their cattle, while swathes of pine trees clung to the mountainsides at impossible angles. This intrigued Cristina, for having spent the last two years nurturing the garden in her house on Piazza Navona, she knew how tricky it could be to get flowers to flourish. You needed just the right balance of light, shade and moisture for each plant, and no matter how many horticultural books you studied, a lot of it seemed to come down to trial and error. And yet here, trees flourished in the most hostile locations. Cracks in rocks which contained no soil had given birth to enormous pine trees; huge overhanging ledges had persuaded some trees to grow into strange contortions, while others balanced precariously in places where acrobats would fear to tread.

Was there some mechanism by which plants could adapt themselves to their surroundings? Cristina wondered. No, it would be absurd to attribute any kind of intentionality to vegetation. Perhaps it was the other way round? Perhaps hundreds of different types of trees had tried to grow in these hostile conditions, and most had failed, but the ones which had survived now thrived. That made more sense — life as a game of chance where living things tried to find the niches that suited them best. Cristina made a mental note to do some more reading on this when she returned to Rome. Next spring would be the perfect time to do some observations … then she checked herself, remembering. Perhaps next spring was beyond her grasp.

No. She couldn't think like that. She must not. She would work on her theory next spring, come what may.

The glorious weather which stimulated Cristina's philosophical thinking only made Tomasso realise that he had wasted money by hiring a mountain guide.

"Disappointed?" he asked, as he rode next to Sigmund.

"The day is young, the Brenner is long," Sigmund replied.

"Surely this is the kind of weather that puts mountain guides out of business," Tomasso said, determined to provoke a reaction.

"Never think you have beaten the mountains," Sigmund warned. "There is nothing the Alps love more than to vanquish arrogance."

It was clear the man had no sense of humour, so Tomasso dropped back and let Sigmund lead. No wonder these guides all insisted on payment in advance.

The weather held, conditions remained perfect, and by the late afternoon, they were through the Brenner and heading down the long, gentle road towards Innsbruck.

North of the Alps it felt as if they were in a different world. Unlike Italy, this landscape was not dominated by the Mediterranean Sea. The air was now filled with the scent of forest and pasture; the soil was moist and dense rather than baked dry; even the quality of the light was different, reflecting off the surrounding landscape.

They parted ways with Sigmund before they reached Innsbruck's city walls, then huddled over the maps to plot their route north.

"Pick a city, any city," Domenico said, as Dante placed rocks around the edge of the map to stop it from scrolling up.

"Most of the convoys have been attacked in the north," Cristina said. "The one that ended up in Chigi's mansion was coming from Magdeburg, so that seems as good a place to start as any."

Tomasso studied the map. "You're sure you don't want to start with one that's a bit closer?"

"In the long run, it's quicker to go straight to the heart of the problem."

"Well, it'll certainly give us a chance to enjoy the German landscape, sir." Dante was trying to remain upbeat.

"I think it's mostly trees," Tomasso replied without enthusiasm.

"There's nothing wrong with trees," Cristina said. "We'd be lost without them."

"I'll work out the best stopover points, sir." Dante pulled out a pair of compasses and started taking measurements on the map.

"We should try and avoid the cities, as far as possible," Cristina suggested.

"Too much bureaucracy?"

"We'll have to deal with permits and taxes, meet the local princes who will be keen to know what a delegation from the Vatican is after. The fewer people who know about our mission, the better."

Tomasso nodded. "We don't want to alert the criminal gangs that we're coming."

It made strategic sense, but as they continued on their journey, it also meant that most of their days were spent riding along bridleways and paths that ran through dense forests; hour after hour staring at trees was enough to test even the hardiest spirit.

Cristina knew that in Roman times, trees covered nine tenths of this land, and even though there had been some clearances for farming, dense woodland still dominated life here. It had seeped into the German soul, with countless folk tales depicting the forests as a place of magical powers and evil spirits. The woods were where children went missing, wolves were fought, and paths to the underworld appeared. This was where the struggle between good and evil played out, and where one step off the well-trodden path would take you across the threshold that separated the known from the unknown.

The taskforce continued north through this ominous landscape for eight days and finally entered the Harz Mountains. These hills were relatively low and covered in spruce woods, but the paths became very narrow.

Tomasso pulled the convoy to a halt. "This is perfect territory for an ambush," he said to Dante.

"Should we change formation, sir?"

"Put a scout upfront, have the rest follow in staggered pairs, and put three men at the back as a rearguard."

"Very good, sir." Dante rode forward to organise the troops.

An hour later, Tomasso realised what a good decision he had made when they heard the sounds of battle nearby, muffled by the trees: musket shots, the clash of swords, horses snorting in distress.

"Defend!" Tomasso commanded.

Immediately the taskforce regrouped their horses into a circle and drew their weapons.

They waited, braced in all directions, eyes straining for any sign of movement in the surrounding forest.

More shots rang out … followed by a terrible silence.

What was happening in the darkness of the forest?

Suddenly they heard the sound of horses galloping away.

Dante looked at Tomasso. "Do we stay, or advance?"

Tomasso concentrated intently on the sounds of the forest.

There — a man's voice.

Muttering incoherently…

In panic…

In pain…

In fear.

Tomasso's eyes locked on the path ahead…

A figure staggered out of the darkness.

He was half-naked, covered in blood and trembling uncontrollably.

Both his hands had been hacked off.

He saw the taskforce lined up across the road and sank to his knees.

"For the love of God…" he gasped. "Kill me!"

"Hold the circle!" Tomasso commanded.

Everybody kept their positions, weapons poised. All eyes focused on the desperate man who knelt motionless in the road ahead of them.

"We have to help him," Cristina whispered to Tomasso.

"He might be bait." Tomasso glanced around, searching for threats. "What do you think, Dante? Is he bait?"

"Difficult to say, sir."

Tomasso weighed the risks in his mind.

"He'll bleed to death," Cristina urged.

"Very well. Bring him in. But be quick."

Dante leapt from his horse and ran towards the survivor, crouching low all the while, as his men covered him with their muskets. Dante scooped the man up, slung him over his shoulder and hurried back to the safety of the troop, where he laid him on the ground.

While the rest of the soldiers held the protective circle, Tomasso, Cristina and Dante knelt by the man to assess his injuries.

"Kill me," the man gasped again. "Before the demons return. Kill me!"

"He's delirious," Tomasso said.

"We must stop the bleeding." Cristina looked at the gaping stumps where the man's hands should have been. "Have you got tourniquets?"

"We can cauterize the wounds with gunpowder," Dante replied.

"No."

"It's what they teach us at the academy."

"Well they're wrong!" Cristina insisted.

"Gunpowder stops the bleeding and prevents infection."

"It's the opposite. Burning creates more tissue damage and increases the risk of infection."

Dante looked to Tomasso for guidance; the deputy nodded. "Get the tourniquets."

Cristina leant over the survivor and looked into his eyes. "I'm not going to lie. This is going to hurt."

"Save me from the demons!" the man wailed.

"Brace yourself." Cristina looped the first tourniquet around the man's right arm, then pulled as hard as she could.

The man's scream tore through the forest with such vehemence, Cristina thought he was going to pass out.

"Whoever's out there certainly knows we're here now," Tomasso muttered.

Cristina looped the second tourniquet around his other arm. "One more time, then we're done." She pulled it tight and closed her eyes as the second scream rang out. "It's done. It's done," she whispered. She opened her eyes, looked at the man's wrists and was relieved to see that the flow of blood had reduced to a trickle — the arteries had been squeezed shut.

"They will devour you!" the survivor shouted at Tomasso. "Save your souls! For God's sake!"

"Get me some wine," Cristina said to Dante, who reached into one of the saddlebags for a flask.

Cristina splashed wine over both the bloody stumps, then swigged a mouthful herself and handed the flask back to Dante. "Try to get some down his throat. It'll calm his nerves."

Dante cradled the man's head in his hands and started dribbling some wine into his mouth. "Easy now. This will help."

Cristina took a few moments to draw breath, then studied the man. He was strongly built, in his thirties with a bushy brown beard, and two parallel lines shaved into his close-cropped hair. She ran her hands over his torso, feeling for other injuries, but there were none. "All the blood must have come from his own wounds."

"Or from other people," Tomasso said grimly. He brushed the leaves and twigs from the man's trousers to reveal embroidered gold strips down the side of each leg. "He wears the uniform of the troops who guard the Indulgence money. Another one must have been ambushed."

Cristina tilted the man's head towards her. "What happened? Tell me what happened?"

"The gates of Hell opened."

"Who attacked you? Was it soldiers?"

"Demons! The demons are here! They've come to drag us down to the inferno!"

"Did they steal the gold? The Indulgence money?"

The man looked at her with crazed eyes. "All the gold in the world will not save you from damnation."

"Who were they?"

"The forest…" The man raised an arm to point to the trees, then saw the maimed stump where his hand should have been. Horror creased his face and he started to weep. "Death came from the forest! Evil is out there!"

Dante put the flask to the man's lips again. He gulped the wine greedily, then his eyes rolled back, and he lapsed into unconsciousness.

Gently, Dante lowered the man's head, then turned to Tomasso. "Will he live?"

"With those catastrophic wounds?"

"We've stopped the bleeding," Cristina said.

"But he's lost too much blood. His skin is grey. And his mind is shot to pieces."

"We can't just wait for him to die," Dante said. "We're too exposed out here. And we can't leave him like this."

"Then we should take him to the nearest monastery," said Tomasso. "They can give him the last rites and bury him."

"The monastery is a good idea," Cristina agreed. "But not to bury him. The monks must tend his wounds and nurse him back to strength."

"It would be cruel to make him live with those injuries."

"That is not your decision."

"Cristina, at best he'll live out his days in an asylum."

"We must cling to life with every fibre of our being. Never give up."

"But —"

Cristina locked eyes with Tomasso. "You made *me* promise. Why does it not apply to this man as well?" She looked down at the broken figure. "There may be a wife, children waiting for him back in Italy."

"Very well," the deputy conceded. "Dante, prepare a stretcher and slung it between two horses." Tomasso took one of the maps out of the leather document cannister and unfurled it. "By my calculation we're about here —" he pointed at the map — "and there's a convent quite close, Walkenried Abbey. If you get him there, we'll join you before sunset."

"What are you going to do?" Dante asked as he attached either end of the stretcher poles to the horses.

"We're going to find out what's around that corner," Tomasso pointed down the road along which the man had staggered. "There may be others who need help."

"I should come with you, sir."

"No. It'll be fine." He looked at the injured man. "Get him to safety. If he lives, and if his mania eases, maybe he can give us some useful information."

Tomasso strode back to his horse and swung himself into the saddle. "We're going forward. Keep your weapons ready."

Cristina climbed back into her saddle and prepared to ride out, but Tomasso looked at her anxiously. "I don't know if you're safer holding back or coming with us."

"You're not getting rid of me that easily."

"Very well." Tomasso snapped his reins, moved to the front of the troop, and led Operation Danube to confront whatever horrors lay on the road ahead.

10: CARNAGE

The horses knew.

With every step, they became more fearful. Nostrils flared, heads reared back, pulling against the reins, they whinnied and snorted as they tried to warn each other. But the Apostolic Guards were well trained, and the convoy pressed on, following the narrow road as it arced through the forest … until the full horror was revealed.

At first glance, nothing made sense. Tomasso had to concentrate to unscramble the visual chaos of deconstructed bodies. When he did, he wished he hadn't.

Men, horses and dogs had been killed. Not just killed … slaughtered. It was like a ghastly parody of a butcher's shop, with cuts of human flesh hanging from the branches of trees or set out for the wild animals of the forest to feast upon.

The weapons which should have prevented this massacre were scattered in disarray. Pikes were snapped like twigs, swords scattered like useless cutlery; all the muskets appeared to have been taken.

Tomasso and his troops were silent.

Many had been in battle, but none had encountered such cold-hearted inhumanity, such cruelty, and no-one knew what to do. There were no protocols for atrocity.

Cristina detached her mind from her emotions. She had encountered violated bodies of the dead before. Only by detaching could you see beyond the horror and start to glimpse the mind of the killer; from there, maybe you could outthink him.

Who would murder like this? Not wolves or wild animals, there was too much order in the carnage. And not common bandits — they would have stolen everything of value and fled. Someone spent time and energy butchering these bodies. This was death as theatre, intended to shock. And it had worked — the troops seemed paralysed.

"Tomasso!" Cristina glanced at the soldiers. "They need to do something."

The deputy blinked, then shook his head to break the spell. He glanced at Cristina, then at his troops. "You two — ride to Ellrich."

"Yes, sir."

"Head back along the road we came on, then go east at the crossroads. Alert the Captain of the Watch. We need assistance, urgently."

Grateful for an excuse to get away, the two soldiers spurred their horses and sped down the road.

"You three, secure the perimeter. Check we're not being watched."

"Sir!"

"Everyone else, search the debris. Maybe someone is still alive."

The soldiers knew it was a futile search — no-one could survive this, but they did as they were ordered.

Cristina dismounted and started to comb through the carnage. Only method could make sense of the madness, so she ignored the morbid theatrics and focused instead on the business of the crime. She found the armoured trunk that had been carrying the Indulgence gold; it was identical to the one placed in Chigi's palazzo, but this one had been smashed open. All the gold had been taken, but this time there was no taunting note or scrawled obscenity.

Cristina found the massive ledger that was used to record the names and remissions of those who had bought Indulgences, but all the pages had been torn out. Instinctively, she looked up, and saw the pages scattered in the tree canopy, fluttering like a strange fruit. "Could someone retrieve the pages for me?" Cristina asked.

The two youngest soldiers put down their weapons and scrambled into the trees. They hauled themselves up and crawled along branches until they reached the lost pages. As they handed the sheets down, a picture started to emerge showing the movements of the convoy.

"They sold a lot of Indulgences in Leipzig." Cristina showed the pages to Tomasso. "Then they moved on to Magdeburg."

"Look at the money they collected." Tomasso ran his finger down the numbers written next to each name. "This was a big operation."

Cristina rifled through the torn pages until she found one that listed the permits by which they operated. "It was led by Johann Tetzel. Grand Commissioner for Indulgences in the German States." She pointed to his extravagant signature. "I've heard of him."

Tomasso looked at the human remains which lay scattered around them. "Do you think Tetzel was one of the victims?"

"I doubt it. He's probably spending his ten per cent in some brothel in Hannover."

"You don't know that. He could have been heading down to Frankfurt to sell more Indulgences."

"Would he really make that journey carrying all this gold?" Cristina pointed to the ledger pages. "Isn't it more likely this was being sent to Rome to be banked?"

"Excuse me, sir?"

Cristina and Tomasso turned round and saw the corporal standing there, with the other soldiers ranged behind him.

"Found something?" Tomasso asked.

"The men have asked … I mean…" His voice trailed off.

"What's going on?" Tomasso sensed trouble.

"The men are worried for their souls. They want a priest, sir. An exorcist."

Cristina stared at the corporal. "How will a priest help us catch the men who did this?"

"What if it wasn't men? What if it was demons?"

"Are we really having this conversation?" Cristina sighed. "Demons as in wings and claws? Just like in the paintings?"

"What humans would do this?" The corporal pointed at the butchered remains.

"And what use would demons have for gold?" Cristina retorted.

"To spend in Purgatory."

Cristina realised it was pointless trying to fight superstition with reason. "Let's settle this with evidence. Spread out and check the ground leading away from here in all directions. If devils did this, they would have flown away. If it was men on horseback, there will be tracks in the dirt." She turned to Tomasso. "Agreed?"

"Agreed." Tomasso split the soldiers into four groups and ordered them to scour the ground following the four points of the compass, looking for tracks and hoof prints.

The search may have been ordered to prove a simple point, but it ended up revealing much more. The bandits had arrived in a single large group, possibly as many as twelve; they lay in wait for some time — that much was evidenced by the pattern of horse droppings. But after the heist, they split up and scattered in three different directions.

"If one group was caught, only one portion of the gold would be lost," Tomasso suggested.

"So, they must have planned to meet up somewhere else," Cristina added.

They tracked the hoof prints through the woods. To the north and east, they got as far as a wide brook, then the tracks vanished. "Most likely they rode into the water to wipe out their trail," Tomasso explained.

To the west, they followed the tracks until they came to a part of the forest blanketed in a dense mass of pine needles, where the horses left no hoof prints. "These men knew exactly what they were doing," Tomasso acknowledged. "This spot was carefully chosen for an ambush."

"Why did no-one ride south, along the road?" Cristina asked. "It would have been the quickest escape route."

"Because they would have run straight into us," Tomasso replied.

"But how did they know we were coming? Had someone tipped them off?"

The possibility made Cristina and Tomasso uneasy. If they were now heading into a territory where their security had already been compromised, where details of their operation were being leaked, what chance did they have?

At least the corporal and the rest of the soldiers seemed reassured — the tracks had proved that this was the work of men rather than devils. But for Cristina, that made the crime even more shocking. This butchery was the work of men who had human souls, but the hearts and minds of devils.

"Monsters walk among us," Cristina said quietly to Tomasso. "If we don't catch them, they will devour us all."

*

They waited until the Captain of the Watch arrived from Ellrich, with a dozen guards and two waggons to take the human remains away. Tomasso briefed him about what they had witnessed, and what they had deduced, but the captain was neither shocked nor surprised. "This sort of thing is becoming more common," he said wearily. "Only a fool goes into the forest nowadays."

With nothing more to be done at the scene of the attack, Cristina, Tomasso and the Apostolic Guards made the short ride to Walkenried Abbey to discover if the sole survivor was still clinging to life.

The convent comprised an impressive set of buildings, with a huge abbey towering over a vaulted courtyard, surrounded by a labyrinth of cells, workshops and farm buildings. Yet despite the grandeur, it struck Cristina that the whole complex had an aura of disrepair. The gardens were overgrown and tangled with weeds, dozens of roof tiles had slipped out of place, and grass sprouted from the gargoyles' orifices at humiliating angles.

"The nuns don't appear to be on top of the maintenance," Cristina observed.

They soon discovered the reason for the disrepair. The abbey, which had once been home to over two hundred, was now reduced to six Cistercian nuns and an abbess, who rattled around inside the grand buildings, clinging to memories of former glory. Yet despite the gloomy presentation, the Apostolic Guards were given a warm welcome.

"This is such an honour for us!" Abbess Gisela exclaimed as she hurried out of the gates to meet them. "From the Vatican to Walkenried — who could have imagined? Welcome, welcome!" She was a petite woman in her late thirties, fired with an enormous sense of energy. "Lieutenant Dante said you were coming, and we have prepared everything."

"Thank you, Reverend Mother," Tomasso said, bowing his head respectfully. "Is the injured man still alive?"

"Indeed, he is. I have dressed his wounds with clean bandages and applied some healing ointments. But whoever put the tourniquets on saved his life."

"That would be Cristina."

Abbess Gisela turned to her. "You did an excellent job. Do you have medical training?"

"No, but I read widely," Cristina explained.

"Well, before I came here, I worked in the military hospital in Dresden, so I can spot a good medic. You've missed your true vocation. His wounds were terrible, but with careful nursing I am certain he will live."

"When can I question him?"

The abbess shook her head. "At the proper time. Right now, you need to make yourselves comfortable."

"I'd rather speak to him first," Cristina pressed.

"He is sleeping now," the abbess insisted. "And you'll know from your reading that the best medicine is rest."

Cristina let the matter drop; it was clear the business of hospitality was particularly important to Abbess Gisela.

"Follow me, and the sisters will show you where everything is." Gisela led the way into the abbey, where six elderly nuns were waiting.

Because Walkenried Abbey was so depopulated, accommodating the taskforce was easy. There was plenty of room in the stables for the horses, and though unused, the workshops still had tools for carrying out maintenance and running repairs. As for sleeping, the soldiers could have had six rooms each. It was all hands on deck for the nuns when it came to dinner, for they hadn't fed these many mouths in years. After much sweating and toiling in the kitchens, they ferried great bowls of *bohnen frieusieren mit speck* — fried beans with bacon — onto the long table in the dining hall. It smelled good and tasted even better, but the soldiers were more intrigued by the side dish of *sauerkraut*, finely sliced fermented cabbage. Naturally, the food was served with a mountain of black bread.

The elderly nuns sat on their own, keeping a respectable distance from the troops, but Abbess Gisela made a point of sitting next to Tomasso. Throughout the meal, she asked about Rome and the Vatican, and was enthralled by his answers; when she wasn't listening with wide-eyed fascination, she was laughing at his witty observations.

Cristina may have been sitting just opposite, but she felt strangely excluded from their conversation. It irked her, in part because she was impatient to get on with the business of interrogating the survivor. But there was something else … a sense of anxiety, like a pressure in her heart. She didn't like it, but she felt powerless to rationalise the feeling away. She caught Tomasso's eye at one point, but he just smiled at her, as if he was enjoying all the attention.

"So, what happened here?" Cristina asked the abbess, cutting across the conversation.

"Excuse me?"

"Why did the glory days of Walkenried end?"

The question came over more aggressively than Cristina had intended, but Abbess Gisela was adept at handling people. "'End' is a very emotive word," she replied. "I think of it more as a lull. A temporary lull. Fortunes come and go; it's a normal part of life."

"But yours seems to have gone." Cristina pointed to the ceiling where once beautiful frescoes were now cracked and peeling.

"Walkenried used to be the most affluent convent in the German states," the abbess said with pride. "We had estates across Europe, from the Rhineland to Pomerania. It wasn't just farming, we had mining and charcoal works, and a library that drew scholars from as far away as Paris. But the Black Death hit us hard. As the economy failed, our wealth collapsed. The sisters died or left, women found better prospects in the world beyond the convent walls. But Walkenried will rise again, I'm sure of it. It is what Great Orders do."

Cristina glanced at the six elderly nuns huddled at the far end of the table. "I'm not sure they would agree, Reverend Mother."

"Which is why they are not in charge." The abbess put her hand on Tomasso's arm. "And I am sure that when you tell the Holy Father how much we have helped your mission, he will look kindly on us. Is that not right, Deputy?"

So that was what this was all about — a charm offensive to save Walkenried through papal generosity, and Tomasso had swallowed the bait.

"We will be sure to mention you in our report, Reverend Mother," Tomasso said warmly.

"On condition the only witness we have doesn't die," Cristina added pointedly.

"Oh, he won't," the abbess responded. "I have made him my personal mission. And unlike you, I am a practising nurse."

"I really would like to question him now," Cristina pressed.

"At this hour?"

"Just in case the night proves too long for him. You never know."

Abbess Gisela looked hurt by the implication. She turned to Tomasso. "And you agree, Deputy?"

Caught between the two women, Tomasso gave a nervous laugh. "Well, if it's not too much trouble, there is no time like the present, is there?"

11: DEVILS

Like all sickrooms, this one exuded a sense of melancholy.

Gisela had put the injured man into one of the many empty cells in the abbey: it had scrubbed walls, a hard bed, a small table with a jug of wine, and a huge crucifix hanging on the wall, allowing Christ to gaze down on the patient. The man lay perfectly still, eyes closed, breathing heavily; the bandaged stumps where his hands should have been lay outside the sheets. But what struck Cristina most was how chilly the room was, as both window shutters were wide open.

"Doesn't he find it cold?" she whispered.

"Fresh air is the most important thing for good health," the abbess said enthusiastically. "An open window clears the room of all unhealthy miasmas. The worst thing anyone can do is sleep with the windows closed."

"Even in winter?"

"Especially in winter. That is when we are most vulnerable." The abbess scrutinised Cristina. "But you must know all about that? Isn't Rome the embodiment of open-air life?"

"It depends. In the height of summer, people often close their shutters to keep the stifling air out."

Gisela shuddered at the thought. "A stuffy room is an ungodly room."

It was clear the windows were remaining open, so Cristina buttoned her jacket tighter, pulled up a wooden stool and sat next to the bed. She looked at the man as his chest rose and sank, his body trying to come to terms with the traumatic injuries it had sustained. For a moment, Cristina wondered if this might be her before the year was out, as the disease ravaged her from the inside.

She shook the morbid thought from her mind and focused. "Has he spoken yet?"

"Not coherently. Just some ramblings about..." The abbess hesitated.

"About what?"

"Blasphemies. Things of darkness."

"Specifically?"

"He keeps talking about witchcraft. Devils and demons."

Cristina nodded. "That was what he told us when we found him." She touched the man's shoulder, and his eyelids fluttered open. "What is your name?"

"Is my mother safe?" he mumbled. "Can I see her?"

"Where is she? Where is home?"

The man gazed up at the ceiling as his mind travelled back to happier times. "Montelibretti."

"I know it," Cristina smiled. "It's in the Papal States. I've stopped there several times. There's a tavern..." She tried to remember the name. "Osteria de something."

"Osteria dell'Uva," the man whispered.

"Yes! That's it."

"Ah ... so many times we played outside the dell'Uva as children..." He mused to himself. "So many games ... until my mother called us in for supper."

"What did your mother call you?"

"Salvatore, when she was angry. But normally, Toto."

Now Cristina had a route to his memories, she could start building. "When was the last time you saw your mother?"

Salvatore struggled to focus his mind. "Christmas. Last Christmas. Before we set off."

"To come here, to the German states?"

Salvatore nodded.

"And has the mission gone well? Did you encounter any hostility?"

Salvatore frowned. "People need salvation. They are grateful for God's mercy. They welcomed us."

"That's good," Cristina soothed. "And you sold many Indulgences?"

"Many, many. We are retuning with so much gold … the Holy Father will be delighted … but the journey ahead…" His body tensed as he relived the passage into the forest. "They came at us so fast…"

"Who, Salvatore? Who came at you?"

He screwed his eyes shut. "Devils, from the darkness of the woods."

"So, these were men, dressed in black?"

"No! Devils! With horns on their heads and blood in their mouths!" He writhed on the bed.

"It's all right, Salvatore, you're safe now."

But he was back in the horror. "We screamed at them. Cursed them. But they were relentless … without mercy…"

"Yet they showed *you* mercy," Cristina said.

"Not mercy. They chose me to be their witness. They tied me to the side of the waggon. Arms stretched, like Christ on the cross. And I had to watch as they slaughtered the living…" Salvatore's body started to shake as he broke down.

The abbess stepped forward and lay her hand on Salvatore's forehead, trying to soothe his nerves. "It's all right. Hush now." She turned to Cristina. "We must let him rest."

"No. We must keep going."

"Look at him!" Gisela hissed.

"We need his testimony." Cristina poured a fresh beaker of wine and held it to his lips, helping him take a few sips. "Toto, how did you escape from the Demons? Did you fight them off?"

Salvatore drew a heavy breath. "You cannot fight a devil."

"Then how did you survive?"

"When they had finished killing, they cut me down. Not by cutting the ropes which held my arms … but by cutting off my hands." He lifted his arms from the bed so that he could see the savaged stumps. "And now I can never touch my mother's face again." Tears ran down the man's cheeks.

"Enough!" Abbess Gisela snapped. "That is enough. He must rest." She chased Cristina away from the bed and pulled a tincture bottle from her tunic pocket.

"What are you giving him?"

"Laudanum. To calm his nerves."

"But I need him to remember."

"Please! That is enough." Gisela pointed to the door, and Cristina withdrew from the cell.

There was a frosty tension between Cristina and the abbess as they walked away from the sick room; both women were accustomed to getting their own way, and compromise felt like failure.

"How much laudanum has he had?" Cristina finally asked as they approached the great hall.

"Exactly as much as he needs to keep him numbed, or the shock might kill him."

"But it is making his testimony unreliable."

"Why question him if you refuse to believe him?"

"Reverend Mother, there are no such things as devils in the forest. The trauma of the attack has flooded his mind with fear and confusion."

"You assume too much. And you don't know these German forests."

"We've been travelling through them all week."

The abbess stopped walking and turned to face Cristina. "This attack is a warning. If you are wise, you will turn back."

"Out of the question. We're pressing on to Magdeburg."

"A person should recognise when God is talking to them."

"With all due respect, if God had a message for me, he wouldn't send it by massacring innocent men."

"Perhaps He had to resort to desperate measures because you are not listening?"

"My mind and ears are always open."

"What about these?" The abbess took Cristina's hands and lay her fingers on the swelling. "Is this illness not a message?"

Cristina flinched and pulled her hands away.

"You see? He is talking to you, but you refuse to listen."

Abbess Gisela plucked a lantern from the wall and walked away into the gloom of the great hall.

12: TETZEL

The soldiers of Operation Danube were understandably reluctant to leave Walkenried Abbey and head back into the forest. Here they had good hospitality and the protection of high walls with sturdy oak gates; back on the road, who knew what horrors lay waiting in the deep shadows of the woods?

But Cristina and Tomasso were keen to reach Magdeburg as soon as possible, so the following morning the taskforce moved out. This time they used a different formation: the two scouts who rode ahead stayed in the trees on either side of the road, muskets ready to fire warning shots. It meant they were more likely to discover hostile forces preparing an ambush, but it made progress much slower.

Mercifully, there were no more violent encounters, and they rode into Magdeburg on the afternoon of the second day. They knew that Johann Tetzel and his team were based inside the castle, which sat on the left bank of the River Elbe, in the shadow of a magnificent cathedral with soaring twin towers dominating its western face. But what struck Cristina most forcibly was the extent of the construction work being undertaken. The old city wall was being expanded with extra sections, and an entirely new secondary wall was being created. Vast defensive ditches were being dug around the city, and heavy new gates and gun towers were almost complete.

"I assume it's no coincidence that Tetzel makes his base in a city that is very security conscious," Cristina said as she watched a new cannon being hoisted into the battlements.

"A lot of cities are doing this now," Tomasso explained. "Defences that have held strong for five hundred years are no match for gunpowder. Every year more powerful weapons are being developed."

"Surely there's a limit to how large weapons can become before they blow themselves up?"

Tomasso shook his head. "It's not that simple. They're experimenting with different blends of powder, and different metals for the weapons. Apparently, there's a gunsmith in Vienna who's discovered that carving a groove inside a gun barrel adds spin to the musket ball. Makes it go further and fly truer."

Cristina nodded. "I've read something about that; they call it rifling. Isn't it amazing how there is always money for research that discovers better ways of killing people?"

Not content with the city's fortifications, the team of Indulgence sellers had created their own secure area within the fortress. To get inside, each member of the taskforce had to have his papers checked, and all their weapons had to be put into a special cage in the armoury.

"Tetzel certainly knows he's not the most popular man in the German states," Cristina whispered to Tomasso as their Vatican warrants were being verified.

Yet after all this, Tetzel wasn't even there. "When will he be back?" Cristina asked one of the guards.

"This evening. He's not gone far. He's conducting a Benediction Ceremony in the town hall."

"What's he blessing?"

"No, no. That's what he calls it when he sells Indulgences."

"Sounds very spiritual."

"Which is precisely the point."

Magdeburg Town Hall was half a mile north of the castle, and Cristina decided to walk the distance; it made a pleasant change from sitting in a saddle, and it gave her the chance to get a feel for the city. The original town hall had burned down, but been rebuilt even more splendidly, and it now dominated the cobbled market square. She asked the whereabouts of Tetzel and was told that he had hired the entire basement, which was the only part of the original thirteenth-century building to survive the fire.

If Cristina had expected to find a pious and solemn ceremony, what she discovered was anything but. Johann Tetzel, Dominican friar and Grand Commissioner for Indulgences, stood on a raised platform at one end of the room, with an assistant on either side of him. Seated on benches before him, mesmerised by his every word, were two dozen affluent burghers of the city, accompanied by their fur-clad wives.

"Who here would be so foolish as to risk his immortal soul for the sake of a few coins?" Tetzel thundered. "Though God is great and his bounty merciful, nothing can be taken for granted. St Augustine reminds us of the moment when Christ considers the two criminals being crucified alongside him." Tetzel raised his arms high as if channelling theological wisdom. "*Do not despair; one of the thieves was saved. Do not presume; one of the thieves was damned.* Our lives hang in that delicate balance. Every moment teetering between damnation and salvation. Which is why what is happening in this room today is so important. The Holy Father is reaching out to offer God's forgiveness to each and every one of you." Tetzel pointed directly at the audience, letting his gaze wander across the faces and fine silks ranged before him. "The Holy Father, heir to St Peter who was at Christ's side as he was nailed to the cross, is giving each of you a chance to wash your sins clean; a chance to avoid the terrors of Purgatory, and to be embraced by the sweet caress of Heaven. And this, my friends, is not just for sins you have already committed, but for sins you may *yet* commit in the future. Think on that!" He pounded his fist into the air. "Think. On. That! The glory of God knows no greater generosity than to forgive *in advance*."

There was a ripple of expectation as the audience considered the lust and greed lurking in their own hearts. Would forgiveness in advance mean they could carry out their sinful plans with no fear of the consequences?

Tetzel picked up a cloth and dabbed the sweat from his face, for although he could have been no more than fifty, he preached with such passion it was physically gruelling. Cristina was intrigued by a small tuft of hair which survived as an island on Tetzel's bald head — why didn't he just shave it off and be done with it?

"And that is not all," Tetzel resumed. "There is so much more." He waited to let the expectation build. "The Indulgences that are in my gift have power which reaches *beyond* the living. Oh yes, my friends, beyond this mortal coil." For a moment his gaze drifted off into the distance, as if he were contemplating the afterlife. Then his eyes turned back to his audience once more. "Do you have a loved one who has already passed over? Is one of your parents languishing in Purgatory at this very moment? Have you endured the agony of an infant dying before they were baptised? Fear not. Fret not. For today you can set their souls free by purchasing an Indulgence. What you do right here in this room can transport their souls into everlasting peace. Friends, citizens, penitents, if you remember just one thing today, let it be this: *as soon as the gold in the casket rings, the rescued soul to Heaven springs*."

A wave of grateful applause broke across the room, and Tetzel bowed like a showman. "All this lies just a few short steps away." He pointed to a red velvet curtain at the side of the room. "The solemnity of the Benediction, like the solemnity of confession, is a moment of spirituality between priest and supplicant. I will withdraw to become the servant to your souls." Tetzel left his podium and disappeared behind the curtain with a flourish. Immediately, his assistants formed a protective phalanx to restrict access, which triggered a rush of burghers to get to the front of the queue.

Cristina studied the upstanding citizens of Magdeburg as they lined up to receive salvation, chattering like excited children waiting for sweets. These people in their fine clothing and glittering jewellery believed that they could buy anything, and because it had worked for them in this life, they assumed it would work in the hereafter. And Tetzel had read them perfectly — with dagger-sharp rhetoric he had cut open their purses.

Cristina waited patiently until the last man — beaming the smug smile of redemption — emerged. As he hurried away, Cristina pulled the curtain aside and entered the small anteroom.

Tetzel sat behind a desk. In front of him was a pile of Indulgence certificates, some sticks of sealing wax, and an official Vatican stamp. On his left sat a clerk, the pardoner, who recorded every indulgence and penitent in a huge ledger. Under the desk was a wooden trunk reinforced with metal straps.

"I will need your name, and the nature of the Indulgence you desire," Tetzel said. "Past or present; living or dead. Each has its own price." He pointed to the trunk. "The money goes straight into the strongbox."

"Actually, I have a question," Cristina said.

"Proceed."

"I have come directly from the Holy Father, Pope Leo."

For the first time, Tetzel looked up. There was anxiety in his eyes. "Ah. You must be Operation Danube. Cardinal Riario's letter arrived two days ago."

"Do you really think this is how the will of God should be presented to people? Like a circus act?"

Tetzel stared at her coolly. "The Pope is delighted with the work we are doing here. He has written to me personally to offer his congratulations."

"Is that so?"

"What is your business here?"

"Another question." Cristina reached into her satchel and pulled out some of the pages she had rescued from the trees at the site of the ambush — they were exactly like the pages in the pardoner's ledger. "What happens to the redeemed souls if the gold never actually reaches the Holy Father?" She put the pages on the desk.

Tetzel's eyes ran down the list of names. "Another theft?"

"Another massacre," Cristina replied.

Tetzel's head sank into his hands. "May God help us all."

13: LEGENDS

Cristina watched Tetzel's assistants haul the trunk onto a carriage. They secured it with chains and padlocks, then loaded the velvet curtain, the desk, and the podium. The theatre of the Benediction Ceremonies was clearly a well-oiled and highly mobile operation.

A clerk from the town hall hurried over with a bill for the hire of the basement, which Tetzel settled immediately from his own purse, then he opened the carriage door for Cristina. "Please."

"Actually, I think I'll walk," Cristina replied.

"That is not a good idea."

"It's not far to the castle, and I need the fresh air."

"I'm afraid I must insist," Tetzel replied firmly.

"Why does it matter so much?"

"You have seen for yourself, we do not take matters of security lightly," Tetzel warned. "All these measures have been put in place to keep us alive so that we may continue to do God's work. But we must be on our guard around the clock. There have now been ten appalling raids in the forest; the perpetrators could feel emboldened to attack us anywhere." He cast a suspicious glance at the narrow streets leading away from the marketplace. Reluctantly, Cristina climbed into the carriage.

Although the distance was short, the journey back to the castle was slow and uncomfortable, for the roads were congested with market traders packing up for the day.

Cristina studied Tetzel as he took a comb from his tunic pocket and groomed the bushy sides of his tonsure. "Were the mistakes deliberate?" she asked.

"Mistakes?"

"In your homily. St Peter was not present at the Crucifixion. After he denied Christ three times, he fled. John was the only apostle who actually witnessed the execution."

Tetzel shrugged. "I need to connect Pope Leo directly to Christ, and the best way to do that is through St Peter. It makes it more real for ordinary people. These Germans are a solid race. They like solid things."

"I see." Cristina nodded. "There is also the matter of selling Indulgences for the remission of the dead. That is not Church doctrine."

"You're getting bogged down in the details," Tetzel replied irritably. "The principle is sound: forgiveness in exchange for penance. What greater proof of a penitent heart could there be than giving up your hard-earned gold to build the greatest church in Christendom?"

"Yet it's important not to sell a lie."

Tetzel was starting to get irked. "In any case, theology is not in the remit of Operation Danube. I suggest that you focus on catching the bandits, while I'll focus on selling Indulgences. Agreed?"

"Very well."

Tetzel listened pensively as Cristina briefed him about the most recent attack, as well as Salvatore's feverish testimony.

"Is there any truth in what he says?" Tetzel asked finally. "Could this be the work of demons?"

"Absolutely not."

"You sound very sure, but these German forests are primeval."

"The attacks are the work of humans, not the Devil," Cristina insisted. "Spirits would not ride off with the gold in three directions and choose routes to outwit trackers; they would just vanish into thin air. Demons wouldn't need to hack their victims to death; they would kill with a single touch."

"Yet bloodshed instils fear, which is the point."

"If I was a demon who wanted to terrify people, I would attack in the most crowded place, in the full light of day, to show the world that I was unassailable."

"Then what did Salvatore see? Was he just hallucinating?"

Cristina hesitated. "Untangling truth from delusion is not always easy. Perhaps … perhaps we are searching for bandits who dress their crimes in the theatre of the supernatural."

"To what end?"

"Showmanship," Cristina replied pointedly.

"Well, whatever they are, the pressing question is how are you going to stop them?"

"Actually, I think another question needs to be answered first," Cristina countered. "Why won't the German authorities take action against the bandits? Why has the Holy Father been forced to send his own troops to uphold the law in the German states?"

"The authorities have tried."

"Obviously not hard enough."

"You will not find it such an easy task," Tetzel warned. "The perpetrators have mastered the element of surprise. They materialise from the forest, they strike, they vanish. There is no pattern to their attacks. They cannot even be pinned down to one province, which makes people feel as if no road in the German states is safe."

"Someone must know something," Cristina insisted. "Ten attacks by well-armed gangs. Who is equipping them? Who is hiding them? Where do they stable their horses? Where do they get their intelligence about the shipments? Who has become suddenly rich?"

Tetzel looked out of the window at the gloomy streets of Magdeburg.

"You seem uneasy," Cristina said.

"I did not want to talk about this for fear of incurring the Vatican's wrath, but..." He trailed off.

"Johann, withholding information could jeopardise the entire mission."

Tetzel fiddled nervously with the tuft of hair above his forehead. "How is your German?"

"Passable."

"*Gerechtigkeit für Deutschland.* You know what it means?"

"Make Germany fair?"

Tetzel nodded. "And that is the problem. A legend is growing around these attacks. Whether it is the work of men or spirits, ordinary people believe that whoever is committing the atrocities is on their side."

"How on earth does that make any sense?" Cristina's brow furrowed. "It is ordinary people who are being slaughtered."

"No, it is Italian mercenaries who are being killed, while they are escorting money back to Rome to enrich the Vatican at the expense of the German people."

"Indulgences are not a tax. They are bought freely. People can choose."

"You saw my customers," Tetzel patted one of the ledgers on the seat next to him. "They are not the poor. Peasants need every coin they can get simply to put bread on the table. It is the merchant classes who pay to save their souls; they have more money and more guilt."

"But the poor are not benefitting from the bandit raids —"

"On the contrary," Tetzel interrupted. "The taverns are full of strange stories. Almshouses receiving large, anonymous bequests. Labourers waking to find a purse of gold has been left on their kitchen table in the night. Nameless well-wishers sending doctors to cure sick children. Larders being filled while peasants are working in the fields."

"This really happens? You have seen it with your own eyes?"

"Not as such. But we have all heard the stories."

"So, the bandits steal from the affluent and give to the poor?"

"Apparently. And meanwhile, the souls of the rich will rot in Hell. From the point of view of the peasant, it's a perfect crime."

"Except the bandits aren't stealing from the rich," Cristina corrected. "They're stealing from the Church."

Tetzel shrugged. "Is that so different? They have a very earthy phrase for it here: *den Sumpf trockenlegen.*"

Cristina rummaged through the German vocabulary in her mind. "Drain the swamp?"

"Most apt for a nation of forest dwellers."

The carriage lurched to a halt, nearly throwing Tetzel and Cristina from their seats. She looked out of the window and saw that they had arrived at the security checks by the main castle gates.

"I hope you remembered to bring your identity papers," Tetzel warned, reaching into his own pocket and pulling out some official documents. "Or it will be an uncomfortable night sleeping on the streets."

"This is a very bad idea," Tomasso grumbled.

"The reconnaissance? Or the clothes?" Cristina quipped.

"Both. I feel like a dry goods merchant." Tomasso faced the large mirror in his room in the castle barracks. Gone was the striking uniform of a commander in the Apostolic Guard, replaced by a coarse linen shirt, a faded doublet and hose, and a battered leather jerkin.

"That is precisely the point. Blending in." Cristina adjusted the jerkin so that it sat properly on Tomasso's shoulders, then looked him up and down. "Definitely a Konrad. Or an Ehrhart."

"With a grumpy wife … and six children."

"And a mother-in-law who has never liked you."

Tomasso allowed himself a smile, but it didn't last long. "Tetzel spent all that time explaining the security protocols, and now you want to just toss them aside?"

"I need to know what the feeling on the street is, and if we go out in uniform or with guards, people will simply clam up."

"You seriously think the bandits are hiding in Magdeburg?"

"No. But if Tetzel is right, they may well have sympathisers in the city. And that could give us a lead." She took a leather cap from the wardrobe and placed it on Tomasso's head. "You know, in all these years, I've barely seen you out of uniform. Not too shabby."

"Really?" Tomasso turned back to the mirror, wondering if Cristina was teasing him. "But I hate not having my weapons."

"On that we agree." Cristina took Tomasso's sword and dagger from the hook on the door and handed them to him. "The baggy jerkin may look drab, but it will hide these."

Magdeburg had not yet woken up. The shops were shuttered and the street stalls empty, save for a few stray cats which glared at them with thinly disguised contempt.

"Perhaps we should have got something to eat before we left," Tomasso said wistfully.

"I didn't think it would be this quiet." Cristina was feeling light-headed from lack of food. "Maybe there'll be something at the livestock market."

This was the reason they had started out so early, to catch the animal auction in full swing, because farmers were notorious for being permanently unhappy and not shy about expressing it.

A terrified squeal cut through the still air and echoed off the buildings. Cristina and Tomasso froze.

"What's going on?" she whispered.

A moment later another squeal rang out, followed by the sound of trotters clattering on the cobblestones. They looked up to see an enormous pig with a spotted snout running towards them down the centre of the street.

"*Halt!*" a voice shouted. "Stop him!" A wiry young man burst out of an alley in pursuit of the runaway pig. "Stop him!"

Tomasso looked at the pig hurtling towards him and decided to step back rather than intervene.

"*Nein!*" the wiry man yelled. "*Schwein!*" He gave Tomasso a furious glare as he thundered past in pursuit of the rogue animal.

Cristina watched them disappear around a corner, then pointed in the direction from which they'd come. "I assume the livestock auction is that way."

The market square had been transformed. All the stalls had been cleared away, replaced by a network of temporary pens that were heaving with restless animals. Hundreds of men were milling around, exchanging gossip, inspecting animals and haggling with each other. The four taverns on the square were not only open, but they were also packed with farmhands who were consuming vast quantities of beer and sausages. There was the rattle of gaming dice in leather beakers, jeers and groans as winning hands of cards were revealed, and the sound of buskers playing folk songs.

Cristina and Tomasso bought two piping hot *bratwursts* sandwiched between chunks of bread and headed into the throng.

At the epicentre of all the activity, standing on a raised platform in the middle of the square, was the auctioneer. He was speaking German, but at such a pace, and using such strange farming patois, that Cristina couldn't understand a word. He waved his arms, pointed to the animals, nodded at farmers as they made bids, scowled, smiled, raised his voice in excitement, then finally brought the hammer down. As each animal was led away, another immediately entered the arena, and the whole performance started again.

Cristina was fascinated to see how intensely the buyers and sellers focused on every gesture and twitch of the auctioneer; each time the hammer struck to conclude a sale, there would either be smiles of jubilation or scowls of disappointment.

Tomasso yawned widely.

"You look like you should still be in bed."

Cristina and Tomasso spun round and were confronted by a man with a ruddy face, bushy grey eyebrows and unruly hair pointing in all directions.

"We're just trying to work out what he's saying." Cristina pointed to the auctioneer.

"Good luck with that. Took me ten years."

"Are you buying or selling?" Tomasso asked.

"Sold. Twelve head of Black Pied cattle."

"Get a good price?"

The man gave a smug grin. "Always do."

"So why aren't you in the tavern celebrating like all the others?" Cristina asked.

The man shuddered. "Don't do that anymore. Six years ago, I sold my entire flock of sheep. Then I went to Fritz's." He pointed to one of the taverns on the square. "Had a drink, got into a game of dice … next thing I know, the landlord's kicking me awake to lock up for the night. Purse was empty. I'd even managed to gamble away my boots. When I finally got home, my wife didn't speak to me for two months."

"What's your name?" Cristina asked.

"Nikolaus."

"Cristina and Tomasso." She reached into her purse and pulled out a few coins. "Perhaps you would show us round the auction? Tell us how it all works?"

Nikolaus eyed them warily. "Perhaps. But you'll have to speak quietly."

Cristina was confused. "Everyone else is shouting."

"But everyone else isn't a foreigner. People round here only like what they know."

"So why are you talking to us?"

"My wife is Polish, so I can't really criticise foreigners."

"Cannot? Or dare not?"

"What difference does it make?" Nikolaus took the coins and led them to a pen in the far corner of the square, where a dozen farmers were standing round a huge bull, arguing fiercely.

Cristina tried to follow the discussion, but the men were talking too quickly and with strong accents. "What are they arguing about? Money?"

"Purity of the breed," Nikolaus replied. "What are the marks of a true German bull."

Cristina eyed the massive animal, hoping that the rails of the holding pen were strong enough to contain the beast. "He looks pretty sturdy to me."

Nikolaus pointed to a man with a ginger beard. "He thinks the hump behind his head is too big. But that one —" he pointed to a younger man with pockmarked skin — "thinks it's the perfect size, indicating ideal muscling."

"What about him?" Cristina indicated an elderly man who was crouched down at the back of the bull, gently cupping its scrotum.

"Large testicles and a tight sheath are signs of good fertility. That's what really matters in a bull."

Cristina watched anxiously as the man weighed the bull's testes in his hand. "Is that really wise?" she whispered.

"How else are you going to find out?"

The old man withdrew his hand, stood up, then gave his judgement with a disapproving scowl and a gabble of farming patois.

"He says the German purity of this bull has been corrupted," Nikolaus explained. "He thinks it's been crossbred with Lakenvelder from the Low Countries."

"Who's right?" Tomasso asked.

"Depends on who you want to get into a fight with."

"I thought crossbreeding was a good thing," Cristina interjected. "Introducing new strains keeps a herd healthy?"

Nikolaus gave a sharp intake of breath. "You don't want to go saying that round here. You'll get into a fight with everyone."

They moved on from the arguing farmers and ended up at a side auction for pigs. "I recognise that one," Tomasso said, pointing to the pig that was currently under the hammer. "Looks like his bid for freedom failed after all."

Cristina recognised the spotted snout and felt a pang of remorse. "You could always put in a bid, Tomasso. He'd make a nice pet."

"You'll never outbid that butcher." Nikolaus pointed to a muscular man in an apron who was leading the bidding. "Biggest butcher in Magdeburg. He knows what he's doing when it comes to choosing animals."

"*Zum ersten, zum zweiten, zum dritten…*" the auctioneer cried. "*Und verkauft!*" He banged his hammer, and the butcher beamed with joy.

"You could be eating that pig before the week is out," Nikolaus commented. "If you stay in town that long."

Cristina looked at Nikolaus; he seemed more thoughtful than many of the farmers here, so perhaps she could trust him. "That all depends on whether there are any more bandit raids."

"I thought as much." Nikolaus spat into the dirt. "Why else would you come up here except to chase Vatican gold?"

"We're not chasing money. We're trying to prevent any more murderous attacks," Cristina replied.

"Is that what they've been telling you? Blood and guts in the woods?"

"It's what I've seen with my own eyes."

"Well, I haven't seen anything like that, and I've lived here all my life."

Cristina blinked, unsure how to counter such a stark denial of the truth. "So what do *you* think is going on?"

"A load of merchants are trying to buy their way to salvation. Some German patriots have said enough is enough and are taking the money back. Giving it to the people from whom it was stolen. *Gerechtigkeit für Deutschland!*"

"And that justifies butchering soldiers?"

Nikolaus shook his head. "There have been no murders. That's just lies put about by the authorities."

A terrible squeal rang out as the pig was led away by the butcher — it was as if the animal suddenly realised that this was to be his last day on earth.

"Do you actually know of any school or hospital that has been gifted by the bandits?" Cristina pressed.

"Course not," Nikolaus scoffed. "They can't actually say that, can they? Anything built with stolen money would be illegal."

"Very convenient. The nature of the lie prevents it from being called out as a lie."

"Look, we all know what's going on. Facts are facts."

"Repeating each other's rumours is what's going on. It has nothing to do with the facts."

Nikolaus spat on the ground at Cristina's feet. "I've been very patient. But I think it's time you were on your way."

A couple of the farmhands standing nearby sensed the rising tension and moved either side of Nikolaus to show their solidarity.

"It's all right. Everything's good." Tomasso rummaged in his pocket, pulled out some more coins and pressed them into Nikolaus' hand. "This is for your time."

Nikolaus looked at the coins. "Makes a change for money to come *out* of Rome."

14: LUTHER

"Just keep walking." Tomasso took Cristina's arm as they turned away from the simmering resentment of the farmworkers.

"Ordinary people defending criminals and protecting murderers?" She wrestled herself free. "What is wrong with them?"

"When people are hurting, they lash out."

"What exactly are they hurting about? They're prosperous farmers with money in their pockets and food in their bellies."

"There's always something to resent."

As they left the market by the western gate, they saw a group of people crowding into *Zum Goldenen Schwan* tavern.

"I wonder what's going on in there?" Cristina veered towards the tavern, but Tomasso swerved in front of her.

"Looks like a locals-only event to me."

"Which is exactly where we need to be." Cristina called out to a group of university students who were hurrying towards the tavern in their long blue coats and yellow stockings. "What's happening in the Swan?"

"Luther's preaching!" one of them replied without breaking his stride. "He's going to stick it to the Pope!"

His fellow students laughed and started chanting, "*Deutschland den Deutschen*!"

"Better be quick before he gets arrested!" the first student said with a laugh as they joined the throng pushing into the tavern.

Cristina turned to Tomasso. "We need to see this."

"Is there any point trying to dissuade you?"

"As long as we keep quiet, we'll be safe."

"But when were you ever able to say nothing?"

For a moment, Cristina looked offended.

"I meant that as a compliment," Tomasso added. "Even though it may get us killed."

"Don't worry, I'll be the picture of restraint." And she led them into the Golden Swan.

The room was already crowded, and still more people were arriving. A small circle had been cleared around a raised dais, and four minders were ushering women and students to the front, while the men were told to stand further back. The elderly and infirm were told to listen from the beer garden at the side of the tavern. When there was no more standing room, the minders helped people climb onto tables and perch themselves on the rafters, which added to the sense of anticipation. Cristina wanted to get as close to the front as possible, but Tomasso managed to keep them within striking distance of the door, just in case they needed to make a swift exit.

There was a commotion in the crowd as two drummers and a piper pushed their way into the tavern. When they reached the dais they struck up a rousing marching rhythm, which soon had everyone clapping and stamping their feet. As the noise built to a crescendo, the crowd parted, and Martin Luther strode into the middle of the space.

There was a huge cheer as he took to the dais and waited for the applause to die down.

Silence filled the tavern. All eyes focused on Luther.

Cristina studied his face — he was in his mid-thirties, with a thick neck, penetrating eyes, and a mop of tightly curled hair. In many ways, he reminded her of the bull they'd just seen at the auction. Luther wore a monk's habit, with the gown of an academic draped over the top, and despite his awkward appearance, he seemed at ease surrounded by the crowd.

When he finally spoke, his voice was rich with authority. "I give you this thought: if there is a Hell, then Rome is built upon it!"

A roar of approval went up from the crowd.

"What madness has descended on the world," Luther continued, "when a Pope demands that honest German people must pay to build a basilica that celebrates his own vanity?"

"Shame! Shame!" came cries around the tavern.

"Why does this Pope not build St Peter's with his own money? He is a Medici prince, after all."

Mocking laughter erupted.

Cristina leaned toward Tomasso. "I thought Tetzel was good at rhetoric, but he is nothing compared to this man!"

"I think he's a troublemaker."

But Cristina was fascinated by Luther's technique. "He's studied Cicero. He's using all the tricks of rhetoric: anaphora, repeated phrases; pathos and logos — emotion and reason. It's a potent mix."

"Friends, shall we talk about the House of Medici?" Luther resumed, quietening the crowd with the promise of juicy revelations. "They are bankers! Dealers in gold and silver. They borrow and lend. They count and hoard. They squeeze every last ducat from every situation."

A low hiss rippled round the room.

"But what did Jesus say about the moneylenders?" Luther opened his arms to invite suggestions. "Did he admire them?"

"No!" answered the crowd.

"Did he politely doff his cap to them?"

"No!"

"*And Jesus entered into the temple of God, and cast out all those who sold and bought in the temple, and overthrew the tables of the moneychangers.*"

There were cheers from the crowd.

"And he said unto them, my house shall be called —" Luther beckoned to the crowd.

"The house of prayer!" they chanted.

"But ye make it —"

"A den of thieves!" came the response.

"I see you paid attention in Sunday school." Luther smiled, and the room broke into applause. He waited for them to fall silent, then resumed in a quiet voice. "What greater theft is there than these Vatican Indulgences? What a shameless trick they are. When you are facing the divine judgement, God will not be looking at the bits of paper you clutch in your hands. He will not be checking the Vatican ledgers to see how many blocks of marble you have bought for Pope Leo's folly. No, my friends. God will only look into your heart, and he will see whether your faith is true and your love for Him pure. Faith alone can save us, and faith lies within each and every one of us. You do not need gold to buy faith. You only need to commit yourself to God. That is what He desires of us, and only that. And how do I know this? Because I have studied the only book that matters."

Luther held out his hand and one of the minders handed him a huge Bible. He held it up as if it was one of the stone tablets Moses brought down from Mount Sinai. "Amen!"

"Amen! Amen! Amen!" the crowd responded.

"This book and this book alone has the power to renew the spirituality of the Church!"

Cristina glanced around the room — everyone was nodding their approval; the women gazed at Luther with adoring eyes, the students seemed inspired. In truth, Cristina couldn't disagree with Luther's sentiments — she knew all too well how often the politics of the Vatican worked against the spiritual mission of the Church.

"I know the truth revealed in the Bible because I have studied Latin and Greek. But you, who only have the German tongue, you are locked out of its wisdom. I ask you, is that fair? Is it just? Or is it an attempt by Rome to control us, to keep us ignorant so that we can be manipulated like the sheep in the field? Well I, Martin Luther, declare before you today — *enough*!" He handed the Bible back to the minder, who gave him a leather document folder in return.

"I have a confession to make," Luther said with an impish smile. "I have defied the authorities." He opened the folder and took out some sheets of paper covered in handwriting. "I am translating the Bible into German!"

An enormous cheer went up as Luther waved the papers in the air. "A solid, honest language, for solid, honest people! See for yourselves..." He started handing out sheets of his translation to the audience. "*Und Gott sprach: Es werde Licht! Und es ward Licht!*"

Eagerly the people passed pages from hand to hand, marvelling at the first sight of God's words in their own language.

"Now there is no separation between you and I," Luther continued. "Priest and parishioner are as one. No longer do you need me to intercede on your behalf. Through these pages you can forge your own relationship with God."

Some of the pages came to Cristina. As she glanced at them, she recognised key passages. "These are good translations," she said to Tomasso. "He's quite a linguist."

But Tomasso was far more concerned about the volatility of the crowd; it felt as if they were spoiling for trouble.

"Some of you may be frightened," Luther resumed. "I understand that. Some of you may fear the wrath of the priests. But fear not. No-one should ever be afraid to hold the word of God in his hands. The Church may condemn us as rebellious troublemakers —" he brandished some pages in the air — "but we are following the word of God. And the word of God is the word of love!"

The crowd burst into applause and Luther basked in their adulation.

"All this talk about love," muttered Cristina as she handed Tomasso the pages. "But we haven't seen much of it since we've been here."

"Cristina, you promised you would keep quiet," the deputy warned.

"You think his inflammatory words and the murderous attacks are unrelated?"

"I think we should get out of here."

"No! I want answers."

Tomasso's fingers tightened around his sword grip as Cristina raised her hand. Luther saw she was eager to say something and pointed a fleshy finger at her. "Speak, sister! Tell us what is in your heart."

"You speak of love, but was it love that butchered soldiers in the forest just sixty miles from here?"

There was a moment of shock in the crowd, then the hecklers turned on her.

"Not true!"

"It never happened!"

"I saw it with my own eyes!" Cristina declared.

"False news! False news! False news!" The chant of the crowd united everyone against her.

Instinctively, Tomasso checked the exits, but they were now surrounded by the agitated mob.

"Be calm, brothers and sisters!" Luther commanded. "Do not give the Church authorities the satisfaction of your anger."

As the chant died down, Luther nodded to the minders, who converged on Cristina and Tomasso.

"Don't touch us!" Tomasso warned, drawing his sword.

"Peace, brother! Peace!" Luther said.

The minders grabbed them both and started bundling them towards a door at the back of the room.

"Take your hands off us!"

Tomasso tried to brandish his sword, but one of the minders wrestled his arm behind his back.

"This is for your own safety!" Luther bellowed.

Moments later Cristina and Tomasso were bundled through the door and found themselves in a storeroom lined with shelves that sagged under the weight of plates and cutlery.

"We're leaving now! Let us go!" Tomasso glared at their captors.

"*You* can go," one of the minders replied. "She stays."

"No! We're leaving together."

"Luther wants to see her," the minder replied with an undertone of menace. "Understood?"

"It's all right, Tomasso," Cristina tried to ease the tension. "You go — I'll meet you later."

"I'm not leaving you, Cristina."

"Luther's a priest. A man of God. What exactly do you think is going to happen?"

Before Tomasso had a chance to reply, the minders bundled him out of the tavern.

15: LIGHTNING

Cristina waited in the storeroom for almost an hour. Guarded by two minders, all she could do was listen to the muffled sounds of Luther preaching, and the fevered reactions of his audience.

She heard them pray in earnest, and taunt with mocking chants. She heard them laugh at Luther's satirical observations, then listen in rapt silence as he painted a picture of possibilities. She heard the thunderous power build in his voice as he imagined a world where the will of God was the only force that mattered. Finally, the crowd gave Luther a long, adoring ovation, then tumbled out onto the streets of Magdeburg to spread the word.

A few moments later, the storeroom door opened, and Luther entered.

A sheen of sweat covered his face and his breathing was heavy. Cristina thought he looked less like a priest and more like a prizefighter after a bareknuckle brawl.

One of the minders placed a bowl of warm water on the table, and Luther plunged his face into it, using his hands to rub the water through his hair. When he stood up, the minder handed him a towel, while the other hung a clean smock across the back of a chair, and then helped Luther unbutton the sweat-drenched shirt he was wearing.

Cristina had seen many priests at work, but none had ever performed like this. The amount of energy Luther put into preaching was extraordinary, as if he had channelled the Holy Spirit through his own body and given himself up entirely to the drama of the Passion. It was a far cry from the cautious and calculating sermons she so often heard in Rome, where every word was a move in a game of church chess.

She waited as Luther went through his post-performance rituals, seemingly oblivious to her presence. When he finally settled, Cristina spoke to him in German, so as not to appear at a disadvantage. "And there was I thinking that we Mediterraneans were passionate people."

Luther gave a small chuckle and replied in fluent Italian. "You are just more flamboyant. Your passion comes from waving your arms. Ours comes from here." He laid a hand on his chest.

"You certainly have a gift for languages." Cristina was genuinely impressed by his Italian.

"Your language was the most useful thing I acquired from my time in the peninsula."

"What about all the brilliant art?"

"Distractions from the truth." Luther beckoned to one of his minders, who placed the large Bible in his hands. "Anything that takes people's eyes away from the words in this book is wrong."

Cristina realised she was in the presence of a radical thinker: where she saw art and culture, Luther saw evil and corruption. "What about art that brings the Bible to life for ordinary people? Paintings which show Christ's ministry surely bring us closer to God?"

Luther shook his head. "The reason ordinary people feel cut off from the Bible is because they are only allowed to hear it in Latin or Greek. Hence…" He pointed to the far side of the storeroom where one of the minders was carefully reassembling the pages of handwritten translation.

"But the truth is," Luther continued, "Rome does not want ordinary people to read the Bible, because they will ask questions, and the Pope fears that will undermine the authority of the priesthood."

"I agree with you that knowledge should be freely available and widely distributed," Cristina said. "But the way you are going about it, well, you are starting a fight that you cannot win."

"I did not start it," Luther insisted. "By stifling criticism and debate, the Pope has forced disagreement onto a more radical path. I am what happens when you try to silence people. Power wants to speak freely but refuses to listen. Power demands obedience through a tyranny of silence."

"Once again, I agree. You and I are not enemies, Luther, even though I do come from Rome. When I die, if I am refused entry to Heaven because of my quarrelsome nature, I will ask God: 'Why did you give me an inquiring mind if you didn't want me to ask questions?'"

"My point exactly," Luther replied. "But I don't want to wait until I'm dead to have that discussion."

Cristina scrutinised Luther, trying to work out how far their common ground extended.

"Come to one of my services," Luther suggested. "Conducted in German, not Latin. Minimal ceremony and more time spent studying the Bible."

"To be honest, right now, I have more pressing concerns."

"Ah, that gold." Luther gave a knowing smile. "Judging from your question, I assume you have been sent from Rome with a troop of soldiers to secure Pope Leo's extortion racket?"

"I wouldn't put it in quite those terms, but yes."

"You are trying to fight something that is far greater than anyone can imagine." Luther stood up and walked to the door that led to the tavern. The minders who had looked so intimidating as bodyguards were now meekly straightening all the tables and chairs.

"Murder and theft?" Cristina pressed. "Surely it is your duty as a priest to help stop these appalling crimes."

"But they are not just crimes. They are crimes which halt the flow of gold from honest, hardworking Germans to a decadent pope in Rome who wants to finance more lavish parties."

"The Indulgences are to finance the building of St Peter's."

Luther scoffed. "Is it not true that when Agostino Chigi, the man who created those Indulgences, last threw a banquet in his palazzo on the Tiber, he instructed his guests to throw their gold plates into the river to spare his servants the work of cleaning up?"

"Chigi is not the pope. Neither is he St Peter's Basilica."

"But he is part of the machine. That makes him part of the problem. And his behaviour will not be financed by the German people any longer."

"And yet that is not the full story. During the day, before his guests arrived, Chigi had his servants spread nets across the bottom of the river. The next morning, they hauled in the nets and retrieved the gold plates. It was all theatre. In poor taste, admittedly. But it was not corruption."

"That Chigi thought it was amusing to display such decadence is sin enough." Luther reached into his pocket, pulled out a few coins and gave them to the tavern owner who was checking that everything had been put back in order. They exchanged some warm words, then Luther patted him on the shoulder and returned to the storeroom to confront Cristina. "That is why your mission will fail, because Rome offends ordinary people."

"How can you be so certain?"

"These bandit raids are part of something much larger. There is a powerful groundswell, hungry for change. You cannot feel it because you are a creature of the mind. This is something of the guts."

Cristina hesitated. "You have a talent for manipulating the mob, Luther. You can rouse the rabble. But cheap tricks to whip up a crowd … that is not a groundswell. It is the stuff of showmen."

Luther loomed towards Cristina until their faces were just inches apart. "Can you not see? God is in the excitement of that crowd. He moves among us through the emotions of the people. Their tears and laughter are His. Their joy and anger are divine!"

"You are disingenuous. I've read Cicero. I know the triggers."

Luther clasped her head in his strong fingers. "Stop using this! You cannot *think* your way to God. You must use this —" he placed his hand over her heart — "you need to surrender to find Him."

Cristina backed away.

"I apologise," Luther said quietly. "I didn't mean to… You clearly have a fine intellect. But you are following the wrong master."

"And you are the right one?" Cristina challenged.

"Twelve years ago, I was a law student. On the 2nd of July I had spent a few days at home with my parents and was returning to the University of Erfurt when a violent storm erupted. The wind was lashing rain into my face. I put my head down, determined to ride through it, but even my horse was struggling. I remember a blinding flash, brighter than anything I had ever seen. The next moment I was blown from the saddle and hurled to the ground. A bolt of lightning had struck a tree just yards to my right.

"I tried to crawl to safety, but lightning was now striking the ground all around me. And I realised I was going to die in that forest clearing. Alone and overwhelmed by fear, I cried out, 'Help! St Anna! Help me! Save me and I will become a monk!'

"I screwed my eyes shut and I prayed. Lying there on the wet earth, surrounded by thunder and lightning, I prayed for salvation. Eventually the storm subsided. I looked up and saw my horse emerging from the trees. He came over and nuzzled me, as if urging me to get up. I clambered to my feet and found myself under a blue sky. God had spared me. And I knew then that I had to honour my promise. It was my destiny. That very week, I left the university, sold my law books and entered St Augustine's Monastery in Erfurt. Ever since, I have followed the signs God has given me."

Cristina studied Luther's sombre face. "You really think God was speaking to you through a thunderstorm?"

"Of course! Without a doubt! God is all around us. In the pulse of life, in the trees and the wind, in every living creature. It is a primal force that you feel in your very being." Luther looked at Cristina and gave a sad smile. "But feelings aren't your strong point, are they?"

Cristina resented being judged. "Are you refusing to help me catch a gang of murderous thieves?"

"If you asked me to help you stop the tide from coming in, I would refuse. This is no different."

"Then why are you holding me prisoner?"

"Prisoner? No, no. You are free to go." Luther stepped aside from the door. "You always were."

Cristina walked out, and then turned to face him. "You are a clever man, Luther. But you are not wise."

Luther gave a small laugh. "I was just thinking the same thing about you."

The moment Cristina stepped out of the tavern, Tomasso rushed to her side. "Are you all right? Did they hurt you?"

"No, I'm fine."

"Let me look at you." Without waiting for an answer, Tomasso grasped her shoulders and turned her round, assessing her body just as soldiers checked each other on the battlefield.

"Please, Tomasso. Let's just get back to the castle."

She seemed pale and tired, so rather than walk back, Tomasso picked up a carriage for hire along Jakobstrasse.

As they bumped and swayed on the uneven cobbles, Tomasso didn't ask Cristina any questions. He knew that she would talk when she was ready. After a while, he noticed that she was massaging her right hand.

"Does it hurt?" he asked.

Cristina looked confused.

"Your hands? You were rubbing them."

Cristina glanced down. "Oh … not really. It's more like pressure than pain. But it's constant."

"Have you found anything in your medical books?"

She hesitated. "Not yet." Cocooned by the intimacy of the carriage, Cristina lowered her defences. "Maybe I never will."

"Don't say that."

"But it's a possibility. We have to face it."

Tomasso reached out his hand and laid it over hers. There was a time when she would have pulled away, but now she took comfort from this simple human touch.

As they rolled through the castle gates, Lieutenant Dante ran up to the carriage.

"Tetzel's on the warpath, sir." He grabbed the horse's bridle. "He wants to know why you went out without his authority."

"We don't answer to him," Tomasso said as he swung open the door and clambered out. He and Cristina headed straight to the kitchens to grab some food, only to find Tetzel already waiting for them. The cooks hadn't arrived yet, as it was too early for lunch preparations, so they had to rummage in the larders and help themselves while Tetzel bombarded them with questions about where they'd been. When Cristina mentioned the private audience with Luther, Tetzel blanched.

"You do know the man is a troublemaker? He will end up like all heretics — tortured then burnt at the stake."

"And yet, I find him strangely compelling," Cristina replied.

"Luther is the enemy of the Pope!" Tetzel declared.

"He wants spiritual renewal, so do I. He wants an end to the waste and decadence of the Church, so do I."

"Left to Luther, the basilica you have worked so hard to create would be torn down. The Germans are philistines. Why do you think I've devoted my life to Rome?"

"You cannot dismiss a whole people, Tetzel."

"Even if I am one of them?"

"Please, enough," Tomasso interrupted. "This isn't helping. We need to keep our focus on breaking the criminal gangs."

Tetzel poured himself a beaker of wine from a jug in the larder, while Cristina finished off her plate of black bread and ham. "You know, Luther was quite cryptic when I asked him about the thefts."

"You think he's involved?" Tetzel sat down opposite her.

"No."

"But he knows something?"

"Possibly."

Finally, Tomasso felt they were getting somewhere. "Then we should arrest him. Question him."

Tetzel shook his head. "An excellent idea … if you want to start a riot and watch Magdeburg burn."

"Luther's a strange man, full of contradictions." Cristina stood up and took her empty plate to one of the sinks. "He is dry and academic, yet he can whip a crowd into a frenzy."

"There is nothing mysterious about that, it is simply a matter of technique." Tetzel shrugged. "It can be learnt."

"But he is the exact opposite of you." Cristina poured some water over the plate to wash it clean. "Like a shepherd, you herd the crowd towards the moment when they put gold in the coffer. But Luther … he showers them with sparks and waits to see which one starts a fire. And when one catches, he fans the flames. Watching him, it wasn't clear whether *he* was in control, or the *crowd* was." She dried the plate, stacked it on the side and returned to the table. "It's the same with his story about the lightning. One minute he is a lawyer in control of his destiny, the next he has surrendered himself completely to God. He allowed his whole life to be changed by a thunderstorm."

Tomasso nodded slowly. "So how does that help us?"

"Maybe we should also surrender control."

"But we aren't in control!" Tetzel was exasperated. "That's why these thefts are happening."

Tomasso saw a familiar smile flutter across Cristina's face as disparate ideas fell into line.

"We have come to Germany to hunt the bandits," she explained. "To gather evidence, track the criminals down, give chase. But rather than pursue, why don't we surrender?"

"What do you mean?" Tetzel asked.

"I mean that we stand still and let the bandits come to us."

Tomasso frowned. "How can we set an ambush if we don't know where or when they're going to strike?"

"Not an ambush. We make ourselves the prize."

Tomasso and Tetzel exchanged a baffled glance.

"Plants are rooted in the ground. How do they spread their seeds?" Cristina continued.

"By attracting bees," Tomasso answered.

"Exactly. We must become the pollen. We must become the next convoy carrying Indulgence gold, so that the bandits are lured into attacking us."

Suddenly one of the back doors clattered open and a kitchen porter shambled in, ready to start work.

"Not now!" Tetzel boomed.

"But I have fish to skin."

"They can wait. And so can you. Outside."

The porter shambled back out of the kitchens, grumbling to himself.

When they were alone again, Tomasso turned to Cristina. "This is a terrible idea. You saw what happened to the last convoy."

"It is the only way to come face to face with the bandits," she insisted.

"Our mission is to hunt them down, not be slaughtered by them."

"The German forests are vast, Tomasso. We could be chasing them for the rest of our lives. And we'd be fighting at a permanent disadvantage. The only way is to *become* the gold."

"I cannot in good conscience ask my men to do that."

"If we plan it carefully, we can control every element of the bandits' attack."

"This is not a theoretical exercise!" Tomasso was losing patience. "While you do the planning behind thick castle walls, my men will be out there in the forests, exposed to danger on all sides."

"Firstly, I will not be hiding, I will be right next to you."

"Don't be absurd!"

"Second, this is the last thing the bandits will be expecting. They've struck ten times. Ten successes. They have no reason to change their tactics. But their complacency will be the key to our success."

16: BAIT

The planning began immediately.

Inside Magdeburg castle, Tetzel made the usual arrangements for sending a trunk filled with gold back to Rome. He acquired a secure waggon, assembled a small arsenal of weapons and ammunition, and selected a sturdy team of horses. The crucial difference this time was that all the troops accompanying the shipment would be undercover Apostolic Guards.

While the transport was being prepared, Cristina and Tomasso rode south on horseback, along the network of roads which led through the forests, hoping to deduce where the bandits would be most likely to strike. To give the impression that they were keen to avoid another ambush, they decided to take the convoy along a different route, which led southeast towards Leipzig.

"Trying to get into the mind of a German bandit is certainly a first for me," Cristina said, studying the maps of the forest.

"They showed us their strategy in the last attack," Tomasso replied, looking at the contours of the forest which enveloped them. "They'll choose a point on the road which isn't far from a river, so they can use the water to throw off trackers."

Cristina's fingers traced the course of various tributaries which ran into the River Elbe. "That narrows it down a little. But not much."

"They'll also choose a spot that's within striking distance of a large town, so they can melt away into anonymity."

"Okay, that also helps."

Tomasso peered over her shoulder at the map. "Which section are you looking at?"

Cristina ran her finger along a five-mile stretch of road.

"So, we need to ride that section, identify where the forest gets really dense, and where the track is at its narrowest. They'll choose a spot where it's impossible for the waggon to turn around. Makes escape more difficult."

They spent the rest of the morning surveying the road and eventually identified a half-mile stretch near Eickendorf.

"If I was a violent bandit, this is where I'd choose," Tomasso said.

Cristina peered into the forbidding gloom of the trees on either side of the road. "So, how will we survive an attack?"

"That is the question." Tomasso scrambled up the embankment on the eastern side to get the lay of the land. "We can't have any troops lying in wait. The men we're up against are professionals, maybe even mercenaries. As soon as they know a gold shipment is leaving Magdeburg, they'll do exactly what we're doing — ride the route to find the best spot for a heist. Any troops we have hidden here will be discovered."

"And remember, we need the bandits to get close to the waggon, or it won't work," Cristina added.

Tomasso felt a shiver up his spine as he imagined the violence of the ambush. "You saw what happened last time. My men will face an onslaught."

Cristina sensed how heavily it pressed on him. "Look, as soon as the attack begins, the men can retreat. Run for their lives."

"Too suspicious. The bandits are expecting resistance. If they don't get it, they'll know they're walking into a trap."

"Can we have reinforcements riding behind?" Cristina suggested.

"Just what I was thinking. The bandits will have spotters waiting for the transport's approach. Maybe two bends in the road behind? That's probably as close as we can risk."

Cristina knew how much Tomasso hated using his men as bait. "It's a dangerous strategy, but how many more men will be slaughtered if we don't stop these bandits?"

Tetzel made a point of preparing the waggon in the castle's main courtyard because he wanted knowledge of the shipment to leak out. Given the groundswell of sympathy for the bandits, he was sure there were several weak links among the castle servants — which is why the most critical part of the plan was being prepared deep underground, away from disloyal eyes, in the lower wine cellars.

Cristina and Tomasso entered the gloom and saw Lieutenant Dante working by the light of flickering wall torches. He was preparing a wooden box that was the same size as the official trunk, but this one was a prop. It was constructed from pine which had been stained to look like oak, and Dante was now painting some grey stripes on the sides to simulate iron straps; he had even fixed some real padlocks to the lid for authenticity.

"Nice work, Dante," Cristina said as she examined the box.

"Still a way to go," he replied.

"Really? It looks good to me."

"I want it to be perfect."

Tomasso knocked on the side of the fake box. "Sounds pretty flimsy."

"It's thin wood, only held together with a few nails," Dante replied. "Won't put up much resistance."

Cristina lifted the lid and looked inside. There was no gold. Instead, the trunk was filled with pebbles which had been packed around two small barrels of gunpowder.

Dante picked up a coil of specially treated hemp. "This is the important part. The match cord."

"What's the burn rate?"

"Once lit, three feet a minute." Dante measured a length with his outstretched arms and cut the fuse. "If we go with this, it will give us one minute to get away."

Tomasso frowned. "That's tight."

"I can make it longer, but the longer it burns, the greater the risk of it being discovered."

"The bigger problem is where to get away *to*," Tomasso said. "The waggon will be under attack from all sides."

"Do you really think any of the men will volunteer to light the fuse, sir?" Dante asked.

"I wouldn't blame them for saying no."

"They don't need to volunteer," Cristina said. "I'll do it."

"Absolutely not!" Tomasso exclaimed.

"It's not up for discussion. I've decided."

"Well, you'll have to undecide! I won't let you do it, Cristina."

"And I won't let any of your men do it," she replied. "I'm older than your soldiers. I have less to lose."

"A soldier knows he might have to put his life on the line when he signs up."

"But let's face it, Tomasso, I'm less likely to live anyway."

"Please don't say that."

"It's the truth. We both know it." Instinctively, Cristina rubbed her right hand. "Maybe this can help us after all."

An awkward silence filled the cellar.

Finally, Dante spoke. "It still doesn't solve the problem of where to run once the fuse is lit. You'll be inside a waggon that's surrounded by violent thugs who would kill you as soon as look at you."

Cristina started pacing around the box, thinking hard. Suddenly she picked up a lantern and strode across the cellar to the real armoured trunk. She inspected it, then opened the lid, clambered inside and curled up. "This is the answer. Both chests are loaded onto the waggon — the real one and the false one. Anyone who sees them will just think Tetzel's had a particularly good month."

Tomasso strode over and peered down at Cristina as she knocked on a side panel. "This is solid — it will protect me from the blast."

"Are you completely mad? Not at such close quarters." Tomasso moved around the chest, knocking on the wood, trying to assess its strength.

"It's three inches of solid oak."

Tomasso turned to Dante. "What do you think?"

"I think we should test it first."

"And let everyone in the castle know what we're planning?" Cristina objected. "Only the three of us can know what's happening in this room."

"It's too risky without testing," Tomasso insisted. "We don't know how strong the wood is."

"They build warships from timber like this," Cristina replied. "But if you're worried..." She clambered out of the box and strode to the far side of the cellar where some armour had been stored. She rummaged through the pile, selected two shields and placed them inside the treasure chest, creating a metal lining. “Better?”

“How can we possibly know?” Tomasso said. “No-one’s ever done this before.”

“Well, we’re just going to have to put our lives in God’s hands.”

17: ATTACK

Two days later, at first light, Cristina clambered into the trunk and curled up. She checked the ventilation hole which had been drilled into the side, then reached for her leather water pouch. "All good — close the lid."

Tomasso looked down at her. "Surely you don't have to get in so early? It could wait until we're on the road."

"We can't take the risk. Whoever has leaked information about the route may still be in the castle, watching. We don't want to alert them to anything suspicious."

"Very well," Tomasso said reluctantly. "Remember, when the attack starts, hold tight. You'll hear me give the whistle for retreat; that's your cue."

"Understood."

"Good luck, Cristina."

"I think you're the one who needs the luck," she replied. "Promise me, no heroics. Just lure them in, then get to safety. Don't take any unnecessary risks."

Tomasso gave a wan smile. "I think it's a bit late for that." And he closed the lid of the trunk.

Cristine shut her eyes and relaxed her body. The more she tried to fight the claustrophobia, the worse it would become; she had to embrace the discomfort.

A few moments later she heard footsteps enter the cellar, then with a jolt the trunk was lifted off the ground. As the soldiers carried the trunk up the narrow steps of the cellar, Cristina was thrown from side to side, forcing her to wrap her arms around her head to cushion the blows. Finally, they made it up to ground level and she felt the chest being carried across the courtyard to the waiting waggon. Outside, Cristina heard the rattle of steel as swords and muskets were strapped to horses, and the Apostolic Guards saddled up.

The trunk was loaded onto the armoured waggon and pushed along the floor, then the troops slammed the heavy wooden doors shut. Cristina heard the metal bolts being slid into place. There was no going back now, the plan was in motion.

She strained to hear what was going on, but the world outside sounded muffled. She heard Tomasso give the command to move out, then everything jolted into motion.

Listening closely, she heard the clatter of hooves … a heavy metallic rattle as the portcullis was raised … a jumble of hawkers' cries as they rode through the streets of Magdeburg … the creaking groan of the waggon's suspension … and the chink of hammers on stone as they passed the construction work on the new city walls.

Eventually, the rattle of carriage wheels on cobbles gave way to a softer sound, and Cristina realised they must have left the city and were now on the dirt road leading south towards the forest. She waited a few more minutes, then pushed open the lid of the chest and climbed out.

She was inside the waggon, about six feet by eight feet wide, which swayed wildly as it rolled through deeply grooved tracks and potholes. The two trunks were the only cargo: the real one from which she'd just emerged, and the false one. Cristina knelt next to the decoy and gingerly lifted the lid — the bomb was now primed. Two kegs of gunpowder were linked by a short fuse, while a longer fuse ran from the powder out through a hole in the lid, and was draped on the floor. The chest had been filled to the brim with pebbles. Under different circumstances, Cristina might have been intrigued by the colourful patterns in the different stones, but being this close to something so destructive made her feel uneasy.

Next to the end of the fuse was a tinderbox. Cristina snapped it open and checked the contents: flint, firesteel, curls of kindling, a wick match.

The only way of seeing outside the waggon was through a small hatch that had been cut into one of the side walls. Cristina slid it open and peered out. She saw trees rushing past and caught glimpses of the guards riding alongside the waggon. On horseback it had taken an hour to reach the attack zone, so it would be longer in the convoy, but even now the guards had their weapons drawn.

Cristina closed the hatch and leant against the wooden wall, settling in for the journey.

She clasped her hands together and instinctively started massaging the cluster of tumours. Without doubt, the swelling was getting worse. She hadn't been entirely truthful with Tomasso — it was more than just pressure; for most of the day she was in pain and had been applying an ointment of white willow bark to try and ease the discomfort.

Cristina frowned. Why hadn't she packed one of her medical books in the trunk? This journey would have been the perfect opportunity to continue the hunt for a cure, but now the time would be wasted. On the other hand, the textbooks were too valuable to risk damaging in battle. Then again, if the bandits got close enough to damage the books, Cristina would no longer have any need of them, because she would more than likely be dead.

After a while, the steady rocking of the waggon lulled her into acquiescence, and Cristina's mind calmed. She had to accept that she was no longer in control. She was stuck inside this waggon, she couldn't see where she was going, and she had no control over when the bandits would strike. Worse, she had put her life in the hands of other people: the carpenter who built the original trunk; Tomasso, who had to time his retreat perfectly; and Dante's calculations about the fuse.

Surrendering control did not come naturally to Cristina. She knew the theory — you couldn't cross the oceans by fighting the powerful forces of wind and tide. Instead, you had to allow your ship to be taken by them and use ingenuity to ride what you could not control. Instinctively, though, Cristina preferred the idea of an oared galley, where complete mastery lay in your own hands.

But as the miles passed, her mind started to shift, and she found it strangely liberating to surrender. Perhaps this was what it felt like to be an animal in the wild, where power came from reacting rather than controlling.

A terrifying howl rent the forest air.

Cristina was jolted forwards as the waggon abruptly stopped.

She strained her ears. Moments later, the howl came again. It wasn't a wolf — it was something much worse.

Cristina slid open the hatch and peered out — the guards trained their muskets into the forest on either side of the road. The horses bridled and rooks took flight from the treetops.

Another animalistic cry went up, as if in answer to the first, then more howls joined from different parts of the forest.

And then, all at once, they stopped.

Silence.

A horse snorted nervously.

Bridles chinked as the animals shook their heads.

Suddenly there was a faint whistling sound as a volley of arrows was fired from the trees.

Thunk. Thunk. Thunk.

Arrows embedded into the side of the waggon.

Cristina glimpsed one soldier slump forward, blood pumping from his neck as he tumbled into the dirt.

Another man was crushed as his horse collapsed under him, three arrows piercing the animal's chest.

Before anyone could react, the charge began. Figures on horseback stormed out of the forest on all sides and hurtled towards the convoy.

They looked more like demons than men. Dressed in black, wearing grotesque masks with horns, they howled like wild animals as they attacked.

Within seconds, all Cristina could see through the hatch was a chaos of close-quarters fighting. It was savage and frenzied. Blood arced through the air as men slashed with swords.

Another wave of arrows came in like a curtain of death, cutting men down and thudding into the wooden walls of the waggon.

An arrow whistled through the hatch so close to Cristina that she felt it skim her hair. It jolted her into action.

She slammed the hatch shut and scrambled across the floor to the pebble-bomb.

Cristina grabbed the tinderbox and snapped off the lid. She picked up the flint and tried to strike it against the firesteel, but her fingers were trembling so much she kept missing.

"Come on!" she muttered. "You've done this a thousand times."

She struck again and again, until finally a shower of sparks tumbled into the kindling. She crouched low and gently blew onto the glowing embers until a small flame jumped into life.

Clunk.

Cristina spun round and saw a split appear in the wooden wall of the waggon. The bandits were attacking with axes.

Clunk. Another split appeared.

Cristina turned back to the tinderbox, but the flame had died out.

"No!"

She struck the flint again.

Sparks showered … and caught.

As soon as the flames jumped from the kindling, she held the wick match above them until it was burning steadily.

She was ready to light the fuse.

Clunk. The split opened wider. She could see a sliver of daylight. She had to light the fuse now, or it would be too late.

But Tomasso hadn't sounded the retreat.

Or had she missed it in the confusion?

Was he even alive?

Cristina looked at the coil of fuse. If she lit it now, there would only be one minute until the explosion.

Clunk. More daylight through another split.

Furious sounds of fighting engulfed the waggon. The guards were fighting for their lives.

Why weren't they retreating?

Clunk. The split was now an inch wide. In the next strike they'd be through. Cristina had no choice.

She held the wick match to the coil of fuse until it fizzed into life.

Then she watched the flame eat its way up the cord for a few moments, just to be sure it wouldn't sputter out.

Cristina scrambled back into the armoured trunk and slammed the lid shut.

She waited.

Agonising seconds passed.

Still the sounds of fighting outside. Why hadn't Tomasso sound the retreat? They had to get out now!

Crack. Axes tore the wooden slats from the side of the waggon with a dreadful splintering. The bandits were in.

"*Zwei! Es sind zwei!*" a voice growled, as he realised there were two trunks instead of one.

And then, finally, a shrill whistle rang out to signal retreat.

Cristina heard hooves thundering on the road as the Apostolic Guards fled, followed by the mocking jeers of the bandits.

Cristina braced for the blast…

Suddenly her own trunk jolted as it was slid across the waggon. The lid was flung open, and she found herself staring up at a devil.

A black leather mask covered its face.

Horns curled out of its wild hair.

It raised a hand and slid the mask aside, trying to understand what it was seeing.

And Cristina found herself looking into the eyes of a bandit.

"*Was zur Hölle?*"

And then it didn't matter anymore.

A blinding light seared Cristina's vision as a thunderous boom exploded the air around her.

The lid was blown shut, and Cristina curled into a tight ball.

She heard the clatter of pebbles firing in all directions.

They hammered into the waggon walls.

They split the trunk and dented the metal shields.

The bandits screamed as they were cut down by the stones.

Horses whinnied in terror and bolted for safety.

Cristina heard the strange patter of hundreds of pebbles raining down around her.

Then silence…

…except for the pitiful groans of men dying.

18: INTERROGATION

Cristina blinked up at Tomasso as he lifted the lid of the trunk. "Is it safe?"

"Best to close your eyes." He extended a hand to help her out.

"No. It was my idea. I need to see everything." But as she clambered from the trunk, Cristina was stunned by the savagery of the destruction. The walls of the waggon had been reduced to shredded wood; the bandit who had peered down at her just moments before had been decapitated by the force of the blast. Other bandits lay around the remains of the waggon — all had been grossly maimed, some were dead, others were groaning in agony. The only survivors were the ones who were furthest from the bomb. The Apostolic Guards roamed among the bandits, pulling masks off their faces, looking for signs of life. Dante tended to his own troops who had been injured in the first wave of the attack.

So this was what it meant to surrender control and abandon yourself to a greater force. Cristina felt sick.

Tomasso saw her sway and just managed to catch her before she stumbled. "We had no choice," he reassured her. "It was us or them."

"Maybe there was a better way. If we'd searched harder —"

"No. Don't think like that. You said it yourself: remember all the innocent lives we've just saved."

Cristina turned and looked at the trunk in which she'd hidden. Pebbles had pummelled it with incredible force, smashing through the wood and only stopping when they hit the metal shields.

Tomasso slid one of the shields out and examined the cratered surface. "You were lucky. We all were."

"So what happens now?"

"We sort the living from the dead. We take them back to Magdeburg. We dress their wounds. And then we interrogate them."

It was a sombre convoy that rolled back into the city.

Although the walls of the waggon had been destroyed, the chassis was still intact because the force of the blast had sent the pebbles sideways and up into the air, not down. It meant the bandits could all be loaded onto the remains of the vehicle for the journey, the living rubbing shoulders with the dead.

Emergency surgery was carried out as soon as they arrived at the castle. Despite that, another two bandits died from their wounds before sunset, which left four survivors. Initial questioning established that the bandit leader was among them: Wulf Wagener.

Tomasso led Cristina and Tetzel into the cell where Wagener was manacled to the wall by his hands and feet. He had a pale, round face and hooded eyes set too deep.

When Wagener saw the visitors enter his cell he spat a bloody globule of phlegm onto the straw-covered floor. "You'll excuse me for not getting up."

"I'd be more surprised if you did," Tetzel replied. "Mass murderers are not known for their good manners."

"From what I saw, *you* are the killers," Wagener replied. "I was just riding through the forest with my men when you ambushed us."

Cristina held up a pair of animal horns. "Just riding through the forest … dressed as demons?"

"It's a German tradition. You wouldn't understand."

"And is ambushing papal convoys also a German tradition?"

Wagener shrugged.

"What about chopping the hands off witnesses?" Cristina continued. "Or stealing Church gold? Are they also traditions."

"No," Wagener conceded. "But they should be. They sound amusing."

"Scum!" Tetzel muttered.

Cristina ignored the interruption and focussed on the prisoner. "Is yours the only gang of bandits, or are there more?"

"I was riding through the forest with my men —"

"Where are they based?"

"I was riding through the forest —"

"How do you get your information about the convoys?"

"I was riding through the forest —"

"Who is protecting you?"

"I was riding —"

"Enough!" Tetzel barked.

Wagener looked at him innocently. "Strange tone for a man of God."

Tetzel turned to Tomasso. "Can't you see? He is mocking us?"

Cristina crouched down until her face was level with Wagener's. "I don't think you realise the gravity of the situation. You have been caught executing a violent robbery. One of many, in which dozens of innocent people have been killed and maimed. Damnation awaits you, Wagener."

"Maybe I'll just buy an Indulgence to save my soul."

"Go to Hell!" Tetzel spat. "I wouldn't sell you one if you were the last Christian on Earth."

"You have only yourselves to blame!" Wagener rattled his chains violently, startling his interrogators. "These raids are happening because St Peter's is gorging itself on gold! It is the face of greed. It is a monster."

"Do not add heresy to your crimes," Tetzel warned. "As you're soon to be hanged, now is not a good time to be excommunicated."

"Heretic? Me?" Wagener chuckled. "I love St Peter's. And I love the Pope. His vanity has unleashed a river of gold for us to bathe in."

"If you love the Pope so much, then you won't mind being tortured in his name, will you?"

Cristina turned toward Tetzel. "We're not doing that."

"It's not up to you."

"This is my operation."

"But they are *my* shipments he has been attacking." Tetzel raised his boot and deliberately tipped over the prisoner's water jug. "Oops."

Wagener gave a contemptuous sigh. "Pathetic."

"You will be executed," Tetzel said grimly. "You cannot avoid that. But before you are killed, you can either talk freely, or after hours of agonising torture. The choice is yours."

"You have quite a way with words, don't you?" Wagener commented.

"Even an ignorant thug like you will have heard of the Inquisition. So you will know that we have mastered the art of inflicting pain. Of pushing heretics to the threshold of death, then bringing them back again to endure yet more pain. That is what you face."

Wagener looked at Cristina. "And you wonder why ordinary people hate the Pope? Do what you want with me, my message remains the same. I shit on St Peter's. I shit on the Pope. And I shit on Rome."

The Indulgence seller snapped and launched himself at Wagener. Tomasso leapt across the cell to stop the assault and pinned the Tetzel's arms behind his back."

"Let me go!" Tetzel cried out.

But Tomasso wrestled him out of the room and away down the corridor.

In the silence that followed, Wagener looked at Cristina. "You are on the wrong side of history. But I think you already know that."

Cristina left the prison cell and started searching for Tetzel; she had to convince him that she could break Wagener's will without resorting to violence.

She checked the Grand Commissioner's office, then scoured the castle library, but eventually found him crossing the great hallway towards the main doors.

"Johann, please don't do this," she said, chasing after him.

"The methods are effective and efficient." He didn't even break his stride.

"At least give me a few more days to question him. We cannot torture in God's name!"

"You won't need to be present."

"That's not the point."

"In any case, the decision is no longer ours." He pushed open one of the great doors and emerged into the main courtyard. "It's his." Tetzel pointed to a magnificent carriage as it rolled into the castle under the portcullis, escorted by six richly liveried outriders. As the carriage lurched to a stop, servants leapt into action, securing the team of horses and wheeling a set of steps into position.

"Who is it?" Cristina asked.

"The Most Reverend Albrecht von Brandenburg," Tetzel cooed. "Archbishop of Magdeburg in Saxony, Sovereign of the Electorate of Mainz, Archchancellor of the Holy Roman Empire … and my patron."

The carriage door opened and a fresh-faced youth with pouting lips stepped out and drew a deep lungful of air. "Nice to be home," he said to no-one in particular.

"Is that his son?" Cristina whispered.

"No. That is Albrecht."

"So many titles at such a young age?"

"He may only be twenty-seven, but with youth comes vigour," Tetzel enthused. "He has been a great advocate for the Indulgence scheme. He knows that the more gold he sends to Rome, the brighter his star will shine in the Vatican."

Albrecht saw Tetzel waiting for him and strode over with a confident gait. "I didn't expect a welcoming committee, but it's always nice to get one."

Tetzel bowed low. "Your Grace."

"How goes the world of soul-saving?"

Cristina was surprised by Albrecht's unruffled charm, which seemed to be at odds with all his weighty titles. Perhaps his ease came from his entitlement.

"We have had a breakthrough, Your Grace," Tetzel announced with relish. "Whilst you were away, the bandits attacked another convoy, but our ingenuity has turned the tables. We now have four of the bandits in the dungeons, including their leader."

"Indeed?" Albrecht nodded. "Well, that's excellent news. These thefts have been plaguing us." His gaze settled on Cristina. "Were you something to do with all this?"

Cristina opened her mouth to reply, but Tetzel was quicker.

"Signora Falchoni is part of the delegation from the Vatican. Offering strategic support."

"Ah yes," Albrecht nodded. "The Holy Father wrote to me about that. Well, has this leader … what is his name?"

"Wagener."

"Has he confessed to everything?"

Tetzel frowned. "Unfortunately, the man is reluctant to talk."

"Well, I'm sure we can persuade him. We Germans have ways." Albrecht glanced at Cristina. "Ways which we learnt from the Italians, of course."

"Your Grace, if I may," Cristina began.

"Please."

"Wagener is not a man who is amenable to pain."

"Oh, come now. All men are amenable to pain."

"If you will allow me to question him, Your Grace, I believe I can find other ways to make Wagener co-operate."

"It won't save him from the hangman."

"Nor should it. But I believe it will salve our consciences."

"Is that so?" Albrecht looked from Cristina to Tetzel. "Well, I'm curious to know more. But first I need to bathe. Travelling is so uncomfortable." He glanced lovingly at his carriage. "She's got all the latest features: double-strap leather suspension, pivoting fore-axle and oak beam chassis, but travelling is still a bugger on the back."

"Perhaps we could talk this evening, Your Grace?"

"Has Tetzel shown you my relics yet, Signora Falchoni?"

"No."

"Then you're in for a treat." Albrecht gave them both a cheery wave and headed into the castle.

The reliquary wasn't just a room, it was an entire wing of Magdeburg castle. The major relics were kept in rows of glass cases which lined the walls, while minor relics were stored in the compartments of six huge wooden cabinets which were dotted along the gallery. Further storage was provided on shelves which were only accessible with stepladders. Light came into the space from a series of small windows built high up in the walls, which kept the hurly-burly of daily life out, whilst letting narrow shafts of sunlight in. Everything about the reliquary encouraged contemplation of the divine.

Cristina peered into a large silver casket which looked like a miniature temple. Held in suspension between the small pillars was a glass chamber which contained a single tooth. An inscription on the base identified it as the tooth of St Peter.

Had this tooth really chewed the bread which Christ passed to his Apostles during the Last Supper?

"It's discoloured over time," a voice said.

Cristina glanced round and saw Albrecht approaching from the far end of the reliquary.

"At first, I wondered if St Peter didn't brush his teeth very well. But experts have assured me the discolouration is the effect of sunlight, which is why we keep this room in shade."

Cristina gestured to the scale of the chamber. "This is more impressive than any collection I've seen in Rome."

"Eight thousand, one hundred and five relics, and forty-two Holy skeletons. If that doesn't buy me peace in the hereafter, I don't know what will."

"Are they all genuine?" Cristina moved onto the next display cabinet.

"Hard to know. Some are genuine, some are genuine fakes." Albrecht pointed to a small, crudely fashioned surgical knife. "The scalpel which circumcised the baby Jesus? Perhaps. But that…" He directed her gaze to a small glass cylinder with gold caps on either end. "The scholars have assured me that really does contain tears shed by Christ when he mourned Lazarus."

Cristina gazed along the length of the room. "Are you the only one who sees these relics?"

"Of course not!" Albrecht seemed hurt by the implication. "One relic is chosen on every saint's day and taken to the cathedral. Relics play a vital role in worship. Ordinary people can focus on them to feel the Holy Spirit." Albrecht took a moment, then resumed his nonchalant manner. "You are a sophisticated person, Cristina. You can connect to the divine through art, but German peasants need something more visceral."

"Like the foreskin of St Anthony?" Cristina suggested, pointing to a shrivelled piece of brown skin in a silver box.

"I've been offered worse," Albrecht replied with a chuckle.

Seeing that his equanimity was restored, Cristina decided to press the archbishop a bit harder. "Talking of offers, Your Grace, given your devotion to the Holy See, perhaps one day you hope to be offered the papacy itself?"

Albrecht looked suitably humble. "There hasn't been a German pope in five hundred years."

"Which surely makes it long overdue?"

"That is not for me to say. But did you know that it was actually my idea to sell Indulgences to finance St Peter's? I suggested it to the Holy Father three years ago."

"So these bandit raids must have really enraged you?" Cristina studied him closely, but Albrecht was firmly back in control of his emotions.

"I have long believed that greed is the Original Sin. It is the one which fuels all others. Thanks be to God you now have the men responsible in captivity." Albrecht pointed to a splinter of wood held in a jewelled locket. "A fragment of the Holy Crib, by the way."

"Makes a change from the True Cross."

"I've got one of those as well."

"There is a professor in Sapienza University who has calculated that if you gathered all the fragments of the Crucifix together, you could build an entire fleet of war galleys."

Albrecht laughed. "All that proves is they pay professors far too much."

"Your Grace, do you think these thefts will ends with Wagener?"

"Why wouldn't they?"

"The bandits are extremely well organised. It feels to me as if they are being helped by…" Cristina hesitated. "People in power."

"Such as?"

Cristina shook her head. "You know the politics of the German states better than me, Your Grace. I just wondered who might be interested in protecting them?"

For once, Albrecht did not have a glib response. He leant over one of the cabinets and pretended to study a twig from the Crown of Thorns. "You have captured the bandits," he said finally. "Wagener does not need to confess, and there is no need to torture him. At least not yet. Hold him for another week — if the raids stop, you'll know that there are no accomplices, and that it begins and ends with him."

Suddenly Albrecht seemed bored. "Now, if you'll forgive me, there is a mountain of correspondence waiting on my desk."

As the archbishop hurried away, Cristina once again found herself alone with the relics. She turned back to study the phial containing the tears of Christ. *Were they real?* she thought to herself. *And if so, what extraordinary powers did they contain?*

She felt the swelling in her hands. Christ had shed these tears shortly before he raised Lazarus from the dead. Could they offer her a miracle as well?

There was a sudden chirruping. Cristina looked up and saw that a robin had found its way in through one of the high windows and was now perched on a ledge. The bird started whistling a beautiful, intricate song, as if it was singing just for her.

Cristina listened…

And for a few moments, the richness of that summer evening seemed to flood into the reliquary.

She closed her eyes and remembered the summers of her childhood … chasing grasshoppers through the gardens in Frascati … swimming in the lake with Domenico … lying on the grass, watching sunlight dappling through the blooms of the great magnolia tree.

And with the memories came a sense of longing. She did not want this to be her last summer. She was not ready for that.

Cristina felt a small pulse of energy reminding her to refocus on the medical textbooks and find a cure. With the bandit leader now in captivity, there was nothing to distract her. She would eat a light supper, then spend two hours studying.

She crossed herself as a sign of respect to the relics — holy or not — then whistled a reply to the robin … who fluttered away into the gloaming.

19: 5TH COLUMN

It was the slops boy who made the discovery.

Early the following morning, he went down to the dungeons as usual, carrying some chunks of black bread and a water flagon. He would normally receive a barracking from the prisoners who enjoyed jeering and mocking him, but this morning the cells were eerily silent.

He unlocked Wagener's cell and pushed open the door … only to find it empty. The boy blinked, confused. The heavy chains dangled from the wall, the cuffs still padlocked. It was as if the bandit had disappeared into thin air.

The boy dropped the bread and water and ran to the adjacent cells, fingers fumbling with the keys. They too were empty. All the bandits had gone — vanished into the night.

The boy ran to the bell and frantically hauled on the rope.

As soon as she heard the alarm toll, Cristina scrambled from her bed, threw on a jacket and some boots, then hurried downstairs.

In the courtyard, castle guards were running onto the ramparts and manning the cannon, but Cristina had an uneasy suspicion that the threat wasn't coming from outside the walls. Her fears were confirmed when she entered the dungeons and saw a soldier berating the slops boy.

"What have you done, you idiot?"

"It wasn't me, sir, I swear! They were already gone when I unlocked the cells."

"Are you all right?" Cristina asked.

The boy nodded. "It wasn't my fault."

"Where are the prison guards?"

"Gone, miss," the boy whimpered. "They were gone when I arrived."

Cristina entered Wagener's cell. She looked at the chains discarded on the floor, but the moment she saw that the cuffs were still snapped shut, Cristina realised this was far more than a simple gaolbreak.

"Is it true?" a furious voice demanded.

Cristina spun round and saw Albrecht von Brandenburg storming into the dungeons.

"I'm afraid so."

Albrecht's easy charm was nowhere to be seen. "I want the gaolers arrested and flogged until they confess!" he raged.

"That won't achieve much," Cristina replied.

"This is no time for your moral qualms! My authority has been challenged! It must be met with brute force, the only thing peasants understand."

"It won't achieve much because the gaolers have vanished," Cristina continued.

The archbishop was stunned. "What?"

"Wagener and the other bandits are gone. The gaolers too. The doors and gates were all locked behind them. I wouldn't be surprised if the key-man in the gatehouse has also disappeared. Everyone who witnessed the escape has vanished."

"This … this doesn't make any sense," Albrecht stuttered.

"Unfortunately, it does." Cristina pointed towards the prison cell. "No scratches on the cuffs. They were unlocked with a key, then snapped shut again. No signs of the door being forced. No sign of a struggle. Wagener and the other bandits simply walked out of the castle."

Albrecht looked pale. "That is impossible."

"And yet it happened."

They heard footsteps running down the corridor, and moments later Tomasso burst into the dungeons.

"Are any horses missing?" Cristina asked.

"No. All accounted for."

"So they can't have gone too far?" It was the first piece of good news, and Albrecht latched onto it. "We'll recapture them."

"I've sent men to question the guards on the city gates as well as the night watch."

"Wagener would have been caught at the gates — so he must still be in Magdeburg," Albrecht concluded.

"I doubt that very much," Cristina replied.

"Flood the city with troops!" Albrecht ordered, ignoring her. "Search every house. Break down every door if you have to. I will not have my authority mocked!"

"That will only make the situation worse," Cristina argued.

"A show of strength will force people into obedience!"

"The more troops who flood the city, the more impotent you will seem," Cristina replied. "Wagener has long gone."

Albrecht scrutinised her. "How can you be so sure?"

"The men vanished from a secure castle. That could only happen if they had help from inside."

"Traitors?" Albrecht whispered. "In my household?"

Cristina held up one of the chains. "Who controls the keys? Who commands the men? Who can open locked gates and cover their tracks?"

"I am the power in this castle!" Albrecht snapped. "I am the authority."

"Then perhaps you are complicit?"

"How *dare* you accuse me!" Albrecht's voice cracked with rage.

"I wasn't accusing; I was asking."

"You think I would engineer my own humiliation? Perverse reasoning may be normal in Rome, but the German people do not have twisted minds. We say things as they are."

"I am glad to hear it."

"Never question my integrity again!" Albrecht glared at Cristina coldly. "And the next time you overreach your authority, you will be finished."

Cristina caught Tomasso's eye — he was silently urging her to say nothing.

"I am going to put every available soldier on the streets of Magdeburg," Albrecht continued. "We will find Wagener and his accomplices and execute them." He looked at Cristina and Tomasso. "Until you can make a more constructive suggestion, stay out of the way. Both of you."

With that, Albrecht swept from the dungeons.

"I think this is going to make it tastier," Tomasso said.

"Really?" Cristina sounded sceptical. "Won't it just make it burnt as well as indigestible?"

"Have a little faith." Tomasso had rigged up a wire grid in front of the fire in his room and hung a couple of slices of black bread on it. "Did you know, it was the ancient Egyptians who invented toast?"

Cristina and Tomasso had retreated to the seclusion of their rooms after Albrecht's outburst. Rather than forgo breakfast, they had helped themselves to some bread, pickles and sour cherry jam from the kitchens, and were now trying to wrangle the food into a meal.

"Do you think Albrecht protested his innocence a little too forcibly?" Cristina said.

"It's understandable."

"His manner is normally so unruffled. His outrage seemed a little … forced."

"You think he's involved?" Tomasso turned the bread to toast the other side.

"Albrecht is an immensely powerful man, especially in his own territory. He arrives here in Magdeburg, then a few hours later, Wagener vanishes. It's quite a coincidence."

"But why would he humiliate himself? It only undermines his own authority."

"I don't know. But I'm convinced the bandits are being protected by some powerful forces, that's how they've got away with their crimes for so long. And those same forces have now rescued Wagener before he had a chance to betray them."

Cristina felt a rising sense of unease. Who could still be trusted?

A wisp of smoke curled up from the bread.

"I think that's done," she said.

Tomasso saw that the bread was on the verge of burning and whipped it off the wire hooks. He spread a thick spoonful of jam over each slice, then handed one to Cristina.

"If these powerful forces were worried about Wagener confessing, they could have just murdered him in his prison cell," Tomasso said, munching his toast. "Easier than breaking him out of the dungeons."

"But a dead bandit can't steal any more gold. And I think whoever is behind this wants the thefts to continue."

"So, it's all about the money."

"Why else would someone in power protect violent criminals?"

They ate in silence as it dawned on them both that their entire mission could be in jeopardy. So instead, they focused on the food — at least that was tangible.

Tomasso licked his fingers clean. "What's the verdict? On the toast?"

"Surprisingly nice. You've found a way of making black bread palatable."

"I wonder why that is?" Tomasso mused, hooking another slice of bread onto the wire. "Why does the flavour improve when you toast bread?"

But Cristina's mind had moved on. "Perhaps this applies: *amicus meus, inimicus inimici mei.* My friend, the enemy of my enemy."

"But we don't know who our friends really are."

"We do know that the bandits are the enemy of the Pope. And if the German people see the Pope as their enemy, then the bandits become their enemy's enemy — their friend."

"But how many Germans hate Pope Leo?" Tomasso asked.

"According to Luther, many thousands, all across the region."

"Which doesn't really narrow the list of suspects."

Cristina crossed the room and rinsed her hands in a bowl of water. "You know, it was a grave error of judgement to make ourselves the target. We surrendered control of the investigation."

"We still caught Wagener."

"Only for twenty-four hours. Because we didn't really understand their operation. We lured the bandits into a trap, but if we'd hunted them down with logic, we would have uncovered every link in the criminal chain. We would have discovered every layer of complicity and corruption. Instead, we surrendered control and let the bandits come to us. That was my mistake."

Tomasso's pride at what they had achieved crumbled. He consoled himself with another pickle. "So what's our next move?"

"From now on, we do things the way we've always done them: we stick to logic and facts. Fact one: whoever freed the bandits wants the thefts to continue."

"So we should follow the money."

"That was how we broke the people-smuggling ring all those years ago."

"The problem is, in this case, no-one seems to know where the money is going," Tomasso frowned. "An awful lot of gold has been stolen, but into whose pockets has it disappeared?"

"That is where we must focus our efforts," Cristina said. "Who has become very wealthy in the last few months? Inexplicably wealthy? Who is suddenly living a lavish lifestyle, or throwing magnificent banquets?"

Tomasso helped himself to one last pickle. "You know, I was talking to one of the stonemasons working on the new city walls. He said there's a building boom in Saxony. Maybe that's where we start, by compiling a list of grand new buildings."

Cristina nodded. "Let's go to the town hall and check all the records."

"That might alert the very people we're trying to track down. We don't know how high this conspiracy reaches. The traitors may be embedded in the city's bureaucracy."

"So where else can we find the information?"

"I don't know how many dealings you've had with builders—"

"Too many," Cristina replied, remembering all the arguments she'd had with contractors about her walled garden.

"Then you'll know that the one thing builders love to do is complain," Tomasso continued. "And once they start, they just won't stop."

"This is a good thing?"

"For once, yes."

20: STALLED

"What's better, oak or pine?" Tomasso asked.

"Ah, well, that depends on who you ask," Herr Hopfen replied with a weary air.

Cristina and Tomasso were in the office of *Hopfen Baustoffhändler*, one of three builders' merchants on the outskirts of Magdeburg, which traded in stone, timber, iron, cement, slate, paint, plaster, and any other material that a busy builder might need.

They had come here posing as wealthy Italian aristocrats wanting to build a summer retreat in the Harz mountains, and while Tomasso distracted the owner with technical questions, Cristina gazed through the office door into the warehouse beyond, where looming racks of timber stretched to the ceiling. She was astonished by the variety of cuts: some wood had been left as raw trunks with the bark still on, while other timber had been dried and shaped. Carpenters with measuring tools inspected beams, joists, planks and slats, like connoisseurs selecting fine wine.

"Oak is the classic choice for timber framed buildings," Hopfen continued. "It's strong, won't decay, and won't get eaten by insects."

"Perfect. Let's go with oak," Tomasso agreed.

But Hopfen sighed again. "Of course, oak is expensive. And with a large building like yours…" He shook his head gravely. "Pine, on the other hand, is more affordable and easier to work with."

"Very well." Tomasso nodded his approval. "Let it be pine."

"Of course, pine is prone to cracking, which shortens its life."

Tomasso was anxious to break this cycle of pessimism and get the man out into the warehouse. "Hang the expense. Let's go with oak."

"An excellent choice. And yet…" Anxiety returned to Hopfen's face. "We can't get oak this year. Next spring at the earliest."

"Whyever not?"

"Demand. Everyone wants oak."

"This is really very disappointing," Tomasso complained, slipping into the role of grouchy patron. "Everywhere I look, something is out of stock."

"I feel for you," Hopfen lamented, "but we simply can't keep up. Material flies out of the warehouse faster than we can restock."

"Well, at least you're turning a good profit."

But even the thought of money didn't cheer Hopfen up. "The grief we get every day. Regular customers expect to be given priority. New customers try to bribe us. To be honest, it's a nightmare."

Cristina had heard enough. "Why don't you look at some samples," she suggested to Tomasso. "Then you can make a decision and get things started, even if we can't build this year."

Hopfen obliged and led Tomasso out into the warehouse. As soon as she was alone in the office, Cristina started rifling through the orders on the desk, then through the drawers until she found a set of ledgers. She placed the most recent ledger on the desk and started leafing through the pages. The *Baustoffhändler* was supplying construction material to dozens of building sites: a new monastery at Helmstedt; the expansion of the city dungeons in Halle, a hunting lodge on the Schloss Hundisburg estate, numerous townhouses, a charitable hospital for the poor —

Cristina stopped. If the bandits were stealing from the rich to give to the poor, what better gift to win hearts and minds than a charitable hospital?

She followed the cross-reference and turned to the accounting pages detailing the materials supplied. Judging from the extensive list of stone and timber, the hospital was a huge building project, soaking up vast quantities of cash.

Maybe this was where the Vatican's gold was ending up.

The hospital was being constructed north of Magdeburg, two miles beyond the city walls. It was only a short ride on horseback, but it puzzled Cristina. "Don't you think it's strange to build a hospital out here, when most of the people are inside the city walls?"

Tomasso shrugged. "It's a hospital for the poor. The countryside is full of poor people, labouring on farms, sleeping rough under hedgerows."

A few minutes later, they crested a shallow hill and saw the building works laid out below. A large area of land had been cleared, foundation trenches had been dug, and the skeleton of one wing had been created from a timber frame. The site itself, however, was deserted. Not a single builder could be seen. What should have been a bustling construction site, full of noise and activity, was eerily silent.

Cristina and Tomasso tied their horses to a lonely doorframe that had not been connected to any walls, then wandered through the site.

House martins had nested in piles of abandoned stones; spiders had taken over the timber frames and spun large webs between the joists; an army of weeds had invaded every corner of the site, and there was even a fox path threading between the trenches.

"What happened to all the materials that were sent here?" Cristina wondered aloud.

"You must have made a mistake. This site has been abandoned for months."

"I saw the lists, Tomasso."

"How old were they? Did you see dates?"

"The last order was put through two weeks ago." Cristina looked around, but nothing here was fresh or new. "I think we have stumbled upon some huge fraud," she muttered.

Suddenly they heard a clatter of stones behind them. Tomasso spun round and drew his sword. "Who's there?"

Silence.

A scurrying sound, this time to their right.

"There!" Cristina glimpsed a shadow darting behind a small mountain of gravel.

"Stay behind me," Tomasso whispered. He crept forward, sword ready to strike. But as they arrived at the gravel mound, the footsteps scampered away again.

Tomasso darted to his left and saw a small figure running inside one of the foundation trenches. "It's just a child."

"Out here? On their own?"

Cautiously, they followed the trench until they reached a makeshift tent which had been rigged inside the shell of what should have been a room. Two children huddled beside a weather-browned woman who was clutching a knife. "Leave us alone!" she spat. "There's nothing for you here!"

"We don't want anything from you." Cristina waved at Tomasso to put his sword away. "We just want to ask you some questions."

"Who sent you?"

"Nobody. We're not with the authorities."

"How do I know?"

Cristina reached into her purse and pulled out a handful of coins. She laid them on a pile of granite slabs, then backed away. "Please. For your troubles."

The woman snatched up the money. She scrutinized Cristina and Tomasso. "Leave your sword there." Then she beckoned them to follow her into the tent.

Reassured by the money, the woman told them of the disaster which had befallen her family. Her husband, Olaf, had been a prosperous carpenter in Magdeburg, with a flourishing trade and many satisfied customers. Out of the blue, a consortium offered him the chance to bid for the contract to build a charitable hospital. It was the opportunity of a lifetime. Olaf had long dreamed of being more than just a carpenter, and he spent weeks preparing his bid, carefully working out costings and schedules.

"When he won the job, he threw himself into the work, body and soul," the woman continued. "It was to be the making of us. Olaf hired the best workmen in Saxony, men he knew and trusted. He ordered the finest timber and stone. You have to understand, this wasn't just a job, it was to be Olaf's legacy. The consortium was supposed to make payments every month, so that we could pay the workers and suppliers. But it never happened. From day one, they started making excuses. The lawyers needed to finalise the paperwork. One of the trustees wasn't available to sign off the contracts. The shipment of silver had been delayed by a storm. One excuse after another.

"I told Olaf to close the build down. Stop everything until he was paid, but he wouldn't. He said it was just the normal complications of business, and if he let the workers go, he would never get them back. Month after month, the excuses came, but the money didn't. Olaf used our savings to keep things going, but eventually, he ran out.

"Then everyone turned on us. Creditors, craftsmen, men who had been Olaf's friends for years. In desperation he rode into Magdeburg to confront the consortium, but they had vanished. Offices closed down. No-one knew where they'd gone. And that was when we fell into bankruptcy."

"Did he have no recourse to the law?" Cristina asked.

"What lawyer would touch a bankrupt? Lawyers work for money, not justice."

"Where is your husband now?" Cristina asked. "Can I talk to him? Perhaps we can help in some way."

The woman nodded absentmindedly. "You have no idea what money worries do to a man. How it eats away at his soul, undermines who he is. Every day, Olaf was made to feel like a failure, even though he was blameless. And the worst of it was, he bottled it all up, trying to be strong, trying to protect me and the children. In the end, it was too much. I only understood how truly desperate he was when I found his body."

The woman drew a ragged breath, trying to hold in her grief.

"I'm so sorry," Cristina whispered.

"I couldn't even lay him to rest him in the churchyard. The priests wouldn't allow him to be buried in consecrated ground, even though he was a God-fearing man. A good man. So now … we're a family of untouchables."

Cristina took out her purse and pressed it into the woman's hand. "It doesn't even begin to replace what you've lost. But take it anyway."

*

As they rode away, Cristina and Tomasso paused on the crest of the hill and looked back at the empty building site.

"I think this country is falling into chaos," Cristina said. "People talk about helping German peasants, while the real peasants are left to rot in poverty. Those in power can't be trusted. Those without power are being whipped into a frenzy of anger. This is how countries collapse into anarchy, Tomasso. And it is happening right in front of us."

21: THESES

Martin Luther worked all night, driven by a compulsion to articulate the unruly thoughts swirling around his brilliant mind.

For months he had preached his beliefs — in churches and taverns, in lecture halls and market squares, and he loved to feel the crowd respond to his words, for their reactions reassured Luther that he was preaching the truth. It was as if he was tapping into a primal force and witnessing the very Will of God. But a day earlier, Luther had realised that preaching was not enough.

On Thursday afternoon, he had been confronted by two parishioners who were returning from purchasing Indulgences from Tetzel. They claimed that they no longer needed to repent, that they didn't have to change their lives or do good works in order to be forgiven, for the Indulgences had washed away their sins and guaranteed them a place in Heaven.

Luther knew that nothing could be further from the Christian truth. The lies that Tetzel was selling were the exact opposite of the example set by Jesus when he walked in Palaestina.

It was time for Luther to strike back.

On Friday morning, he sat down at his desk to put his thoughts into a precise and logical order. Hoping to stimulate a genuinely intellectual debate, Luther decided to write in Latin, the language of scholars.

He dipped a quill into the ink pot and began. *Dominus et magister noster Iesus Christus dicendo, Penitentiam agite, omnem vitam fidelium penitentiam esse voluit.*

'When our Lord and Master Jesus Christ said, "Repent," he willed the entire life of believers to be one of repentance.'

And once he started writing, Luther could not stop. He railed against the Indulgences being sold by the Church. He demonstrated how they discouraged people from leading genuinely Christian lives by performing acts of mercy and charity. He explained how forgiveness could not be bought and sold, it could only come from God's divine grace, and only be bestowed on the truly penitent and faithful.

By first light on Saturday, the ninety-fifth thesis was written.

Luther put down his quill and spent the next two hours reading the document, checking for mistakes and making corrections. Then he picked up a hammer and six nails, pulled on his heavy cloak and left the house. He was heading towards All Saints' Church in Wittenberg.

People often nailed propositions and announcements to the church doors; it was the quickest way to communicate ideas to parishioners, and it did not seem like a particularly radical act. Luther wanted his theology to move out of the taverns and into the halls of the universities, for that was the best way to persuade the Vatican that things had to change.

He placed the two large sheets of closely written Latin in the middle of the right-hand door, checked they were straight, then drove the nails into the oak.

When it was done, Luther felt a sudden wave of exhaustion. All the missed hours of sleep caught up with him, and he went home to bed. Yet while Luther slept, the sound of the hammer blows on that church door grew louder and louder…

The first people to read the *Theses* immediately realised their significance: with scholarly rigour, a lowly monk had dared to challenge the central policy of His Holiness Pope Leo X. A German was taking on the spiritual might of Rome.

Word spread. Friends told friends, and soon a crowd had gathered outside All Saints to read the *Theses*. One enterprising printer sent his clerk to copy the pages, then spent the rest of the day typesetting and proofing. Before he closed his shop for the night, two hundred copies of the *Theses* had been printed and sold.

Merchants took the pamphlets to other cities, where different printers saw that money was to be made and started producing their own editions. Within days, the *Theses* had crossed borders and were being translated into French, Dutch and English.

In the German states, the simmering resentments of ordinary people found their lightning conductor in Luther's words. But rather than sending the currents of discontent safely to earth, the pamphlets connected people to each other, amplifying their grievances, giving citizens the courage to speak up. The shape of reality was starting to change.

Cristina sensed the change the way you sense a thunderstorm approaching — it felt as if the air around her was thickening. Within hours, the status that she had derived from being a papal envoy vanished; now, any connection to the Vatican was a liability.

As the days passed, people started looking at her differently, with a resentment they no longer felt obliged to conceal. Servants in the castle seemed more offhand with her and Tomasso; their rooms were no longer cleaned as thoroughly, and it seemed as if they were now given the less favourable cuts of meat at supper.

Determined to discover how far the hostility had spread, Cristina and Tomasso headed back to the livestock market. They wore unassuming clothes and tried to blend into the crowds, but by now everyone knew who they were. Farmers jostled past them, deliberately bumping shoulders, then glaring at them rather than apologising; a group of drinkers started singing a ribald song mocking the Pope; an elderly beggar even spat at them.

Through the crowd, Cristina saw the farmer Nikolaus, who had previously been so helpful. Now he studiously avoided catching her eye. "Let's go over and talk to him."

"I really don't think that's a good idea," Tomasso said.

"He can't ignore us if we're standing next to him."

"He can. And he will."

"But he knows we're here to track down murderers."

"If we humiliate Nikolaus in front of his friends, who knows how he'll react. That's how riots start."

Cristina let it drop. Slowly she turned on her heel, taking in the sea of hostility which surrounded them. "Do you think this is what Luther intended?"

"That man knows exactly what he's doing."

"So why draft the *Theses* in Latin? That's not the language of the rabble-rouser."

"It allows Luther to pretend he is just a harmless monk, debating points of theology. While in truth…"

Cristina's eyes lit on a tavern on the far side of the market. "Let's see what the mood is in *Zum Goldenen Schwan*."

Tomasso shook his head. "You really think it'll be any better in there than out here?"

"Maybe Luther's going to be preaching there again."

"Cristina, let's just head back to the castle. The streets aren't safe for us any longer."

"What on earth could happen to us in a crowded tavern?"

Tomasso hesitated.

"One drink. Just to test the waters." Cristina smiled persuasively.

The moment they entered the tavern, they knew it was a mistake. They could sense the cold hostility in the glances and mumbled comments. But the more hostile the locals were, the more stubborn Cristina became. Several times she tried to sit at an empty table, only to be told that it was taken. Eventually they found a couple of chairs in the corner furthest from the bar. Tomasso tried to catch the attention of one of the serving women, who managed to look everywhere but at him.

"Something tells me we're going to go thirsty," Cristina said.

"I'll get them myself." Tomasso stood up and jostled his way towards the bar, where he disappeared in the throng.

Left alone, Cristina felt suddenly vulnerable. She lowered her head to avoid making eye contact with anyone.

Ten minutes passed, and still Tomasso had not returned. Cristina stood up and craned her neck, but it was impossible to see though the crowd. Maybe he was talking to someone.

She waited a few more minutes, then set off in search of him.

But Tomasso was not at the serving bar.

Nor was he in the far lounge.

Cristina asked a young woman carrying two flagons of ale but was ignored.

Where had Tomasso gone?

Panic started to rise in Cristina's chest. She spun round, eyes studying the hostile faces, then she stumbled towards the doors and burst out into the street.

"Tomasso!" she yelled, looking up and down the street. "Tomasso!"

How could a soldier vanish in broad daylight?

*

Cristina hurried back towards Magdeburg castle, her eyes scouring the streets for any sign of Tomasso.

Conflicting thoughts raced through her mind. She knew that he would never abandon her, especially with such hostility in the air. On the other hand, she longed to believe that was *exactly* what he'd done, because it would mean he was still safe.

She pictured Tomasso sitting in the castle kitchens, tankard of ale in hand, tucking into a plate of sausages. He would give her one of his wry smiles, then she would scold him for leaving her in *Zum Goldenen Schwan*. Yes, that must be what happened. They'd got separated in the tavern. He assumed she had returned to the castle, so he went there as well. It was all just a misunderstanding.

Cristina clung to that thought all the way back, but when she arrived at the gatehouse and asked when Deputato Tomasso had returned, the guard looked at her blankly. "He left with you, this morning."

"But he came back early."

The guard shook his head. "No, I'm afraid not."

"He must be here." Cristina grabbed the gatehouse ledger. "There's been a mistake." Her eyes scanned the column listing all the people who had entered the castle that day — but Tomasso's name was not among them.

"Is there another way in?" Cristina demanded.

"It's this gatehouse, or you scale the walls," the guard replied.

Cristina thrust the ledger back at him.

What could she do? She just wanted to see Tomasso's face again. She wanted to hear him tell her to stop worrying, that she was making a fuss over nothing.

She hurried across the courtyard and up the steps, then pushed open the doors to the great hall — Albrecht and Tetzel were huddled across the table.

"Have you seen Deputato Tomasso?" she demanded.

Tetzel frowned. "Isn't he with you?"

It was exactly the answer she didn't want to hear. Cristina felt her legs go weak, and she stumbled into a chair.

The two men hurried over. Tetzel poured her some wine, but she pushed it away and told them everything that had happened. She wanted them to offer an easy explanation; to tell her she was imagining danger where there was none.

But they didn't.

Tetzel looked fearfully at Albrecht. "What does this mean, Your Grace?"

"They steal the gold I send to Rome … they abduct my prisoners … they kidnap my guests…" Albrecht's fury broke, and he hurled the goblet across the room into the fireplace. "They are humiliating me! They are mocking my authority!"

"We have to get him back," Cristina pleaded. "We have to negotiate his release —"

"Negotiate with who?" Albrecht thundered. "If I knew that, I would execute them all and this nightmare would be over!"

His helplessness filled Cristina with despair. Albrecht was the absolute power in this city, but if he could do nothing, then they were all at the mercy of lawless gangs.

Albrecht turned to Tetzel. "Flood the city with troops."

"We already tried that, Your Grace, to recapture Wagener. But it yielded nothing."

"Then do it again!"

"No-one would talk to us. No-one saw anything. It was a wall of silence."

"Then put more pressure on our informants. Torture them if you have to. Detain anyone who might be useful. And close down that damn tavern! It's a breeding ground for insurrection."

"But Your Grace," Tetzel ventured, "that will only lead to more resentment."

"It is not your authority which is being challenged!" Albrecht bellowed. "Obey me, or leave this city."

The waiting was unbearable.

Cristina realised it was pointless going out with the troops to search Magdeburg; they knew the city's streets inside out, and she would only get in the way. But staying in the castle was agony.

She tried to read the medical textbooks, but her mind refused to focus. Her stomach was too knotted to eat, and there were only so many times you could pace around the castle courtyard.

Which is how she ended up in Tomasso's room.

She saw the wire grid positioned in front of the now cold fire; a few crumbs of bread still clung to it from the last toasting. On the desk was Tomasso's pistol, partially disassembled for cleaning. His uniform hung in the wardrobe, buttons freshly polished. Cristina lifted the jacket close to her face for a few moments so that she could catch a trace of Tomasso's scent.

Maybe there was a clue to his disappearance in this room? What if he'd been sent a warning, or secret instructions to go to a rendezvous? It was conceivable, and it would explain why he hadn't told her.

Cristina rummaged in the desk, but found nothing, then she picked up Tomasso's leather satchel from the side of the bed and started to rifle through the contents. Inside were his orders for this mission, signed by Domenico and Cardinal Riario; a set of papal warrants with three different Vatican seals, giving free transit across various Italian and German States; a collection of maps in different scales; and a notebook in which Tomasso had recorded a daily log of events, presumably to help him write up a full report when they returned to Rome.

In a side pocket of the satchel, Cristina saw a set of papers that had been tied together with a ribbon. She pulled it out and realised it was the instructions she had written some years ago, setting out how to care for the orphaned Alnaaji. She untied the ribbon and leafed through the pages — Tomasso had added his own notes and witty observations in the margins.

Wedged in the middle was another document, a letter she had written to Tomasso on her return from Tunis, thanking him for the courage he had shown in the investigation to break the people-smuggling ring.

As far as Cristina could remember, these were the only two things she had ever written to Tomasso, but he had treasured them like Holy relics.

She put everything neatly back in the satchel and fastened the buckles. But what now? She didn't know how to ease the pain in her heart, so she lay down on the bed and curled up tightly. She closed her eyes and prayed that Tomasso was safe.

A heavy knocking on the door woke Cristina with a start. She scrambled to her feet and opened the door. Tetzel was standing there, pale-faced and anxious.

"There's been a note, from the kidnappers," he said.

"What do they want?"

Tetzel hesitated. "It's best you see for yourself."

22: RANSOM

They met in Albrecht's study, a room adorned with paintings which verged on the erotic — a strange choice for an archbishop, but right now there were more pressing concerns.

"They've sent their demands," Albrecht said with a grim expression.

"How much money do they want?" Cristina asked.

"I'm afraid it's not that simple. They are threatening to execute Deputato Tomasso unless all the Apostolic Guards withdraw from the German states. Immediately and permanently."

"That's absurd!" Cristina said. "They can't banish the Pope's forces from his own jurisdiction."

"Nevertheless, I think we need to take these men seriously."

"Show me the note." Cristina held out her hand, and Albrecht gave her the letter. It was written in *Kurrentschrift*, an old-fashioned cursive script that was so formal and stylised, it obscured all the idiosyncrasies of the writer. Cristina held the letter up to the light to look at the pattern of the fibres in the paper, but there was nothing unusual. "Who delivered this?"

Tetzel looked embarrassed. "We don't actually know. The guard on the gatehouse left his post for a few moments. When he returned, the note was on the table."

Signs of collusion once again, Cristina thought. She was now sure that their enemy was working inside the castle's circle of trust — someone close must have been betraying them all along.

"I'm afraid there's more," Albrecht said.

"Do we really have to show her?" Tetzel whispered.

"If there's evidence, I need to see it," insisted Cristina.

"It's worse than evidence. It's proof." Albrecht handed her a beautifully carved wooden box which was slightly larger than a deck of playing cards.

Cristina studied the intricate patterns on the wood. Then she slid open the lid … and recoiled.

A severed finger had been placed inside the box, arranged in the folds of a small piece of velvet.

"Dear God…"

Cristina drew a breath, then held the box up to the lantern. Inscribed in small letters on the inside of the lid were the words, *DIGITUS PER DIEM.*

"A finger a day."

"We must assume the worst," Albrecht conceded. "For every day the Apostolic Guards remain in Germany, Tomasso will lose another finger."

"And when they run out of fingers," Tetzel added, "they will take his life."

Cristina forced herself to look at the severed finger. It had a grey pallor, there was dried blood encrusted around the stump, but most chilling of all was the signet ring that had been left in place. There was no doubt it was Tomasso's.

She imagined the pain he must have endured. And the shock. Had they bandaged the wound properly, or was he now slowly bleeding to death? And if this went on, how would he be able to do the job he loved? How could he fire a pistol or grip a sword with maimed hands?

"Appalling as this is, we must think clearly," Tetzel began, "If the Apostolic Guards withdraw without first breaking the gangs, it will leave my Indulgence collectors completely at the mercy of the bandits. They will raid every transport that is sent south." He nodded deferentially to Albrecht. "And since my Lord Archbishop has built his reputation on the river of gold being sent to the Holy Father, you must stay and hunt these criminals down. It is what Tomasso would want."

"How do you know what Tomasso would want?" Cristina replied. "You've barely met him. And it is not your body that is being maimed."

"The failure is mine," Albrecht conceded. "I am ashamed to say that I am no longer able to protect you, Signora Falchoni, or Deputato Tomasso or the Apostolic Guards. Power is shifting in the German states."

"All the more reason to fight rather than surrender," Cristina replied crisply.

"We have tried to fight them. *You* have tried. But all it leads to is more suffering." Albrecht seemed crushed by the admission.

"You are Pope Leo's envoy," Tetzel said to Cristina. "We cannot tell you what to do. That decision is yours. All we can do is advise. But the situation seems clear: you must choose between pursuing the bandit gangs and saving Deputato Tomasso's life."

"And what if I reject that choice?"

Albrecht and Tetzel exchanged an uneasy look. "What do you mean?"

"I refuse to have terms dictated to me by a gang of lawless killers. We must take control of this situation. We must hunt the criminals down and they must face justice."

"But we've tried everything!" Tetzel was exasperated. "The latest search yielded nothing."

Albrecht shook his head. "I'm afraid we have become strangers in our own city, at the mercy of forces I cannot control and do not understand. These criminals are beyond the reach of the law."

"Maybe that was true yesterday." Cristina held up the carved wooden box. "But now we have this."

"We must take their threat seriously."

"I do. But in trying to intimidate us, the bandits have overreached themselves."

Cristina bundled her emotions behind a shield of reason and focused her mind on the facts. She placed the wooden box on the desk in Tomasso's room and gazed at it.

It looked expensive, the work of a skilled craftsman. Why did the kidnappers go to such lengths? They could just as easily have sent the severed finger in a leather pouch. But they hadn't because they were trying to say something with this highly polished box. It was a statement of power. Of intent. Of impunity. In a cold and calculating move, they had dismembered one of Pope Leo's personal security team and displayed the bloodied flesh like a trophy.

Cristina studied the image etched onto the lid of the box — it showed a serpent-like monster entwined in the trees of a forest. She made her way to the castle library, where she eventually found a heavy volume titled *Enzyklopädie der germanischen Folklore, Mythologie und Magie*. She turned the pages until she found the beast depicted on the box. It was a Lindwurm. Sometimes they were shown with huge, clawed forefeet, and occasionally they had wings, but they were always fierce and grotesque.

Their favourite pastime seemed to be terrorizing villages and fighting courageous knights who came to vanquish them. There was also a belief that everything which lay underneath a Lindwurm would increase in size as the beast grew, which gave rise to tales of dragon-like creatures sitting on piles of treasure.

That could be significant. If the kidnappers' demands were met and the Apostolic Guards withdrew from the German states, the piles of bandit gold would certainly grow larger. Was that why they had chosen this particular box for their macabre message?

Cristina closed the book and put it back on the shelf. Whatever the clue in the symbolism, she hoped there were more revealing clues in the wood itself.

Cristina had glimpsed the small carpentry workshop down an alley off the Alter Markt, but she had never actually been inside; now she headed straight there. The sign above the door said *Schneiden und Söhne*, and although the frontage was small, it went back a long way. As Cristina pushed open the door, she was astonished by how many beautifully crafted wooden objects were crammed into the shop. There were trays inlaid with intricate patterns, carved dice, chess sets in every size imaginable, dozens of crucifixes, elephants shaped from blocks of ebony, hair combs, backscratchers, walking sticks and dainty clogs. As for wooden boxes, Cristina had never seen so many, and all beautifully finished with marquetry designs.

At the far end of the shop, a man with a grey beard sat hunched over a heavily scarred bench, working a piece of oak with a small chisel. Behind him were shelves packed with hundreds of pieces of wood, all waiting to be transformed.

"Herr Schneiden?" Cristina ventured.

The man put down his chisel and looked at Cristina with soft eyes. "The original Herr Schneiden was my great-great-grandfather. So I'm not *the* Herr Schneiden."

"But you are a Herr Schneiden?"

The man nodded, picked up the chisel and continued with his work. He had the air of someone whose equanimity could never be shattered.

"These are all so beautiful," Cristina said, picking up a scale model of Magdeburg Cathedral. "You must be a very patient man."

"Well, I trained here as a boy, then did my apprenticeship here. I've been in this workshop pretty much my whole life. So I think I'm finally getting the hang of things."

Cristina smiled at his modesty. "I wonder if I could ask you about this." She put her carved box on the workbench, though she had taken the precaution of leaving the dismembered finger back at the castle.

Schneiden glanced at the box. "It's not one of mine."

"How can you be sure?"

He raised a brow. "You think I would not know something I made with my own hands?"

"The thing is, I had an aunt who left Rome to come and live here in Saxony thirty years ago. But we lost contact. The last thing she sent me was this box. Now I'm trying to trace her, and I wonder if it's a clue."

Herr Schneiden seemed moved by her story. He picked up the box and turned it over in his expert hands. "It's not from any workshop around here."

"What makes you say that?"

"The style of the etched design. And the way the wood is laminated."

"I don't understand."

"It's difficult to show you without damaging the box."

"To be honest, if a damaged box is what it takes to find my aunt after all these years, I think it's a price worth paying," Cristina replied.

"If you're sure?" At a nod from Cristina, Schneiden took an exceptionally fine blade and scored a small square on the side of the box. "This mahogany is just a veneer, to make the thing look more expensive." He slid the blade under one corner of the square and started to prise up a thin layer of dark wood. "You see?"

Cristina peered at the patch of exposed wood, which was a golden yellow.

"Now this, underneath," Schneiden scratched the exposed wood and held the blade to his nose to sniff. "Is hazel."

"Which tells us…?"

"All the hazel trees around Magdeburg were cut down a hundred years ago. Everyone wanted it for basket weaving and fences. No-one thought to replant. 'We'll never run out of hazel!' they said. But they did."

"So where does hazel still grow?"

"Lots of places. But not here. And you need a mature tree to get this sort of wood." Schneiden tapped the box. "So I know it's not from round here."

Cristina frowned. Far from narrowing things down, the box had opened up too many possibilities. Then a thought occurred.

"What about Mainz?" Cristina asked. "Does hazel still grow there."

"It's quite common in that area — Mainz, Frankfurt, Wiesbaden."

"Interesting." Albrecht's full title was Archbishop of Magdeburg in Saxony, Sovereign of the Electorate of Mainz. "And how much would a box like this have cost?"

"It's not as expensive as it looks. Solid mahogany would have been more impressive. But still…" Schneiden studied the box through a magnifying glass. He checked the workmanship at the corners and edges, then opened the lid to see how well the interior was finished. "It's something a wealthy merchant would buy. As a gift, or to put something special in. It's not something to give away casually."

As Schneiden handed her the box, Cristina's mind was racing, pulling together the threads of evidence — which all pointed to one man: Archbishop Albrecht.

The timing of his return to Magdeburg…

The mysterious escape of Wagener…

The access Albrecht had to all aspects of castle security…

Precise knowledge of the movement of his guests…

And now the origins of this box.

Everything made sense … except for the crucial fact that Albrecht was a *victim* of the bandit gangs. It was his guards who were butchered; it was gold collected under his authority that had been stolen.

How could Albrecht be both a victim and a perpetrator?

23: ISOLATED

The last thing Cristina felt like doing was eating, but to turn down the dinner invitation would have aroused suspicion. There were just three of them at the polished mahogany table: Albrecht sat at the head, while Tetzel and Cristina were on flanking sides. As the servants started to set out the food, Cristina felt nauseous.

"I'm afraid I cannot eat," she apologised.

"But you must," Albrecht insisted. "You must keep yourself strong. Eat."

She finally managed a few spoonfuls of *kartoffelsuppe*, a potato and vegetable soup laced with bacon.

While Cristina sipped the spicy broth, she watched Albrecht and Tetzel tuck into a trout baked in pastry. Their appetites seemed undimmed by Tomasso's kidnapping, and while they ate they chatted and laughed. But was that because they were somehow involved in his abduction, or because they were callous men? They said they cared, just as they said they were worried by the theft of the Indulgence gold, but people can *say* anything. What really mattered was how they *behaved*, and right now, Albrecht and Tetzel were sharing jokes as they filled their bellies.

Could the archbishop really be playing such a duplicitous game? All the evidence pointed towards him, but was that enough? It was only circumstantial. Could she be obsessing about a series of coincidences?

Cristina raised the spoon to her mouth and sipped the potato soup. She had spent so many years of her life investigating crimes and unravelling mysteries, she knew that coincidences should never be ignored; more often than not, they pointed the way to truth.

And yet it made no sense. Albrecht had won favour with the Pope by sending gold to the Vatican, so why would he protect the bandits who were stealing it?

The doors opened and servants entered with the next course. They placed a large platter of roast woodcock in the centre of the table, then cleared away the remains of the trout. When one of the servants tried to remove Cristina's bowl of half-finished soup, she held onto it. "This is good for me, thank you."

Thinking that he was being helpful, the servant refreshed Cristina's side plate with yet more black bread.

Motive.

That was the key to all this. What possible motive could Albrecht have for protecting the bandits?

Greed? The deadliest sin, which had haunted all the stages of St Peter's construction?

It would certainly make sense. Albrecht could curry favour with Pope Leo by making a great show of sending Indulgence gold, yet at the same time he could be enriching himself by covertly stealing it.

Did the bandits work for Albrecht?

That was logical, but it wasn't wise; gold may give Albrecht power in the short term, but it was nothing compared to the power he could enjoy from the Pope's favour. Why risk the wrath of the Vatican for a few chests of gold?

Unless…

What if Albrecht's true loyalties were to *another* power altogether? But what could that other power be? What was there in the German states that was more potent than the Pope? Surely Albrecht could not be secretly working for another country — the man seemed too solidly German for that.

"Is the soup not good?"

Tetzel's question jolted Cristina back to the present; she had been so deep in thought, her spoon was hovering in mid-air.

"No, no. I was just…" She made a dutiful show of eating.

The worst of it was, there was no-one Cristina could confide in. To discuss her fears with either of the men sitting at this table might mean she would never see Tomasso again, and never bring the bandit gangs to justice.

Cristina's hand touched the small St Christopher medallion which hung around her neck. Tomasso had given it to her to keep her safe, but now he was the one in peril, and he was also the only person she could trust. That had always been true. Across the twenty years they had worked together, she had never once doubted Tomasso's loyalty. No matter how tangled their investigations became, his integrity had remained unimpeachable. Tomasso was the rock upon which Cristina had built so much.

But now he was gone.

Cristina felt a longing in her heart; she would give anything to see Tomasso walk through those doors right now, sit down at the table and start eating.

Maybe that was the answer. Maybe the only way out of this was to refocus her mission.

She started paying attention to Albrecht's conversation. He and Tetzel were talking about hunting wild boar, trying to outdo each other with their embellished anecdotes. Strip away all the titles, and you could see that these men were not deep thinkers; they were simple men whose morality played second fiddle to their earthly desires. Maybe Cristina should do the same. Maybe she should accept the kidnapper's demands and withdraw the Apostolic Guards in exchange for Tomasso's life. She would have to return to Rome a failure and beg Pope Leo's forgiveness, but at least she would be home, and Tomasso would be by her side.

And yet…

Cristina studied Albrecht's face, trying to glimpse beyond the easy charm. Could she trust this man even to accept her defeat? Given how much she had already witnessed, would Albrecht let her leave the German states alive? Could he risk her telling Pope Leo of her suspicions? Or would she and the Apostolic Guards be slaughtered in the depths of the forests before they made it back to the Brenner Pass?

Who could Cristina trust in this castle? Or in the whole of Magdeburg?

And then her mind settled on Luther. There were many things that made them natural enemies — his rebellion against Rome, his rabble-rousing rhetoric, his willingness to turn a blind eye to the crimes of the bandits. Yet despite that, Cristina couldn't feel hostility towards the man. Like her, Luther valued learning and intellectual endeavour; like her, he wanted to see the spiritual renewal of the Church. He struck Cristina as a man who valued the truth, no matter how inconvenient and troublesome it might be.

The words of a philosopher from ancient Greece came back to Cristina; she couldn't remember his name but had a feeling he was one of the Stoics — *The people to fear are not the Strong, but the Weak. It is the Weak who will break when you are least expecting it, the Weak who will betray you without warning, the Weak who will stop at nothing to save themselves.*

Luther was many things, but he was not weak. He had the strength to openly dissent, to speak out against one of the most powerful institutions in the world.

And if Luther was strong, he could be trusted ... even by an adversary.

Cristina found Luther in the *Johanniskirche*, which dominated the strip of land between the River Elbe and the Alter Markt. She knew he was scheduled to preach in the church two days hence, so there was a good chance he would be staying in the priest's house. When she enquired, she was told that Luther was already rehearsing in the pulpit.

The sun was streaming through the long windows high up in the southern wall, splashing beautiful smudges of colour across the pillars and stone floor. At first, Cristina thought the church was empty, then suddenly a man stood up from behind the pews, startling her. It was Martin Luther.

"Forgive me. Were you praying?" Cristina apologised.

"Not yet," Luther replied. "Still preparing."

"For a game of hopscotch?"

Luther was momentarily puzzled, then saw that Cristina was looking at the piece of white chalk in his hand. "Oh, you mean *Himmel und Hölle*? The children's game? No, no, not in church. That wouldn't be right."

Cristina walked up the nave to see what Luther was doing. "Why are you preaching here and not in the cathedral?"

"I like the *Johanniskirche*. It's a breath of fresh air." He glanced up at the soaring vaulted roof. "It always gets overlooked because of the cathedral, but this church is nearly six hundred years old. You get all the purity and history of the Church, without having an archbishop breathing down your neck."

"And the chalk?"

"It's a trade secret," he smiled. "But as you have such a curious mind..." Luther pointed to the different pools of light falling across the great flagstones. "As clouds move across the sun, these splashes of colour come and go. I use the chalk to mark their position on the floor." He bent down and chalked a small X on the flagstone to demonstrate. "When I preach, I leave the pulpit and walk here, among the people. But I make sure I'm always standing on one of the marks. As the words of God leave my mouth, every now and then a heavenly light illuminates me. It's like a divine blessing endorsing my words. It is most effective. Very moving for the congregation."

Cristina looked down at the series of small crosses on the floor. "It seems quite cynical."

"Not at all. God provides the light; I am merely letting it shine on me if He chooses." Luther patiently marked the remaining patches of colour, then put the chalk into his pocket and dusted his hands. "So, have you finally understood what is going on here?"

Cristina hesitated, but she had sought Luther out because she trusted him, so she may as well tell him the truth. "I cannot win. I was sent here to stop the violent thefts. Soldiers are being butchered like animals. Money is being stolen by criminal gangs who then spread lies about helping the poor. In truth, the only people they are helping are themselves. If ever there was a wrong to be righted, it is this. But now I see that it is an unwinnable battle."

"So you're giving up?"

"Friends are enemies. Those who should be helping me are working against me. Magdeburg is a nest of vipers, and I fear the evil has spread across the German states."

Luther nodded. "Harsh. But not unreasonable."

"I have accepted that I cannot finish what I came to do," Cristina continued. "But at least let me leave without any more violence. Help me rescue Deputato Tomasso from his kidnappers."

Luther blinked. "Why do you think I have anything to do with that?"

"Tomasso is a good man, and I need him back." She pulled the small wooden box from her pocket. "They cut off his finger and sent it to me in this."

"Barbaric," Luther whispered with contempt.

"And it is only the start. They will mutilate him and eventually murder him. I am begging you to intervene."

"You assume a lot."

"You are a powerful man, Luther."

"No, I am just a monk."

"In name, but your influence goes much deeper. We both know that. I do not understand the mechanism that links you to the criminal gangs, but I believe you can help me."

"Cristina, nothing makes sense because you do not realise that you have stumbled into a revolution."

"A very grand name for theft and murder."

"You must understand, in normal times the authorities would hunt down the guilty and punish them. But these are not normal times. In a revolution, all the forces that bind society together realign."

"But a few rabble-rousing speeches do not make a revolution."

"Come with me." Luther led Cristina to a carved plaque on the north wall, depicting Jesus being condemned to death. "The first Station of the Cross. Or the *Via Dolorosa*, as you Italians call it." He pointed to the fourteen carvings that were positioned down the length of the church, showing key moments in the life of Christ on the day of his execution. "On one level, this shows the violent execution of a condemned criminal. On another level, it shows the greatest spiritual revolution in the history of mankind. On this day, allies became enemies, the meaning of good and evil was redefined, families were torn apart and new loyalties forged. When radical change happens, wise people no longer think about how their actions are judged by the old order, but how they will be judged by the order which is coming. That is what is happening in the German states."

"But what is this revolution?" Cristina asked. "I don't see people burning down castles or raising peasant armies."

"You witnessed it in *Zum Goldenen Schwan*."

Cristina couldn't hide her surprise. "*You* are the revolution?"

"I am."

"I thought monks were supposed to be humble?"

"Humility is for those who are unsure of the truth," Luther replied. "But I know that God is speaking through me, because I feel Him in the reactions of ordinary people."

"People react because you use every trick in the book to manipulate them." Cristina extended her foot and rubbed out one of the chalk crosses with her boot. "Take away the tricks, and the emotion vanishes."

"But you're forgetting, God is the one who decides whether or not the sun shines when I preach. It is his endorsement."

"And what if it rains? Is that also a judgement?"

Luther sat down on the front pew. "You see, this is your problem. You are always thinking about logical arguments."

"That's what it means to be human."

"No. Reason is only part of the story. You are a rational person swimming in a river of emotion. That is why you are struggling to understand what's happening. You must allow yourself to be swept away by all the emotions around you."

The thought filled Cristina with dread. She needed to get this back onto her own terms. "God may be mysterious, but I know what He doesn't want. He doesn't want violent gangs cutting men to pieces. He doesn't want theft and terror. That is why I came to Magdeburg, to restore peace."

"No!" Luther exclaimed. "You came here to secure Vatican gold!" He leapt up from the pew, strode to the altar, grabbed two candlesticks and brandished them like daggers. "The Church loves gold. It is obsessed with it. But it means nothing. Gold is spiritually bankrupt."

"The gold I am trying to protect will be used to create the greatest basilica in the world. It will inspire the whole of Christendom."

"Is that so?" Luther gave a sardonic smile and gently reset the candlesticks on the altar. "Well, I will let you into another secret." He turned and locked eyes with Cristina. "I actually want Tetzel to keep selling his overpriced Indulgences."

Cristina frowned. "But you railed against them in your *Theses*."

"I did, didn't I?" Luther said mischievously. "Yet in truth, the more Indulgences they force down the throats of the Germans, the more resentment people will feel towards the Pope. And I will ride that wave of resentment to bring about the spiritual renewal of the Church. Outrage is my friend."

"And what if outrage leads to anarchy?"

"It won't, because God is in control. I am just a mouthpiece for the Divine Will."

Cristina was unnerved by Luther's absolute conviction. This quietly spoken man was a stranger to self-doubt.

"But I am also doing God's work," Cristina countered. "The new St Peter's is a manifestation of Divine Will."

"You believe it is. But you cannot know."

"I have dedicated twenty years of my life to that belief. If God had wanted to stop me, he would have done that by now."

Luther glanced at Cristina's hands. Suddenly self-conscious, she pushed them into her pockets.

"Cristina, there is what *seems* to be going on, and what is *really* going on. These are two different things."

"Do you want to stand in one of the pools of light? It might add weight to your words." Cristina immediately regretted sounding so petulant.

"Last spring, I was unwell," Luther replied patiently. "I was suffering from influenza. I was confined to my bed in the monastery for over a week. One evening, I woke from a fevered sleep to see two bumblebees on the window ledge. They were alive but not moving. It was almost as if they were staring at me. I confess, I was alarmed. One of the older monks had died a few months earlier from a bee sting, and I didn't know what to do. Should I call one of the novices to chase them away? As I was trying to decide, two more bees flew through the window and joined the others. Four bees, sitting quietly on the ledge, watching me. And then I sensed that something special was at work. So I decided to do nothing. I wanted to find out what this strange visitation meant.

"Eventually, I fell back to sleep, trusting that the bees would not harm me. When I woke at dawn, they were still on the window ledge, they hadn't moved. But as the sun rose, they took flight, circled the room, then disappeared through the window, one after the other."

Cristina looked at Luther sceptically. "And you think that was somehow an act of God?"

"Yes and no. A simple mind would see God in the bees. But in truth, God was unfolding in the mechanisms of Nature. When I was back on my feet, I talked to a beekeeper about what had happened. He explained that bees are not strong fliers. They can only fly well in the warmth. The bees that I saw had been lured from their holes by the spring sunshine, but when the sun dropped and the air became chilly, they suddenly found themselves too weak to fly home. Which is why they rested on my window ledge. And as the first bee arrived, it left a marker on the window, so that other bees could follow. All they wanted was to find safety until the sun rose again. Did God visit my sickbed through those bees? No. But was the Divine Will at work through Nature? Absolutely. And that is what is happening with St Peter's. The true meaning of your basilica is quite different to how it appears on the surface."

"Your analogy is ludicrous." Cristina took a step back, but Luther reached out and took her arms.

"You have seen me preach, Cristina. You have witnessed ordinary people listening to the word of God as if hearing it for the first time. Not because they were in awe of some vast pile of stone, but because they could connect with the Divine through their own language. The true purpose of your basilica is to turn people *away* from the old Church and embrace spiritual renewal."

"That is nonsense!" Cristina struggled to break free, but Luther tightened his grip.

"God's Will is to make St Peter's so grand and so expensive, that it will put the entire Church in financial peril, forcing the Pope to sell Indulgences, squeezing ordinary people until they rebel."

"No! Rebellion is meaningless. There is no life outside the Church!"

"There is the new church," Luther insisted. "A reformed church where people are guided by the Bible rather than by wealthy men in distant palaces."

"This is heresy!"

Luther grabbed Cristina's swollen hands and clasped them tightly. Pain shot up her arms.

"Let me go!"

"For all these years you have been doing God's work, but not in the way you thought. It was never about a new St Peter's. It was about using St Peter's to create such division that people would cast off the old church and rediscover Christian spirituality. That is what is happening in the German states, right in front of your eyes. And the part you have played in that rebirth, albeit unwittingly, is the true meaning of your life."

"No!" Cristina pulled back violently, forcing Luther to let go. She looked at her hands and saw the chalk smudges from Luther's grip.

She wanted to turn and run, to get away from this dangerous heretic … but her feet would not move. Instead, she felt all the intellectual constructions that she used to navigate her life start to crumble. Every tool she needed to get leverage on the world seemed to slip from her grasp.

Had she been living a lie for the last twenty years? Was that why she had now become so powerless?

The strength drained from Cristina's legs.

She felt dizzy and nauseous.

For a brief moment, the sun emerged from behind a cloud and a pool of colour washed over her face. Then Cristina collapsed onto the stone floor and her world plunged into darkness.

24: SURRENDER

Cristina's eyes fluttered open. She lay on the floor of a dark cell. It was like a prison, but strangely, the door was wide open.

She hauled herself to her feet, then felt suddenly dizzy and had to reach out and steady herself.

Where was she? What kind of a gaol was this?

"Hello?" she called into the gloom.

No answer.

Tentatively, she approached the open door and peered out. Her cell was in a long, deserted corridor. There were no windows, and the only light came from flickering torches that were mounted at intervals along the walls.

"Hello?" she called again.

Silence.

Cristina drew a breath. The air tasted damp. Maybe she was underground. Cautiously, she started to walk down the corridor, listening for any signs of life. At the end, the corridor split into two — one passage going left, the other right. She chose right, walked to the end, then came to another choice: left or right.

This was bad. She must be in some kind of labyrinth. Best to return to the cell she had woken in rather than get completely lost.

As she made her way back, Cristina looked for clues. She tapped the walls, listening for hollow areas, but found nothing. She ran her hands over the surfaces, feeling for irregularities, but the walls were perfectly smooth. Someone had put a lot of effort into building this, but to what purpose?

She plucked one of the flaming torches from the wall and slowly moved it around — up to the ceiling, then down to the floor, watching the flame to see if it flickered in a draught. But there was none.

So how was air getting in?

Maybe it wasn't.

Maybe this was a tomb.

Her tomb.

This labyrinth was yet another mystery, just like all the others that had been frustrating her ever since she arrived in the German states.

Cristina made it back to her cell and slumped down.

How had she got here?

She cast around in her mind … what was the last thing she could remember?

Luther. Standing in *Johanniskirche.* He was gripping her hands tightly.

Cristina felt nauseous. When was the last time she'd eaten? She couldn't remember. And she didn't know how long she'd been down here.

She took a deep breath. *Focus.*

If Luther was the last person she had seen, did that mean he had abducted her? Had he imprisoned her down here – wherever *here* was. But Luther was a man of God, he would never stoop to kidnap … would he?

She tried to remember their last conversation … Luther's devastating words, telling her that she had misunderstood the purpose of her life.

Suddenly the nausea returned. *Don't think about Luther. The important thing right now is to get out of here. Think! Think of an escape plan.*

But logic was no longer working. It couldn't get any purchase in this place. Cristina closed her eyes and surrendered to the frustration…

Then she screamed.

A loud, primal scream of fear and anger, unleashed from the depths of her being.

She listened to her cry echo down the corridors then fade to nothing. It was astonishing how satisfying it felt.

Cristina drew a deep breath and screamed again, focussing all her rage into her voice. Then she slumped against wall and enjoyed the sense of release.

And then…

A distant voice called back — "Here!"

Had Cristina imagined it?

She hurried back into the corridor and looked left and right. Nothing to see but the torches burning in the gloom.

"Hello? Is anyone there?" she called out.

"I'm here!" the voice responded. It was a faint, but she was sure it was a man.

"Tomasso?" she called as loudly as she could. "Is that you? It's me! Cristina!"

Silence.

Just as Cristina drew a breath to call out again —

"It's about time!"

Relief welled up in Cristina's chest. She sobbed and laughed at the same time.

"Keep shouting!" she called out. "Count to ten! I'll find you!"

"One. Two. Three…" Tomasso's voice was faint, but it was enough.

Cristina wiped her eyes and started moving towards the sound. Every time she reached a fork in the corridor she paused and strained her ears, letting the sound draw her in the right direction.

"Four. Five. Six."

Left … right … right … left. The labyrinth seemed endless, or was she going round in circles? Either way, Tomasso's voice was getting steadily louder, and that was all that mattered.

"Seven. Eight. Nine."

There was an open cell ahead. Cristina stepped cautiously towards it … put her head round the door…

"Ten."

And there he was.

She ran into Tomasso's arms, and they held each other tightly. Finally, here was something that made sense. Something real and true.

Cristina didn't know how long they held each other, but down here time didn't seem to matter. There was no day or night, no clocks or deadlines.

Eventually they let go of each other and sat down on the floor.

"Let me see this." Cristina took his maimed hand in her own and examined it. The bandages had been neatly applied. "Did it bleed much?"

"I think it was done by a surgeon," Tomasso replied. "He removed the finger, then immediately stitched and dressed the wound. They clearly want me to live. At least for now."

"Did you recognise any of them?"

"I was blindfolded the whole time."

"What about the people who brought you here?"

Tomasso shook his head. "In the tavern, someone grabbed me from behind and dragged me outside. They immediately put a sack over my head. I tried to fight, but it was all so fast. And there were too many of them."

"And no-one came to help you?" Cristina didn't remember any sounds of a struggle in the tavern.

"We have no friends here, Cristina. We are foreigners. We are the enemy."

"What happened after that?"

"They bundled me into a cart. We drove out of the city, not too far. They dragged me down here and dumped me in this cell. Told me not to move or they'd kill me. I waited until the footsteps left, then took the sack off my head. They didn't chain me up. They didn't lock the door. But that only means there's no escape."

"I tried to find a way out," Cristina said, "but I was worried about getting lost."

"I've searched as well. There is no way out."

"But who are they?" Cristina asked.

"Since I've been down here, I haven't seen anyone. Not a soul."

"What about the gaolers? Who brings you food and water? Who changes all the torches in the corridors?"

Tomasso shook his head. "Food and water only appear when I'm asleep. I've tried staying awake, but no-one appears when I do. I've even pretended to sleep, but they're not fooled. Somehow, they're watching me. And they're close. But I never see them."

Cristina looked up at the walls and ceiling — there was no sign of a spyhole. "Now there are two of us, perhaps we can sleep in shifts."

"There's no fooling them. We are completely at their mercy."

But what did that mean? Cristina wondered if there was still room to negotiate, or had capturing her changed everything?

"Do you know what they want?" Tomasso asked.

"Withdrawal of the Apostolic Guards from the German states. They want us to abandon the mission and give the bandits free rein."

Tomasso considered the implications, but he knew how wilful Cristina could be. "Will you accept?"

"If they give us another chance, I will," Cristina conceded. "But maybe they're beyond that now."

"They can't just leave us here," Tomasso said. "People will come searching for us. We have the protection of the Vatican."

"I wouldn't be so sure." Cristina turned to look at him. "You just vanished. No clues. No leads. And Archbishop Albrecht … well, let's just say he didn't exactly weep for you."

"Maybe he'd care more if I was a Holy relic."

Cristina gave a wry laugh. "I'm sure he would."

They lapsed into silence for a few moments, until Tomasso said out loud what they were both thinking. "Maybe they want us to die down here. Quietly forgotten."

Eventually, Cristina and Tomasso slept.

When they woke, a tray of provisions had been placed in the corridor outside, just as Tomasso had described. He brought it into the cell and removed the cloth. "Cold sausage, cheese, some wine and…"

"Let me guess — two slices of black bread?"

"Three, actually."

They divided the provisions and started to eat.

"I was hungrier than I thought," Cristina said.

Despite the fact they were imprisoned, and their lives were hanging in the balance, there was a calmness in the cell which gave Cristina another chance to reflect on what Luther had said.

There was nothing illogical about his interpretation of her life, but that didn't make it true. Would God really work in such a twisted way, deceiving those who think they are doing His work? He had certainly done worse. After all, this was the God who sacrificed His own son to save humanity, so building a vast basilica to turn people against the decadence of the Church and embrace spiritual renewal … it was a plan which understood the perverse wilfulness of ordinary people.

Cristina poured some wine into one of the beakers and leant back against the cell wall. "If Luther is right, then I have been a fool."

"That is the one thing you definitely are not," Tomasso said.

"At the very least it means I have to change the way I approach the world…" She hesitated as a heaviness settled upon her. "In whatever time is left."

"Don't say that, Cristina." Tomasso poured himself some wine and shuffled closer to her. "God made you the way you are for a reason — to play a part in the building of St Peter's. You have done that with conviction and passion. And that is all that matters."

"Even if I'm wrong?"

"You're not wrong. It's just that there may have been other forces at work which you couldn't possibly have known about."

"But look where it's brought us." Cristina gestured to the stark walls of the cell. "A dead end. Logic and learning mean nothing in here. They have no traction. There is no debate, no chance to plan or act."

Tomasso sipped his wine. "Soldiers define themselves as fighters. But when a soldier is overpowered, or when continuing to fight would lead to a pointless death, he surrenders. Living to fight another day is a weapon that every soldier has. There is no disgrace in it."

"But how can we surrender when we cannot see the faces of our captors?"

"We need to write them a message," Tomasso suggested.

"Using?"

He unwound a length of bandage from his hand. "Well, this will do for paper."

Cristina glanced around the cell, then she went out into the corridor and returned a few moments later carrying one of the flaming torches. "What's the quickest way to put this out?"

"We need a snuffer."

"What about your jerkin?" She pointed to the folded leather jacket which Tomasso used as a pillow.

"We can try." He picked up the jerkin and wrapped it around his hands, then seized the flame and smothered it. When he took his hands away, the torch was a gently smoking stump.

Cristina licked her finger, dabbed it into the black soot then examined it. "I think this will do." She slid off her belt, dipped the buckle prong into the sooty torch and patiently wrote on the bandage — *Blessed are the peacemakers.*

Tomasso looked at the sentence. It wasn't neat, but it was legible. "Will they understand?"

"Luther will know what it means."

"You really think he's part of all this?"

"Let's find out." Cristina placed the bandage in the corridor, next to the empty tray.

When they next woke, a contract had been left for them, setting out the terms of their surrender. Cristina read the document carefully. "They'll let us go, but we must leave the German States permanently, along with all our troops."

"And in return?"

"They guarantee that one in two shipments of Indulgence gold will arrive safely in Rome."

"Half?" Tomasso couldn't believe how brazen the demand was. "They're going to take half the gold? Who has the authority to draw up a contract like that?"

Cristina handed the paper to Tomasso. "I think they'll all working together: Albrecht, Tetzel, Luther, and the criminal gangs."

"But they all hate each other. Luther rails against the archbishop. Albrecht rails against the thefts."

Cristina shook her head. "They're all preparing for the world that is coming. Whatever form that takes, it will need money."

"But if we sign this, we are giving away half of Pope Leo's gold. That's going to be difficult to explain back in Rome."

"Think of it another way," Cristina suggested. "We are making sure that half the Holy Father's gold is secured."

"Hmm. I think I'll let you do the explaining on that one."

"It's really quite simple. Pope Leo doesn't have a choice. Accept these terms or get nothing."

Tomasso wasn't convinced. "Popes aren't in the habit of being told what to do."

"Well, times are changing. The Vatican needs to get used to it."

Their captors had provided a quill and a small pot of ink with the contract, so this time Cristina didn't have to improvise. They both signed the document and put it outside in the corridor. Now there was nothing to do but wait.

"Of course," Tomasso said, "now they have the signed contract, they could just kill us anyway."

"If they do that, then there never was any way out of this alive," Cristina replied. "We just have to surrender to what will happen."

This time, it was a gentle breeze which woke them.

Cristina sat up. Was she imagining it, or was that fresh air? She hurried out into the corridor and saw that all the torches were fluttering.

"Tomasso! Quickly!"

He scrambled next to her.

"You feel that?"

He drew a deep breath. "They've opened a way out."

Immediately they started heading into the draught. At each junction in the labyrinth, they were guided by the breeze. Turning by turning, it got steadily stronger … until they could see a small patch of light up ahead.

It was an open door at the top of a long flight of steps.

But did it lead to freedom?

25: FREEDOM

"I don't believe it..." Cristina pulled aside the canvas sheet flapping in the wind to reveal the half-finished, abandoned hospital for the poor laid out before them. They were standing in the tent that had only recently been occupied by the widow and her two children, but there was no sign of them now.

"Hello?" Cristina shouted into the deserted building site. She waited a few moments, but no-one answered.

Tomasso shook his head. "This was never going to be a hospital. That was just a cover story. It's true purpose is to be a clandestine base for the gangs. This is where all the building materials went — to construct the underground labyrinth. And this is how the bandits managed to vanish so easily after each attack."

"But we saw no sign of them down there," Cristina replied. "No horses, no men. We didn't hear anything."

"This can't be their only hiding place. There must be others, perhaps all across the province.

"How on earth do you keep something like this secret? Think of the manpower needed to build it."

"By convincing people that you are on their side. Even if you're not."

Cristina and Tomasso could no longer be sure who was an ally and who an enemy, yet they were still glad to arrive back in Magdeburg castle. Albrecht worked hard to create the illusion of a warm welcome, showering them with food, wine, clean clothes, and a visit from his own personal physician. He made a big show of expressing bewilderment and anger that the

Pope's envoys had been treated with such disrespect, and he vowed that justice would be swift and merciless. Cristina and Tomasso knew that Albrecht's outrage was performative, but they said nothing.

The physician told them to rest for the afternoon, after which they were to go to the great hall for a debriefing. As they strode down the corridor towards the huge oak doors, Cristina and Tomasso were still trying to determine the best strategy.

"Are you going to confront them?" Tomasso asked. "It would be good to see Albrecht squirm."

"He's not the squirming type. He'll have a glib answer for every accusation."

"So, we just let them get away with everything?"

"We don't want to find ourselves locked in another labyrinth, Tomasso. Next time, there may not be a way out."

When they pushed open the doors, they discovered Archbishop Albrecht and Tetzel sitting at the far end of the great table, deep in conversation. Both men had numerous questions for Cristina and Tomasso. Ostensibly, they were trying to help identify and capture the kidnappers, but Cristina and Tomasso quickly realised that each question had a subtext designed to reveal how much they had discovered about the city-wide conspiracy.

They answered honestly but cautiously and avoided saying anything that might alarm Albrecht. Finally, Cristina revealed details of the settlement which had secured their release.

"It's a compromise," Cristina admitted, "but at least it guarantees a steady flow of gold to the Vatican."

Albrecht scowled with displeasure. "What does that actually mean in practice?"

"Business as usual. Tetzel will keep selling Indulgences, and half the gold will be safe."

Tetzel was indignant. "So I must simply accept that half my transports will be attacked? That my men will continue to be murdered?"

"No. Half of what you collect gets sent to Rome, the other half…" Cristina studied Albrecht, but he remained stony-faced. "The other half will remain here in the castle, under the protection of the archbishop."

Tetzel and Albrecht looked at each other uneasily.

"So now the bandits will have to attack the castle to get their gold?" Tetzel said.

"That is simply not unacceptable," Albrecht objected.

Cristina studied the two men. Was their bewilderment an act? Or was this really news to them? "The contract merely says that half the gold must stay in Magdeburg. What happens then is down to you."

"Are you insinuating that we know who these criminals are?" Tetzel demanded.

Cristina gave a noncommittal shrug. "From what I have learnt, the different factions in this city are connected in all manner of surprising ways."

There was a very awkward silence. Then, with customary ease, Albrecht gave a charming smile. "Well, I am truly sorry that your mission has been so difficult, but at least you have put an end to the violence and lawlessness which was terrorising our state, and for that we are grateful. And I'm sorry that the Holy Father will have to forgo half his Indulgence gold, but we must all make sacrifices for the sake of peace."

"Indeed, Your Grace." Cristina gave a respectful bow. "As it says in the Gospels, 'Blessed are the peacemakers'."

"Quite."

*

Lieutenant Dante immediately started making preparations to leave, and the following morning Operation Danube rolled through the gates of Magdeburg castle. They were all glad to be leaving the German states.

As they passed the Alter Markt, Cristina saw that a large crowd had gathered to listen to a preacher. A few moments later, Martin Luther climbed onto the makeshift podium and was greeted with rapturous applause. As he basked in the adulation, Luther caught Cristina's eye and raised his hand in greeting. She waved back across the crowd but didn't stop riding.

"I wonder if he's the one we've been fighting all long?" Tomasso mused.

"Maybe."

"It would certainly put a lot of blood on his hands."

"There's always a bloody price for progress," Cristina replied. "The old guard need to have their hands prised from the levers of power."

"Luther isn't progress," Tomasso scoffed. "He's just a radical preacher spreading heresy."

"That's certainly how the Vatican will judge him. They will denounce any movement to reform the Church as the work of evil forces. But underneath all the noise, Luther may have a point. Maybe Christian enlightenment is actually built on freedom rather than conformity. The freedom to think."

Tomasso considered the idea. "But surely, if everyone has a voice, you'll just end up with a cacophony. And without guidance, who will know what is true and what is a lie?"

"That, Tomasso, may well become the question of the age."

*

It was a relief to be back in the Brenner Pass, this time heading south towards the Italian peninsula.

Tomasso was glad he'd hired a mountain guide for the return trip, as a heavy fog engulfed them shortly after leaving Innsbruck, and while other travellers were forced to delay their journey, Operation Danube pressed on. They arrived safely at Castle Reifenstein in the middle of the afternoon, and after a solid meal and a good night's sleep, prepared to strike out for Bolzano, where they would once again enjoy some Italian cuisine under a Mediterranean sun.

While Lieutenant Dante took care of the final preparations, Tomasso went to call Cristina, but she wasn't in her room. He looked in the chapel, then checked the library, and finally tracked her down on the rampart walkway, gazing up at the snowy mountain tops towering over them.

"Are you going to miss the Alps?" Tomasso asked as he walked over to join her.

"They're certainly more impressive than the Apennines. But I'll be glad to be home."

"Me too."

Neither of them could shake off the sense of disappointment at the failure of their mission. They were used to returning to Rome in triumph, but in the German states they had encountered opposition of a different magnitude.

"Remember how confident we felt the last time we were here?" Cristina said. "We had no idea what we were riding into."

"At least we made it back alive. Given what happened, that must count as success."

"I don't think Pope Leo will see it that way. And anyway," Cristina turned to face Tomasso. "You did promise you'd keep me safe. And you are a man who always keeps his word, so being alive is the least I could expect."

Tomasso laughed. "On this occasion, I think it was you who saved me."

"I got myself kidnapped and thrown into the same dungeon."

"But you didn't abandon me, Cristina. Many would have sacrificed me for the good of the mission. You kept looking."

Cristina knew how much this meant to him. "I saw the documents. In your satchel."

Tomasso was momentarily puzzled.

"When you were abducted, I searched your room for clues," Cristina explained. "I saw the letter I wrote to you, and the instructions for looking after Alnaaji. You kept them."

Tomasso's cheeks reddened.

"I didn't realise … if I'd know they meant that much…" Cristina hesitated. "Are those really the only things I've written to you? In all these years?"

"You did once write me a monograph about how quickly dead bodies decompose," Tomasso recalled. "But that was in Latin, so I'm not sure it counts."

She studied his face, and the gentle eyes that regarded her with such tenderness. "You know, I've always seen you, Tomasso. Even though you think I haven't."

"Really?"

"Of course."

"If I'd known that, I would have asked you to marry me fifteen years ago. But I think you'd have turned me down."

"Not because of you. Because of me. I was too obsessed with … with everything."

"And what about now?"

"The obsessions?"

Tomasso shook his head and took her hands in his. "Will you marry me now, Cristina?"

"How can I accept when we both know what will happen?"

"You mustn't think like that."

"There is no cure. I have searched the medical textbooks —"

"No-one knows what will happen in the future. And we must live despite the uncertainty. That is what life is — living for the moment."

"How could anyone want me like this? When there is no future?"

"I want you, Cristina. I always have. And if you want me, then we should concentrate on that and just forget about everything we cannot control."

Cristina gently touched Tomasso's face. "It's because I love you that I cannot inflict this on you."

"That doesn't make any sense."

"We have a wedding just so that you can bury me a year later? How is that fair on anyone?"

"We will all die at some point. But we can't let that stop us from living."

Cristina closed her eyes, struggling to untangle her conflicting emotions.

"Put your trust in me, Cristina. I beg you."

Finally, she opened her eyes. "I will redouble my search. I will talk to every doctor who will listen, and if I find a way to heal myself, then I will happily marry you."

Tomasso folded her in his arms and held her tightly. "You have just saved me again, Cristina. It's a good habit. I like it."

"My search may still fail," she whispered.

"The promise is all I need. That is enough."

26: CONSPIRACY

"Behold!" Isra turned a shiny brass valve on the garden wall, a faint gurgling sound came from some hidden pipes, and then the fountain in the middle of the courtyard sprayed into life.

"Bravo!" Cristina and Domenico applauded, watching with delight as water bubbled out of a bronze pinecone and splashed down into the red marble basin, sending soothing echoes around the Moorish garden of the house in Piazza Navona.

"I was determined to get it finished before you came home," Isra explained.

"Was the builder finally happy when he saw it working?" Cristina asked.

"Of course not. He still thinks we should have gone for a bench."

Domenico wandered among the citrus trees, listening to the effect from all corners of the garden. "It's transformed this space. Just the sound of water makes it seem so much cooler."

Isra turned to Cristina. "Do you really like it?"

"I love it! Thank you for persevering." She leaned forward and hugged Isra, who was taken aback by Cristina's open affection.

"Did you miss Rome?"

"More than you can imagine."

"What happens when there's no rain?" Domenico asked. "Does the fountain dry up?"

"It's a circulating loop of water, driven by the feed from the aqueduct. But the same water goes round and round," Cristina explained.

"I don't follow."

"Let me show you on the plans."

She started back toward the house, but Isra took her by the arm. "Not this afternoon. Today is about welcoming you back to Rome. The library is out of bounds until sunset."

Isra steered them towards a table under the shade of some orange trees, where she had laid out a supper of oysters, salads, pumpkin pie, gilded pastries and all manner of pickled vegetables.

"This looks amazing," Domenico said as he sat down and took a plate. "My sister should go away more often."

Cristina helped herself to a chunk of white bread, still warm from the oven. She took a bite and savoured it with closed eyes. "Now I know I'm home!"

As they tucked in and the wine flowed, the conversation remained upbeat; no-one asked about Cristina's research into a cure for the tumours, and they avoided talking about the rapidly deteriorating situation in the German states.

But as the light faded and dusk settled in the garden, the mood became more pensive. Isra started to clear the table, and Domenico used the moment to hand Cristina an envelope.

"This looks ominous." Cristina's fingers traced the pattern of the Vatican insignia which sealed the letter.

"What's happening in the German states is causing quite a panic."

Cristina opened the letter and read it. "Tomasso and I have been summoned to an audience with Pope Leo and Agostino Chigi." She looked questioningly at her brother. "But we've already put everything in the report."

"They want to hear it from your own mouths."

"If someone has to take the blame, it should be me. Tomasso did everything that was expected of him. And more. I'm the one who agreed to our captive's demands."

"Tomasso was in direct command of Operation Danube. He has to account for what happened."

Cristina read the summons again, but it was impossible to determine the mood of the Holy Father from the formal language.

"Cristina, there's something you need to know before you see the Pope."

Isra glared at Domenico. "Do you have to spoil the evening with politics?"

"Indulge me for a few minutes, then I'll stop. I promise."

"Do I have a choice?" Isra cleared some of the dishes and vanished into the kitchen.

"Events moved quickly while you were away," Domenico explained. "And I'm afraid there is one ally we can no longer rely on. Cardinal Riario has fallen from power."

Cristina gasped. "That's impossible."

"They uncovered a plot by Cardinal Petrucci to poison Pope Leo."

"Petrucci is a child," Cristina exclaimed. "This can't be right."

"He was twenty-six."

"Was?"

"He was strangled in his cell at Castel Sant'Angelo. The Pope took the opportunity to arrest not just the conspirators, but all those he perceived as a rival. Including Cardinal Riario."

"But Riario would never stoop so low. That's not how he does things."

"Under interrogation, Riario confessed to being aware of Petrucci's intentions to murder the Holy Father. He refused to join the plotters, but the fact he did nothing to prevent it was enough to cause his downfall. Cardinal Riario was only spared execution by surrendering his palace and wealth to the Holy Father."

Cristina gazed at the fountain burbling in the centre of the courtyard. It was hard to reconcile the gruesome details of the conspiracy with the serenity of this private space. Part of her never wanted to leave this garden again; the more difficult the outside world became, the stronger the attraction of seclusion and retreat.

"Pope Leo is living proof that the Medici never change their colours," Cristina said quietly.

"I'm afraid it might be even darker than that," Domenico replied. "Cardinal Petrucci was young, intelligent, and charismatic. They say the Holy Father couldn't bear to be in his presence. Which is why there may not have been an assassination plot at all."

"What are you saying? That Pope Leo framed Petrucci in order to dispose of his rivals?"

"That is what some of the inner circle are saying."

"So, an innocent man was strangled to death in order to satisfy the vanity of a Medici Pope?" Cristina shivered at the thought.

Isra emerged from the kitchen carrying a shawl, which she wrapped around Cristina's shoulders. "Maybe it's time to go inside."

Cristina struggled to comprehend the scale of what had unfolded while she had been away. Cardinal Riario had been a constant throughout her life. He was regarded as the man destined to become Pope and it seemed impossible that he had fallen. It felt as if a star had dropped from the firmament.

"If the Holy Father is prepared to frame and kill cardinals, how will he react to the turbulence in the Germans states?" Cristina looked searchingly at Domenico.

"Neither you nor Deputato Tomasso are threats to Pope Leo." He reassured her. "You were sent on a difficult mission. The fact that the German states are facing huge problems is not your fault."

"But losing half his gold is really going anger him."

"If the Holy Father needs to vent his rage, then he should direct his anger at Archbishop Albrecht."

"Maybe. But Albrecht is seven hundred miles away in Magdeburg. Tomasso and I are here."

Cristina stood up, walked to the brass valve on the wall and turned the fountain off. "Perhaps it's best I get an early night."

27: OVERREACH

Cristina and Tomasso stood before the Holy Father in the papal rooms. The report Tomasso had written was sitting on the huge gilt-covered desk, along with the contract they had brought back from the German states; both documents had been heavily annotated in the margins. Pope Leo was enthroned behind the desk, while the banker Agostino Chigi stood respectfully to one side.

Leo finally broke the silence. “It is impossible to overstate my disappointment at the failure of your mission.”

Chigi gave a heavy sigh, echoing the Holy Father’s disapproval.

“Was it really too much to ask that an elite military unit should be able to outwit a gang of German thugs?”

“I am sorry to have displeased Your Holiness,” Tomasso replied, “but power in the German states is moving in strange and unpredictable ways, and across all levels of society. It proved impossible to find allies we could trust. Given the circumstances —” he glanced at the contract — “we were fortunate to secure half the gold and return home alive.”

Pope Leo glared at him. “I can read! What is the point of regurgitating what you have already spewed onto paper?” He slid the report across the desk with contempt.

Mercifully, Chigi spoke up. “If it pleases Your Holiness, I do have a possible solution to this vexatious problem.”

“Speak.”

“This contract was signed under duress, which in the eyes of the law invalidates its integrity. It is voidable. So, we can mount a legal challenge which I believe we will win.”

It was clear from the sycophantic expression on Chigi's face that he was expecting praise. What he actually got was a look of unalloyed contempt. "You talk about mounting a challenge? About legal technicalities? In practice that means sending an army of Papal troops north to suppress the Germans by force. It will provoke a full-scale war! Which no doubt you would be happy to finance with more extortionate loans."

Chigi was unsure how to respond. War was generally good for bankers, but it needed all parties to be fully committed, or the risk of default became too great. "Forgive me, Holy Father."

The room plunged back into silence.

After a few more painful moments, Pope Leo plucked the contract from the desk. "There are many things I hate about this document, but at least it guarantees *some* revenue flow. It gives us a degree of certainty which war cannot."

Chigi glimpsed another opportunity to please. "Then if you are happy to honour the contract, Holy Father, might I suggest a different solution?"

"You might."

"If we are to lose half our revenue, why do we not simply double the number of Indulgences we sell?" Chigi studied Pope Leo's face and when there was no sign of disapproval, he pressed on. "We can recruit more pardoners with more zeal; we can organise twice the convoys and double the number of states we target. I believe that will bring us back to where we started."

A smile slowly appeared on the Holy Father's face. "I knew I kept you close for a reason, Chigi."

The banker looked pleased with himself … until Cristina spoke.

"Forgive me, Holy Father, but that was not the intention behind the contract."

The men stared at her in consternation.

"Intentions are irrelevant," Chigi snapped. "This is a plan which enables everyone to win. More Indulgences sold means for money for the Holy Father and more money for the bandit gangs, as well as their protectors. It is the perfect arrangement."

"Not everyone will win," Cristina insisted. "Ordinary Germans will pay the price. They will be the ones reaching into their pockets."

Chigi shrugged. "So twice the number of peasants will avoid the horrors of Purgatory. Another win."

"You think peasants can afford Indulgences? Most just about survive day to day."

"Then it's high time they started thinking about their souls," Pope Leo asserted. "This life is just a temporary state, unlike the Eternal hereafter. Peasants need to remember what is truly important."

Cristina glanced at the wealth on display in the papal rooms: beautiful frescoes and gold clocks, ornate tapestries hanging behind antique furniture. It was easy to be dismissive of material possessions when you had so many.

"If you squeeze the German people too hard, they will turn away from you, Holy Father. And do you know who really would approve of this plan?" Cristina pressed. "The monk, Martin Luther. Because it will drive ordinary people into his arms."

The Pope frowned. "Luther is a troublemaker and a heretic."

"Do not underestimate him."

"Do not tell me what to do!" The Holy Father slammed his fist onto the desk. "The Church has dealt with countless heretics in the past. We will dispose of this one as well."

"And yet, Luther may be different."

Tomasso nudged Cristina, trying to silence her, but it was no use.

"This man knows how to harness power," she explained. "The power of ordinary people. The power of language. The power of resentment."

"I am power!" the Pope thundered, rising to his feet to command the room. "I am God's power on Earth! Everyone else is merely a pretender."

In the silence that followed, Cristina listened to the ticking of the clocks mounted on opposite walls of the study; they were slightly out, and she wondered how long it would take for them to synchronise.

Pope Leo misread her silence as contrition and softened his tone. "I made a promise to you, Signora Falchoni. When you took on this mission, I gave you my word that the gold would be used to restart building work on St Peter's, not squandered by an architect who has no sense of duty. Focus on the basilica, pull Raphael into line, and leave the troublesome German people to me."

Domenico kicked open the doors to the *camera della passione* in Rome's most exclusive bordello and a squad of Apostolic Guards stormed inside.

Before him, in the candlelight, all Domenico could see was an incomprehensible tangle of limbs writhing on a huge bed.

"Is that him, sir? Over there?" A guard pointed to a divan couch on which a man with pale skin and long golden curls was sprawled; one of the hostesses was massaging oil onto his slim body using just her breasts.

"Hard to believe, but yes."

Domenico beckoned to his guards, who immediately surrounded the couch and hauled Raphael out from under his companion.

"Get off me!" he yelped. "How dare you?"

"Find your clothes and get dressed," Domenico ordered. "You're done."

Raphael glared at him. "You again!"

"I know. We must stop meeting like this."

"You have just signed the death warrant of your career!" Raphael sneered. "When I tell Pope Leo how you have humiliated me in front of my friends —"

"It was the Pope who sent me," Domenico interjected. "I'm here on his direct orders."

Raphael's face paled. "Oh."

"Yes. Oh."

By now, everyone was staring fearfully at the Apostolic Guards.

"Get dressed!" Domenico repeated. He kicked the nearest bundle of clothes across the floor towards Raphael. "You're going back to work."

They marched the artist through the streets of Rome as he tried to fasten the buttons on his velvet doublet.

"Can I at least go home to wash?" Raphael protested.

"No," Domenico replied.

"I cannot meet with the Holy Father like this!"

"Agreed."

"Then where are you taking me?"

Raphael didn't have to wait long to find out. The guards escorted him over the Ponte Sant'Angelo and up the hill towards the St Peter's construction site, where the old and new basilicas jostled shoulder to shoulder. They escorted him along what remained of the old nave and pulled aside the huge tarpaulin that separated it from the active building site, then Domenico bundled the artist into a standalone room that had just been erected next to the northeast pier.

Raphael saw Cristina standing by a large desk. "Ah. I might have guessed."

Cristina didn't take the bait. "A thank you would be nice." She gestured to the walls of the temporary office. All the papers and drawings relating to St Peter's had been brought from Raphael's apartments and filed on racks of shelves; maquettes modelling various stages of the construction had been arranged in a large cabinet, while the detailed architectural drawings were laid out across the desk. "Now there is no need for you to leave site at all. Everything you need is here."

Raphael was determined to be unimpressed. "Maybe if I was an embittered spinster whose only pleasure was denying pleasure to others, I would never have to leave. As it is, I have a life beyond St Peter's."

"Not anymore."

"The Holy Father understands that an artist needs to nourish his soul and —"

"Spare me!" Cristina snapped. "You have no idea what you're talking about! The world is changing. The Holy Father is under immense pressure, and the very last thing he needs is for a petulant, spoiled artist to become an additional headache. So, this is what will happen," Cristina continued with quiet resolve.

"You will put all other commissions on hold. You will focus exclusively on delivering the Holy Father's vision of the greatest basilica in Christendom. And you will ensure that the excesses of your lifestyle no longer encroach on the working day. You repeatedly tell the world you are a genius, now prove it."

Raphael wandered over to the maquette cabinet and picked up the largest model. As he studied it, he gave a strange shrug, almost as if he was casting off an unwanted skin. "The next task is to complete the drum on which the dome will ultimately rest." His finger traced a circle on the model. "At the same time, the carpenters will create the scaffolding to centre the dome, supporting the brick skin as it rises. But the space is so huge, the scaffold will need to be built in sections that can be assembled in mid-air." Raphael looked at Cristina. "Professional enough?"

"Impressive."

"Which is why I am the architect, and you are … to be honest, I don't really know what you are."

"I am the woman who is losing patience." Cristina turned and walked out of the office.

Within days, the building site was once again teaming with workmen. Gangs of masons laboured high up on the vaulting which linked the four piers, raising the drum, quadrant by quadrant. At the same time, master carpenters supervised the preparation of hundreds of beams which would form a wooden hemisphere, supporting the first brick skin of the dome as it went up. It was like creating an enormous puzzle in three dimensions.

But to lift the hemisphere to the correct height required a huge additional wooden scaffold rising from the floor, and it was this part of the structure that preoccupied the carpenter Giacopo.

Even though he had only just turned thirty, there was precious little Giacopo didn't know about wood. After completing his apprenticeship in Pisa, he had travelled around the Italian states, working on everything from palazzos to warehouses to municipal buildings. Like thousands of others, he had been lured to Rome by the thought of a job that might last ten years or more, which would mean his young family could finally enjoy some stability.

But when Giacopo gazed up at the vast hole that had to be enclosed by the dome, he wondered if it was physically possible. Had anyone ever bridged such vast spans, so high up in the air? The weight of timber pressing down on the feet of the scaffold could only be spread so far, since gaps had to be left for the movement of men and materials. And when he thought of the immense pressure on the diagonal braces…

Once the scaffold was buttressed in place, the basilica walls could take some of the weight, but to get up to that height, it would need to spend several weeks as a freestanding structure. It was this worry that kept drawing Giacopo back to the scaffolding plans, much to the annoyance of the carpentry foreman.

"Just cut to the templates I give you and leave the rest to me," he said impatiently.

"Yes, *capo*. But I wondered…"

"You don't get paid to wonder, Giacopo. You get paid to saw and hammer and keep your mouth shut."

"I know, *capo*. But I was thinking, given the weight, shouldn't we buttress the scaffold to the piers?"

"We're tying it to the piers."

"That will give stability, but it won't take any of the weight."

The foreman drew a breath and stared at Giacopo. "So, you think my drawings are wrong?"

"No, *capo*."

"You think you know better?"

"That's not what I'm saying."

"Do you know how many carpenters knock on my door every day asking for work?"

"I'm sorry, *capo*. Forget I mentioned it. Won't happen again."

"It had better not."

And that should have been the end of the matter…

Except no-one told the laws of physics that they too were supposed to doff their caps to the carpentry foreman.

28: TOUCH

"Dinner is on the table!"

Cristina was still soaking in the warm bath when she heard Isra's voice call up the stairs. Although the housekeeper sounded tetchy, Cristina knew that what she really meant was that dinner was still in the oven, but Isra always made the announcement a few minutes early to give Cristina time to finish what she was doing and get downstairs … which meant daydreaming in the bath could continue for a little longer.

So Cristina slipped under the surface until her head was immersed in the scented water. It was glorious … total immersion, and the world beyond simply vanished.

Slowly she counted to see how long she could hold her breath. At twenty-five seconds her exhale began, sending a trickle of bubbles from her nose, then at thirty-three she broke the surface and gulped in a new breath.

"It's going cold!" Isra called up the stairs.

This was significant. It meant that the plate of food was actually being put on the table. Now she really would have to get out of the bath.

Cristina gripped the sides of the tub ready to haul herself up … and paused. She looked at her hands. Something seemed different.

She released her grip and brought her right hand close to her face … turning it slowly in front of her eyes … examining its shape … gently pressing the areas around her wrist and thumb.

Had something changed?

Was she imagining it?

Or perhaps it was just the effect of the warm water…

*

Isra made a point of clattering the cutlery as she served up the food. She loved working for — and with — Cristina, but if there was one thing she could change, it would be this. The art of cooking was in the timing, culminating in piping-hot delicacies appearing on the table; to miss that moment was a culinary crime. And yet, the number of times Cristina arrived late to the table … Isra shook her head and started eating anyway.

Moments later, Cristina pushed open the door and entered the kitchen wearing a dressing robe. Immediately, Isra could tell that something was on her mind.

"Did you have a nice bath?"

Cristina nodded but said nothing. She picked up her fork, but instead of eating, she held it in mid-air.

"If you're not hungry, I can heat it up later? Give you a chance to dry your hair."

Cristina stretched her right hand across the table. "Look."

"Do you want me to bandage it?"

"No, just look."

Isra took her hand and gently ran her fingers over the skin. "Is the swelling going down?"

"I think it is. And it's not so painful. It feels easier to move my fingers."

Isra put her arms around Cristina and the two women clung to each other, neither daring to speak.

"It must be a miracle," Isra finally said.

Cristina shook her head. "That's absurd."

"No, it's not. It could be God's way of thanking you for saving St Peter's."

"That's not how God touches people's lives."

"You don't know that!"

"Miracles don't exist, Isra. Not in that way. They're metaphors, symbols."

"Then why do you have a book upstairs in your library cataloguing all the known miracles in Christianity?"

"Because it's part of Church history."

"You need to keep a more open mind." Isra started walking towards the kitchen door.

"Where are you going?"

"To get the book."

"What about our 'no studying during meals' rule?"

Isra was already climbing the stairs. "For this I'll make an exception!"

A few minutes later, the large leather-bound *Libro dei Miracoli* was open on the table in front of Cristina, who turned the pages as the two women ate supper.

"There are so many to choose from," Cristina said, glancing at the numerous categories. "Appearance of stigmata … bodies of saints which never decompose … casting out of demons … prophecies…"

"Focus on medical miracles," Isra suggested. "There must be a section on miraculous cures."

Cristina flipped through the pages. "Here we go … Saint Cuthbert of Lindisfarne. His reputation for healing led to people giving him the name the Wonder Worker of England." She turned a few more pages. "A deaf-mute was healed by placing wax tablets on the tomb of Saint Otmar. And another mute was healed after blood gushed from his mouth."

"Miracle after miracle."

Cristina shrugged. "Could have been a cyst which burst."

"Please, try not to be so cynical," Isra replied.

"Ah … these are closer to home." Cristina smoothed the page and started reading. "Saint Francesca of Rome, just last century. She turned her family's palazzo in Trastevere into a hospital, where she performed over a hundred miraculous cures."

Cristina's eyes spotted another entry. "Saint Peregrine. Aged sixty, he developed an infection in his right leg that became so bad, the doctors realised it was actually a tumour. They decided to amputate. He spent the night before the operation praying under a fresco of the Crucifixion. At some point, Peregrine fell into a deep sleep and had a vision of Jesus descending from the Cross and touching his leg. The next day, the doctors arrived to amputate but found the tumour had vanished." Cristina looked up from the book.

"Where is this fresco?" Isra asked.

But Cristina didn't respond. She was recalling the moment when Martin Luther clasped her hands just before she passed out … when he was telling her that God had been working through her in ways she had not understood. Cristina remembered the intensity of Luther's grip … the warmth of his skin … the chalk dust left imprinted on her wrists.

"What is it? What are you thinking?"

"Luther's touch." Cristina looked at her own hands.

"You think something happened in that moment? Something miraculous?"

"Luther is tapping into a power that is far greater than himself. That's why people follow him. He talked about it. But…"

Isra reached across the table and clasped Cristina's hands. "I have prayed for you every day since that terrible moment at the hospital. Every day and every night. Finally, God has answered me."

Cristina shook her head. "Prayers are not for God; they are for us. To focus our minds."

“Not true.” Isra refused to back down on this one. “The power of prayer is real. If prayers don’t work, why have people been offering them to the heavens for thousands of years?”

“But I didn’t actually do anything to beat the disease.”

“Maybe that’s the point, Cristina. For once, instead of fighting, you surrendered.”

29: REMISSION

Once again, Cristina found herself sitting by the large bay window in her surgeon's office … only this time she dared to hope.

"When did you notice the change?" the surgeon asked, taking her right hand to examine it.

"Yesterday, as I was getting out of the bath."

He gently waggled each of Cristina's finger joints. "So, it changed suddenly? Or has the swelling been going down for a while?"

"The first time I noticed it was yesterday. But it's difficult to say. I've been travelling, things have been complicated."

The surgeon picked up a magnifying glass and studied the contours of Cristina's wrists. He spent a long time searching for signs of irregularity. "Any tenderness in the wrists?"

"Not anymore."

"What about here?" He squeezed the tips of her fingers.

"No. It feels normal."

"Uh-huh."

"That's good, isn't it?"

The surgeon handed her a wooden skittle. "Squeeze this as hard as you can. As if you want to crush it."

Cristina did as she was told, squeezing the toy until her knuckles went white.

"Any pain?"

"No. None."

"You can let go now." The surgeon took the wooden toy from Cristina, then sat back in his chair and scrutinised her.

"Is it true, Doctor? Have the tumours really gone?"

"Perhaps. It certainly seems that way. Your hands, your wrists … they feel normal. You report no symptoms, no pain."

"So, I'm cured?"

"If this is not remission, I don't know what is."

Cristina's heart was racing with excitement, but her mind was hungry for an explanation. "How could this have happened? I don't understand."

"I'm not sure that matters. Just accept the gift."

"But if I don't know why it was given, how can I make sure it will not be taken away again?"

The surgeon got up and started searching through the volumes of books on his shelves. "There are cases of spontaneous remission. They're rare but documented." He selected a volume and started leafing through the pages. "The earliest one we know of is late thirteenth century, a bone sarcoma in a patient called Peregrine Laziosi spontaneously disappeared."

"Saint Peregrine," Cristina interrupted. "I know about him. It was a miracle cure."

"Not according to the medical profession." The surgeon sat down and referred to the textbook. "The case records indicate that he had a sarcoma in the leg, then he suffered a severe infection. When that cleared, it took the cancer with it. Which is interesting."

"But it is still a cure without an explanation. That surely makes it miraculous."

The surgeon considered this carefully. "No-one knows why diseases suddenly occur, but they do. So why can they not disappear of their own accord as well? Perhaps the lesson of Peregrine's life is not that the heavens worked a miracle, but that a faithful man put his life unconditionally in the hands of God; he was prepared to accept whatever happened."

Cristina frowned. "If we all just accepted what happened, there would be no doctors in the world, would there?"

The surgeon laughed. The fact that his patient was so eager to answer back proved that she really was on the mend. "Go and get on with the rest of your life, Signora Falchoni. And don't look back unless you need me."

Cristina went straight to the bustling market at Campo de' Fiori, where she bought the best bottle of wine she could find — a Ricasoli red, freshly shipped from Siena. By the time she arrived at the barracks of the Apostolic Guards in the Vatican, the wine had been joined by a wheel of Grana Padano and a basket of figs.

The moment Domenico saw his sister's arms filled with delicacies, he knew it was good news. They hugged and laughed; they drank and ate, and Domenico loved the impromptu lunch even more because he couldn't remember ever seeing Cristina so relaxed. He had always known her as a woman who was in the middle of some project or other, yet now she seemed to be enjoying every moment simply for itself.

Only when they had nearly finished the Ricasoli did Cristina give any indication that her happiness was more nuanced than it first appeared.

"What if the surgeon has made a mistake, Domenico? What if the tumours have moved deeper into my body?"

"He examined you; he told you they were gone. What more do you want?"

"Half the time, physicians are just guessing. I've read the same books as them, I know how much they don't know."

Domenico laughed. "I bet they love having you as a patient, Signora Self-Diagnosa."

"They have more experience of course, but —"

"Cristina, put this behind you and move on with your life. It's the only way."

Cristina nodded, yet the worry remained. "You remember the lake in Frascati when we were children? It would freeze over in winter and we would creep across it, knowing that at any moment it might crack. That's what it feels like now. At any moment the cancer might return. If not next year, then the year after. I can't stop thinking about it, but how can I live like this? Always waiting for the awful news to break?"

"Soldiers spend their whole lives close to death." Domenico drained the last few drops of wine from the bottle into their glasses. "It's so unpredictable. Some soldiers survive battle after battle; others die the first time they're in combat. But it's not about age or being the strongest or having the best weapons. The men who survive have an unwavering determination to survive which makes them the quickest to adapt as conditions change. They just refuse to be outwitted by the fight." He looked at her. "And that is what you've done your entire life, Cristina. Without even thinking about it, it's who you are. This illness has shocked you, but you need to absorb it."

"What does that mean?"

Domenico tried to find a better way of expressing himself. "I've only seen a whale once in my life. We were on a troop carrier sailing from Valletta to Syracuse. When we were in the middle of the Malta Channel, an enormous sperm whale broke to the surface. It looked at our ship for a few moments, took in some air, then dived back into the depths. But as it curled through the water, I saw all the scars and wounds on its skin, gathered over the years, like trophies of war. Scars can be a reminder of fear and death, but they can also be a celebration of victory. Scars are how survivors map their lives, Cristina. That is how you need to think of what's happened to you."

"It's a good image," she whispered. Domenico's words had touched the anxiety in her heart. "Do you think Luther's touch really cured me? Is that possible?"

Domenico slugged back the last of his wine. "I am not the person to ask about theology."

"But if he did … maybe he was right about everything else. The purpose of St Peter's, the future of the Church."

"That really is beyond my pay grade. Maybe you should ask Pope Leo?"

"I don't think that's such a good idea." Cristina wrapped the Grana Padano in a cloth. "You can share this with the rest of the men."

"But who better to advise on miracles than the Holy Father himself?"

"We didn't exactly part on the best of terms. What about Cardinal Riario?"

Domenico looked bemused. "You want to consult a man living in disgrace?"

"At least there'll be a space in his diary."

"I wouldn't be so sure," Domenico said as picked up what was left of the wheel of cheese and headed towards the mess room. "Riario is leaving Rome any day now. I hear his palace has already been stripped."

"Then I'd better be quick."

30: FALLEN

Normally, Cardinal Riario's lavish palazzo in the Parione district of Rome would be bustling with activity, as priests, scholars and Vatican bureaucrats came to discuss Church matters with the great man. Almost overnight, the nature of the activity changed. Carpenters filled the corridors, crating up Riario's huge art collection; auditors logged the contents and dimensions of each room, compiling lists of which objects counted as fixtures and which as fittings; and removals men arrived to take away the mountains of boxes, trunks and furniture. Now, Cristina and Cardinal Riario sat in the only space that remained unscathed — the magnificent orangery, filled with beautiful plants.

"Of all the things I'll miss about Rome, this garden will hurt the most," Riario lamented. "Present company excepted," he added with a smile.

Cristina gazed at the abundance of plants which surrounded them. There were Salix trees trimmed into perfect spheres and plum trees laden with ripening fruit; there were lilies and roses, honeysuckles and jasmine, as well as a fan of poppies planted to create a vivid rainbow of colours.

"This one," the cardinal picked up a pot containing a young but sturdy tree, about three feet tall, "is an English oak, sent to me by Cardinal Wolsey himself."

"Take everything with you," Cristina suggested.

"To Naples?"

"You cannot rely on whoever Pope Leo gives this palazzo to. They might let everything die, which would be criminal."

"It would. But taking them with me is impractical. The climate in Naples is different, the heat more intense. Many wouldn't survive. Plants are like old men; they don't like to be moved."

Cristina could sense the sadness in the cardinal. "You don't have to leave Rome at all, Your Eminence. The Pope hasn't banished you; he's just taken this mansion. But there are others."

Riario shook his head. "The Holy Father has also confiscated much of my wealth. How could I live in a small townhouse and walk past this magnificent palazzo every day? It would be a constant reminder of how far I had fallen."

"But it could also remind you of how much you have achieved in your life."

The cardinal chuckled. "I appreciate your sanguine philosophy, but it is not for me. Better to change my life altogether. It's the only way to accept what has happened and move forward."

Cristina had seen many once-great men leave Rome in disgrace, but she had never expected to see Riario go that way. "I will miss you more than I can say, Your Eminence. You have been such an important part of the Vatican for so long … you deserved the Papal Throne."

"*Grazie.*" Riario seemed humbled by her words. "But maybe that is precisely why they don't allow women to become priests; because they would put a different class of leader in power."

"Well, I certainly wouldn't have voted for Leo had I been in Conclave."

"Never forget that beneath his charming surface lies a ruthless Medici prince. Cross that monster at your peril."

"Which is why I've come to see you, rather than the Holy Father, about a theological issue."

Cardinal Riario's face lit up. "Please. Anything to take my mind off the aggravation of moving."

Cristina told the cardinal about her encounters with Martin Luther in Magdeburg, about his strange prophecy regarding the true purpose of St Peter's, the moment he clasped her hands, and the mysterious disappearance of the tumours.

"And you believe that was a miraculous touch?" Riario asked.

"There is something about the intensity of Luther's vision … something that feels more potent than just human rhetoric. I can believe that divine forces are working through him."

"The most important thing is that you are cured. That news alone has brought joy to my final days in Rome. I believe you have many years of life ahead of you, Cristina, and I know that you will live them to the full."

"But could it be a miracle, Your Eminence? Is this how they manifest? Not with grand theatrics, but in quiet, unseen moments?"

Riario pondered the question. "Did you feel a great warmth when Luther gripped your hands?"

"I felt pain. And fear. But that was as much from his words as his touch. What he told me was overwhelming."

"The Vatican regards Luther as a heretic. But the central belief of his teaching cannot be ignored. *Sola fide*. By faith alone. A sinner is redeemed and forgiven only by God's grace through trust in Jesus Christ. It is a powerful idea. We are not saved by doing good works, but the doing of good works is a sign that salvation has been granted. It puts redemption into the hands of every man, woman and child. They don't need to win the favour of their priest, and they don't need to fear his wrath. If they put their absolute faith in Christ, that is enough. Which is what makes this such a revolutionary idea. It dismantles the hierarchy of the Church and looks back to those early centuries when Christianity was the religion of the poor, not the powerful."

"You think it is a purer form of Christianity?"

"I think it will grow stronger and stronger, until it is unstoppable."

"Even if they excommunicate Luther?"

"Especially if they excommunicate Luther."

Cristina nodded. "He becomes a martyr to the movement."

"Quite. I'm afraid the push to reform is now unstoppable." The cardinal gave a stoic smile. "Another good reason for me to be out of Rome and a long way from the Vatican."

But Cristina was troubled by the prediction. "You talk as if there will be a schism."

"I'm afraid I think that is highly likely. And it will not be peaceful."

"Surely the Church is big enough to embrace a wide range of different beliefs?"

"But not the belief that you can have a direct relationship with God. That undermines the very foundations of the Church. Christ said to Saint Peter, *I give you the keys to the Kingdom of Heaven.* That authority has been passed down to every Pope for over a thousand years. If Luther refuses to back down, Pope Leo will have no choice but to expel him. Then Luther will lead a new church that splinters from Rome."

Cristina took in the enormity of what was coming. "If everyone who follows Luther leaves the Church … where will it end?"

"Thankfully, Signora Falchoni, that is no longer my problem. The Pope has cast me aside just in time."

The orangery doors creaked open and one of Cardinal Riario's personal assistants entered. "The palazzo is now cleared, Your Eminence."

"Finally. Bravo!"

"Would you care to accompany me as I walk through the rooms for one last inspection, Your Eminence?"

"Why not?" Riario eased himself to his feet. "The exercise will do me good."

Gently he made the sign of the cross on Cristina's forehead. "Now go to St Peter's and light a candle for both of us."

Cristina did exactly that.

But rather than find a quiet side chapel in Old St Peter's to pray, she chose an altar close to the great tarpaulin which screened off the building site, so that her prayers would be wrapped in the cacophony of construction noise.

She lit a candle, crossed herself, then knelt down and composed her thoughts. She didn't want to give thanks for her cure; instead, she asked for forgiveness for any part she had unwittingly played in fracturing the unity of the Church. She prayed earnestly and honestly but didn't offer up any excuses to explain her actions. God had known what was in her heart when she embarked on this mission over twenty years ago. Deep down, Cristina could not believe that God was truly angry with her. He had cured the cancer in her hands; that was not the behaviour of an angry and vengeful God. Perhaps it meant that Christianity was bigger than the Church of Rome, greater and more varied than anyone had imagined; perhaps it meant that true faith went far beyond the Vatican hierarchy and the learned writings of the medieval theologians.

The thought was as terrifying as it was exciting, so Cristina made the decision to keep all these ideas locked in her own mind for the time being; if the German states really did split from Rome, there would be a fierce backlash, and she didn't want to get caught up in that.

"Is it true?" a voice whispered close by.

Cristina opened her eyes and turned to see Tomasso standing behind her, his face illuminated by the bank of flickering votive candles.

"Domenico told me, but I need to hear it from you."

"Yes … I think it's true."

A look of relief washed over Tomasso's face. His lips parted into a smile, his eyes filled with tears, and his arms reached out to Cristina. "Then marry me, Cristina."

She hugged him close, burying her face in his shoulder. "Yes, I will. Now I will marry you."

They held each other tightly, refusing to let go of the joy of the moment.

"You have made me the happiest man in Rome," Tomasso said.

"Just Rome?" Cristina quipped. "Not the Italian peninsula?"

"The whole world!" Tomasso tightened his hug, and Cristina surrendered to it. So much around her was in flux, but the embrace of this man felt secure. Upon the rock of Tomasso, she could build the rest of her life.

A terrible cracking sound split the air. Cristina spun round and stared at the tarpaulin. "What was that?"

There was a pause, then another dreadful splitting sound echoed around the basilica, followed by giant timber beams thundering into each other … and the screams of men.

It was the sound of disaster.

Cristina and Tomasso ran to the tarpaulin, pushed through one of the openings and saw the world collapsing.

The lower beams of the enormous scaffold that was being erected in the centre of the basilica had split and buckled under the weight of timber above. Now the entire structure was collapsing like a child's game of pick-up-sticks.

"Look out!" Tomasso grabbed Cristina and pulled her back, just as a timber beam crashed to the ground inches from where they stood.

Carpenters working high in the scaffold scrambled for safety but were overtaken by the speed of the collapse and plunged into the abyss beneath them.

The floor shook under Cristina's feet as tons of timber battered into the flagstones, sending workmen scampering into the safety of the transepts.

But there was no safety for the falling men. Their screams cut through the clattering roar of the wood, but they were beyond help.

Some survived the drop, only to be crushed by the weight of falling beams.

Others were swallowed up by the tangled mountain of debris that was forming in the centre of the basilica.

Cristina saw one man lying on the floor, unable to crawl to safety because his legs were pinned under an enormous beam.

The horror seemed to unfold in slow motion. On and on it went, as if nothing could satisfy the basilica's appetite for destruction.

Until finally, the last beam smashed onto the enormous pile of fallen timbers.

A terrible silence filled the space.

Cristina stared at the twisted carnage and the clouds of dust rising in shafts of sunlight which punched down through the void. She could hear the screams of men who were still visible, but impaled or crushed by the timber … and then there were the haunting wails of men who were now buried deep in the collapse.

Workmen emerged from the transepts and started clawing at the debris with their hands, desperately trying to reach the victims.

Tomasso started clambering up the tangled mountain of scaffolding that led deep into the chaos.

"No! It's not stable!" Cristina called out.

But Tomasso didn't hesitate. "All the more reason to get them out."

Cristina started scrambling around, looking for survivors, but as she approached the northeast pier, she saw that Raphael's office had been destroyed by falling wooden beams. The breath caught in her lungs — when she ordered the artist to relocate, had she unwittingly sent him to his death?

"Raphael!" She picked her way through the wreckage until she was standing by what was left of the office.

"Raphael!"

The roof of the temporary structure had caved in and taken two of the walls with it. Cristina peered through a gap where the door used to be — architectural drawings were scattered everywhere and most of the maquettes were smashed, but there was no sign of the artist.

"Raphael! Are you in there?"

Silence. Maybe for once, his dissolute lifestyle had saved him, and Cristina found herself praying that he was safe in the arms of some high-class courtesan.

"Help…" a man's voice groaned.

Cristina spun round and saw one of the carpenters trapped under the rubble. His chest had been crushed by a huge beam, his face had a ghastly pallor, and his body was trembling with shock. She knelt next to him and wiped the dust from his eyes, but already they were glazing over.

Gently she lay her hands on the man's head and reassured him that help was coming, that he would be all right. She kept talking to the carpenter until a few minutes later, his life slipped away.

31: GIACOPO

As news of the disaster flashed across Rome, builders everywhere downed tools and ran to St Peter's to help their fellow craftsmen. They were confronted by a scene of fear and confusion.

Drawing on his battlefield experience to try and impose order on the chaos, Deputato Tomasso had organised the Apostolic Guards into three units. He led the first team, which worked on top of the enormous pile of debris, hauling wooden beams out of the tangle whilst trying not to trigger a further collapse. The broken scaffold beams were passed to a second team who formed a human chain down the side of the debris mountain and ferried the material into the transepts. Whenever they discovered a trapped victim, Tomasso blew a whistle and all movement stopped until the man could be extracted from the tangle of wood. This was where the guards with knowledge of battlefield medicine took over — they carried the wounded on makeshift stretchers down to one of the side chapels which had been turned into a triage area. There, Lieutenant Dante examined each victim and made an immediate assessment. The walking wounded were bandaged, wrapped in blankets and given brandy to calm their nerves; the more seriously wounded were stretchered straight to the *Ospedale per Incurabili* for emergency surgery. The dead were taken down into the crypt which had been repurposed as a temporary morgue.

On the other side of the great tarpaulin, Cristina was trying to calm the crowd of anxious relatives who were desperate for news of their loved ones. She had deliberately set the cordon up out of sight of the collapsed scaffold to avoid creating unnecessary distress, but holding back the family members was challenging.

"Let us through!" the wives pleaded. "We can help! Let us help!"

"We're doing everything we can to get the men out safely," Cristina urged.

"We need to see for ourselves!"

"I understand, but it would only slow things down."

"Let us through! These are our men! Our husbands!"

"Please! Just a little more patience." Cristina hated refusing the women, but she knew that if they started clawing at the debris themselves, it could trigger a fresh collapse. So she tried to distract them by compiling lists of names and liaising with Lieutenant Dante in triage.

Whenever one of the walking wounded emerged through the tarpaulin, there would be a shriek of relief as a family member surged forward to embrace their man. But one family's relief meant prolonging the agonising wait for everyone else; secretly, each of the women was praying that death had taken someone else's husband and spared their own.

By the evening, all the living had been rescued, and everyone's attention turned to the dead. Eleven wives, some clinging to young children, were huddled by the great tarpaulin. They had endured hours of torment, witnessing the joy of other family reunions; now they had to face the dreadful truth.

Cristina led the sombre procession of widows down the narrow steps into the crypt, where the shrouded bodies had been laid out along one wall. Two priests from *Santa Maria della Pace* who had been administering the Last Rites during the afternoon, now concentrated on comforting the bereaved.

One by one, the women were led into the crypt to identify their husbands; one by one they slumped to the floor, weeping inconsolably. There was nothing Cristina could say to ease their pain. Men who had left for work that morning, cheerily kissing their wives on the way out, or perhaps grumbling about the contents of their packed lunch, had been cut down in an instant. Death had silenced arguments, annulled promises, made family plans redundant. The priests did their best, praying with the families, trying to offer words of solace, but the raw grief which filled the crypt could not be easily dispelled.

And then Cristina noticed an anomaly: there were eleven grieving families, but twelve bodies.

She walked over to the unclaimed corpse and lifted the shroud to look at the man's face. He couldn't have been more than thirty years old, but his chest had been torn apart, impaled by falling scaffolding.

"Are there no families left upstairs?"

Cristina looked up and saw Tomasso standing next to her. His face was covered in dust, and his hands blistered from the rescue work.

"The whole of Rome knows what's happened," she replied. "Maybe he wasn't married."

"I'll get the foreman." Tomasso went upstairs and returned a few minutes later with one of the carpentry foremen, who looked exhausted.

"Do you know who this man is?" Cristina asked as she drew back the shroud.

The foreman looked at the dead man, hesitated, then started to tremble. Tomasso stepped forward to stop him from collapsing.

"Do you know him?" she repeated.

The foreman nodded. "Giacopo," he whispered. "One of the carpenters."

"Does he have family in Rome?"

The foreman opened his mouth to answer but was suddenly overwhelmed with grief. His shoulders shook as great sobs erupted. Tomasso guided him away from the body and sat him down on the edge of an ancient marble tomb.

Cristina watched the foreman as he buried his face in his hands. Had something happened between the foreman and Giacopo? Was there bad blood between them?

Cristina walked across the crypt and stood in front of the foreman. "Tell me about Giacopo," she said.

The foreman wiped the tears from his dust-streaked face. "He was a good worker. Reliable. Never missed a day."

"Does he have family in Rome?"

"He came from the north, looking for work. Kept himself to himself. Never went drinking with the others."

"Where did he live?"

The foreman shook his head. "How can I know where every worker lives?"

"You don't keep lists? Records of who is working for you?"

"People come and go." The foreman shrugged. "We can't keep track."

"But Giacopo wasn't just anyone, was he? What happened between the two of you?"

"Nothing. Nothing happened. It was a terrible accident."

Cristina crouched down and locked eyes with him. "I don't think you're telling me everything."

The foreman looked away to avoid her gaze. "Trastevere," he said. "I think he lived somewhere in Trastevere."

Cristina walked back to Giacopo's corpse, pulled the shroud aside and rifled through his pockets until she found a key. There was no number or street name engraved on it, but it looked like a house key. She held it up to show Tomasso, who came over and inspected it.

"There's a tent in the yard where the men put their bags before they start their shifts. Maybe there's something there," he suggested.

Tomasso led her up the stairs and out to the yard. When they entered the tent, there were several dozen battered bags of various shapes and sizes hanging from pegs, waiting for their owners.

"Let's look for a name."

The two of them started checking each of the bags, and eventually Tomasso found an old leather satchel with the Giacopo's name inked on the strap.

"I'll take this home," Cristina said, slinging the bag across her shoulder.

Isra emptied the contents of the satchel out onto the kitchen table, and Cristina spread everything into a line.

"Is that it? Just food?" Isra said. "Nothing more interesting?"

"But the food *is* interesting," Cristina insisted. "Most of the construction workers take their lunch into work with them."

"What about the traders near St Peter's?"

"They're much more expensive because the shopkeepers know they have a captive market." She pointed to the food: half a loaf of bread, three slices of salami, and a chunk of cheese. "According to the foreman, Giacopo lived in the Trastevere district. So we can assume these came from local delicatessens. If we can identify them, we should be able to find the door that fits this." She put the key she'd found in Giacopo's pocket onto the table.

"Hmm." Isra pulled up a chair and studied the food.

"What do you think, Isra? Can you identify the shop by the food?"

Isra picked up the bread. It had a sturdy crust with a soft, white interior, and large holes for mopping up sauce. "*Pane casereccio.* Could be from any of a dozen bakeries across the city. Each baker has his own recipe, but they all taste similar." She tore off a piece and popped it in her mouth, concentrating on the flavour. "It's nice, but it doesn't help us."

"What about this?" Cristina broke off a piece of cheese with a fork and offered it to Isra, who sniffed it, then tasted it.

"*Pecorino Romano*, much more distinctive. Made from sheep's milk. It's supposed to be sharp and salty, but that only works if you're sprinkling it on a dish. For eating on its own, people like a softer, more buttery taste." Isra took another bite. "There's a delicatessen on Via di Santa Bonosa that does this sort of cheese. I've bought it from there a few times."

"Good. What about the salami?"

Isra cut off a piece of salami and tasted it. "The garlic overpowers the other ingredients. Could be from anywhere, but the shape..." She held up one of the remaining slices. "Most salamis are round but look at this one."

"Rectangular," said Cristina.

"Each delicatessen will use a different press to shape its salamis. If we can match this shape, we will have the shop."

"And both shops must be close to where Giacopo lived. It's unlikely he would walk past one that was close by."

"Let's go first thing in the morning," Isra suggested. "When the shops are open."

Cristina pulled her coat off the hook. "No. Let's go now."

Armed with the remnants of the food, Cristina and Isra walked across the Tiber to the cheese shop in Santa Bonosa. By the time they arrived, the streets were dark and deserted. From the cheese shop, they started walking systematically down all the adjacent streets until they came to a shuttered shop with a painted sign hanging from the wall: *Carne di Carminio.* Each letter 'i' was depicted as a slice of rectangular salami, just like the ones in Giacopo's bag.

"And now?" Isra asked.

"Now we listen."

The two women stood in silence, listening to the sounds of the neighbourhood: a dog barking … a woman scolding her husband … someone practising the mandolin … nightingales singing in the trees.

They moved to the next street along and listened again: the clatter of someone washing dishes … drunken singing coming from a local bar … the rustling of feral cats rummaging amongst the street rubbish.

And then they heard the faint sound of two young children, crying.

32: ORPHANS

Sister Marianna finished saying her prayers and pulled back the crisp white sheets on her bed. But rather than clamber in, she stood in her cell gazing at the welcoming pillow, relishing the anticipation of the good night's sleep that was about to come.

Marianna had been in charge of the *Ospedale di Santo Spirito in Saxia* for twenty-eight years, and found the work as rewarding now as when she first started. But it was exhausting.

Two hundred and fifty-seven orphaned children were in her care, and almost every day, a young mother in distress would use the renowned 'wheel of the foundlings' baby hatch. Even after all these years, Sister Marianna found it heartbreaking that a mother could be so desperate that she believed her child would have a better life without her. Thank God the orphanage was here and could accept the infants with unconditional love.

The orphanage worked diligently to provide the children with food and shelter, an education, and some vocational training. Where possible, Sister Marianna would also try to find caring families who wanted to adopt, but she was very protective of her children and very particular about the selection criteria.

This small, hard bed in Marianna's cell was the key to the whole operation, for it was here that she recharged herself each night and nurtured the strength to deal with the countless challenges the orphanage presented every day.

Finally, Sister Marianna lay down. She drew a deep breath and exhaled slowly, allowing all the stresses of the day to melt away. Any moment now, she would be embraced by a deep sleep…

There was a knocking on her cell door. "Sister Marianna!" a voice whispered. "Are you awake?"

Her heart sank. For a brief moment she thought about pretending to be asleep, then immediately felt guilty. She never ignored the call of duty.

"Enter."

The door opened and one of the novices peered round. "Forgive me, sister, but we've had a message asking for you."

"Can it not wait until the morning?"

"They said it was urgent."

"I see." One of the many things Marianna had learnt about children, was that when they needed help, they needed it immediately. So she swung her legs out of the bed, wrapped herself in a woollen shawl, and slipped on her sandals. "Where are we going?"

The novice held up a piece of paper with an address written on it. "Trastevere."

It was a relatively short walk from the orphanage, but at this hour the narrow, tumbledown streets were dark and menacing. Underfoot, large potholes filled with foul water dotted the streets; overhead, rickety rooftops loomed over the two nuns at precarious angles.

"Maybe you were right, sister," the novice whispered. "Maybe we should have left this until the morning."

"No," Marianna replied. "*You* were right. A child in need cannot be kept waiting."

When they finally arrived at the address on the paper, the novice shook her head. "There must be a mistake."

"Why do you say that?"

"Look at it, sister. It's a slum." She gazed up at the building which had been all but consumed by wild ivy. The window shutters had rotted away, and the roof consisted of sheets of canvas which flapped in the wind.

"I've seen worse," Marianna replied. "I once had to rescue a child who was living in a pigpen with the animals." She glanced up at the building. "At least this has four walls."

They picked their way up the staircase, trying to avoid the rotten steps, then approached a room at the far end of the landing that was illuminated by a flickering lantern. When Marianna pushed open the door, she saw two young children, about four years old, a brother and sister by the look of it. Their clothes were clean and their hair tidy, which was surprising given the surroundings, but they had obviously been crying for a long time as their eyes were red and their breathing still stuttered. The children were sitting on the laps of two women who looked as if they came from an affluent household.

"Thank you for coming out at this late hour," the older woman said. "My name is Cristina Falchoni, and this is my housekeeper and friend, Isra."

Sister Marianna nodded politely. "What happened here?"

"There was an accident at St Peter's," Cristina explained. "A scaffold collapsed."

The novice crossed herself. "We saw people running in the street. We realised something had happened."

"Tragically, there were some fatalities. But one body remained unclaimed by his family: a man by the name of Giacopo. Immediately we launched an investigation to discover his identity, and ended up here." Cristina stroked the hair of the boy sitting on her lap. "They were inconsolable when we found them. God knows how long they had been crying. It seems Giacopo was raising these two children on his own."

Marianna's brow creased. "You cannot just leave young children alone for a whole day," she said indignantly.

"Maybe his wife died. Maybe he had no choice. There was food and water, and they had some toys to play with."

"Why are you making excuses for him?"

"I'm not. But neither am I assuming. The point is, we found the children in time, thank God. They are safe and well. And now they need our help."

Marianna stepped closer and knelt down so that her face was level with the two children. As she entered their world, all the nun's sharp edges melted away, revealing the gentle soul that had devoted her life to the most vulnerable. She smiled at them. "Hello. I'm Marianna."

They looked back at her warily.

"We're going to make everything better," she said gently. "Get you some food and a nice warm bed to sleep in. Would you like that?"

The children just stared at her with their large eyes.

"What is your father's name?" she asked.

"Papa," the boy whispered.

"Yes, Papa," Marianna said with a smile. "What's Papa's name?"

The boy shook his head and retreated deeper into Cristina's arms. His sister saw what was happening and turned away, clinging to Isra.

Sister Marianna accepted the retreat with good grace. "Are there any aunts or grandparents?"

"Not that we know of. Giacopo came down from the north."

"Then we shall have to make enquiries. There are convents we work with in Florence, Milan, and Turin. I shall write to them tomorrow. In the meantime, we must take these two into the *Ospedale*."

Marianna reached out to take the boy from Cristina's lap, but he turned away. "No! Papa! I want Papa!"

Triggered by the argument, the boy's sister started to cry.

Isra kissed the girl and held her tight, while Cristina stroked the boy's hair and tried to explain. "It's all right. This lady is going to take care of you. She'll make everything better."

The boy screwed up his eyes and shook his head. "No! I want Papa!"

Cristina looked at Marianna, not sure what to do next. But the sister was always prepared.

"Look what I have here…" She took a small pastry from her bag. "A strawberry crostata. Doesn't that look nice?"

Both children looked at the tart, mesmerised by the golden pastry latticed over red fruit.

"We have lots of these in the *Ospedale*. And all different flavours. Apricot, apple, pear. You can have one each, with a glass of hot milk. What do you think?"

Tempting … but not tempting enough. The children turned away and buried their faces in Cristina and Isra.

Sister Marianna was momentarily stumped. She had no more bribes on her, but she didn't want to force the children.

Cristina saw the deadlock … she felt the little boy's heart beating against her own chest … and she closed her eyes to offer up a small prayer. Then she looked at Marianna. "Allow us to adopt the children."

Sister Marianna was taken aback. "You are racing ahead. We must try and trace their family."

"Of course. But if that doesn't work —"

"We'll cross that bridge when we come to it."

"But in the meantime, while you're searching, we can look after them, can't we? Look how calm they are with us."

Marianna looked at the children and couldn't disagree. Yet she knew nothing about these two women.

"The Holy Father himself will vouch for me," Cristina said, as if reading the nun's mind. "I have money, and time. I come from a good family."

"But do you have any experience of looking after children?"

"Of course."

"Children this young?"

Cristina hesitated. She thought about her baby brother Aldo and the pain of his death at such an early age, but over the years she had finally accepted that it was not her fault. Then she thought about Alnaaji, who she plucked from the most dreadful circumstances and guided back to life. She could do this; she could be a mother to these young orphans. "Whatever their age, sister, the most important thing is to give children love. Love and security."

Sister Marianna nodded. This was not just the right answer, it was the only answer she would have accepted.

33: VOWS

Spring finally arrived in Rome with a glorious wave of warmth.

The first three months of the year had seemed to last forever, with the city in the grip of northerly winds which brought relentless rain and freezing temperatures. Cristina had thrown herself into the task of helping Sister Marianna trace Giacopo's family, while secretly hoping that they wouldn't find anyone. At St Peter's, the fallout from the accident brought in sweeping changes, as Raphael insisted new foremen were appointed who put safety on an equal footing with quality. With the most dangerous part of the build still ahead of them — constructing the largest dome in the world — the chief architect didn't want to take any unnecessary risks.

In the second week in April, the winds changed direction. Warm, dry air blew up from Africa; it was hazy with dust from the scorched Sahara, yet it brought clarity on all fronts. A new tranche of funding for the basilica was put in place by Pope Leo, securing the build for the next decade. Two weeks later, just before Cristina's forty-sixth birthday, permission to adopt was finally granted by the *Ospedale*, and Cristina and Tomasso became the proud parents of Leo and Luna.

It was an unorthodox family, but it was a happy one, full of laughter and anarchic energy. To celebrate, Cristina and Tomasso set a date for their own wedding: the 4th of May 1518.

For the venue, they chose Santa Maria della Pace, the same church where Cristina had witnessed the devastating fireball twenty years earlier; it was her way of replacing painful memories with ones that celebrated life.

Cardinal Riario made a special journey up from Naples to conduct the service even though it was not a lavish society wedding. Tomasso invited some of the Apostolic Guards, and Cristina invited a few friends from Sapienza University, but there were no more than thirty people in all.

As Domenico walked his sister up the aisle, he saw Leo and Luna sitting on the front pew next to Isra, clutching beautiful bouquets and beaming joyous smiles. Then he looked at Cristina, whose gaze was fixed on Tomasso waiting at the front of the church. Domenico had never imagined that his sister would find happiness like this, and he felt an enormous sense of pride that she had always lived her life on her own terms, without compromise, and still come out on top.

The reception was held in the garden of the house on Piazza Navona, where Isra had laid on an enormous banquet for all the guests. The garden itself had undergone a transformation over the winter months. Gone was the spiritual retreat — this was now a garden for young children. Ropes had been slung from the top branches of the tallest tree to create a swing; one of the flowerbeds had been removed and replaced with a wooden climbing frame; the walkway by the eastern wall which had originally been designed for quiet meditation was now home to a skittle alley, where Isra and Luna were taking on Tomasso and Leo in a match of boys versus girls.

Amidst all the laughter and chatter of the wedding reception, Cardinal Riario made a point of searching out Cristina. He kissed her on both cheeks. "It fills me with joy to see you like this."

"Thank you for coming all this way to marry us, Your Eminence."

"I wouldn't have missed it for the world."

"I know we're not exactly a conventional family, but it works for us."

"When has being conventional ever interested you, Cristina? All that matters is that you have found happiness." He clasped her hands. "And happiness is the greatest healing force in the world."

She knew exactly what he was talking about. "It's still good. There is no sign of the illness returning."

"And you go to the surgeon regularly?"

"Once every three months, without fail. He conducts a thorough examination."

"Then you are cured."

Cristina gave a cautious smile. "I hope so. Of course, it could return at any time, but that is something I cannot control, so I must accept the uncertainty. And in any case, it focuses my mind on enjoying every day for what it is. Guiding Leo and Luna through childhood, passing everything on to the next generation."

Riario nodded. "As Jesus tell us, 'It is more blessed to give than to receive.'"

Suddenly they were interrupted by a bundle of four-year-old energy flinging her arms around Cristina's leg. "The girls won! The girls won! We beat Papa!"

"Of course you did!" Cristina laughed.

Running towards them was Leo demanding a rematch. "We let them win! Next time we'll play properly."

Cristina offered congratulations and condolences as appropriate and directed the children to help Isra ferry a tray of freshly baked cakes from the kitchen into the garden.

As Leo and Luna ran off, Cardinal Riario studied Cristina. "I must confess, I am surprised by how well you have taken to motherhood. Delighted … but surprised."

Cristina smiled but said nothing, because in truth it wasn't so simple, and she wasn't sure that the cardinal would really understand. From the very outset, she had started carrying a small notebook with her at all times, and as she played or walked with the children, as they talked and joked together and explored the city, she made hundreds of small observations. Then at night, when the household was asleep, she went to her library and wrote up all her thoughts, sketching out an evolving theory of how the human mind develops.

Because although Cristina loved her family more than anything, she still loved her library. It was her safe place, where she felt nourished; that she could now share it with her children only made the library more special.

Everything developed quickly over the months that followed.

Leo and Luna flourished, and it seemed as if Isra was constantly at the market, replacing shoes and clothes that had become too small overnight.

Across the city, the silhouette of St Peter's grew ever larger on the horizon, and in her library, Cristina made steady progress recounting her own involvement in the creation of the greatest church in Christendom. By Christmas, her *Basilica Diaries* were complete. To celebrate, Cristina bought a sturdy wooden trunk from the Campo de' Fiori market and locked the large pile of manuscripts inside. Who knew if they would ever see the light of day?

Dissent in the German states was also growing, and spreading at an alarming rate. Rebellion against the Church had spilled over into Switzerland and France, led by a new breed of firebrand preachers. The cracks that had opened up with Rome were now unbridgeable, and bloody conflict seemed inevitable; the only question was when, not if. The Vatican was horrified by these schisms, and there was a time when Cristina would have shared their fears, but she found it impossible to shake Luther's vision of Christianity from her mind. Violent revolution may be coming, but if they could survive that, perhaps they would discover a world where different traditions of Christianity could co-exist in peace.

When Cristina looked at Leo and Luna, and felt the generosity and love in their hearts, her fears for the future subsided. Somehow, the younger generation would save them.

In the summer of 1519, rapid progress on the construction of St Peter's enabled Michelangelo's *Pietà* to be moved into the basilica's sacristy, where it was always intended to rest. Cristina wanted to be one of the first people to see it in this new location.

The moment she walked onto the construction site, Cristina felt reassured. The new St Peter's had continued to devour the old one, and the great tarpaulin had moved almost three hundred feet further east; soon the nave would reach its full length. The circular drum at the heart of the basilica was reaching ever higher, and the design work on the great dome was now well underway. The whole project had a critical momentum which felt unstoppable, and it was now beyond doubt that St Peter's would be finished; perhaps it would even happen in this century.

Cristina saw that Raphael was deep in discussion with his foremen, so rather than interrupt, she just waved and walked through to the sacristy, where she positioned herself in front of the *Pietà*. She waited quietly, hoping that the emotion captured in the white Carrara marble would reach out to her … and in a few minutes, Cristina found herself moved to tears by the great work of art.

But these tears were different.

The last time she had stood in front of Michelangelo's creation, all she could see was grief and death — the lifeless body of Christ being held by his heartbroken mother. Yet now, Cristina gazed at the same statue and saw love — the intense love of Mary for her son that was so strong, even death could not break it. She imagined what it would be like to hold her own children like this, and how that would test every fibre of her being. And yet Michelangelo had by some miracle channelled Divine Grace through his chisels and into the marble of the *Pietà*. Through this sculpture, the world could now see how even the most unbearable pain could be endured.

"There she is!" Tomasso's voice echoed in the sacristy. "I thought as much."

Cristina turned and saw Leo and Luna running towards her, arms outstretched for a hug. She picked them both up and twirled them round.

"What are you doing?" Leo asked.

"I came to look at this statue." Cristina put the children down on either side of her. "It's beautiful, isn't it?"

But Luna was gazing at her mother. "Why are you crying?"

"Because even though the statue is made from marble, you can feel the love between a mother and her son."

Leo was puzzled. "He looks dead."

"He is dead."

"So … they can't play together?"

"No."

"That's why they're sad," Luna explained.

"Partly," Cristina replied. "But although she's sad, she still feels all the love she had for her son when he was alive. And that will never fade."

Leo and Luna frowned. "That doesn't make any sense."

Cristina knelt down so that her face was level with the children. "It took me a long time to understand. But one day, when you have children of your own, you will also understand."

Luna and Leo said nothing, but they trusted their mother and when they gazed at the marble statue which towered over them, they sensed that they were in the presence of something magical.

Then Tomasso knelt down, kissed Cristina's hair, and folded his family in his arms.

A NOTE TO THE READER

What an epic journey! The *Basilica Diaries* series so far spans twenty-two years and four popes, as St Peter's Basilica moved from being just an idea to a vision in stone created by some of the finest architects of the Renaissance.

Researching this series of books has been fascinating, but what really surprised me is how many themes resonated with life in the twenty-first century. This is particularly true of *Tyranny of Indulgence*, as the Protestant Reformation of the sixteenth century was accompanied by a revolution in power and allegiance that was every bit as disorientating as the shifts in power we are seeing in the modern world. The final act of the story pivots around the fateful moment when Luther nailed his 95 Theses to the door of the Castle Church in Wittenberg. This is a vital beat, but in order to make the repercussions in Rome work, I had to move the death of Cardinal Petrucci by a few weeks — apologies to any timeline purists!

Tyranny of Indulgence was written in the year Pope Francis died and Pope Leo XIV was elected. For the best part of a month the world's media descended on Rome, with all eyes focussed on the Sistine Chapel's chimney, awaiting the appointment of a new pope. It was a vivid reminder of how important the basilica has been for five hundred years, and how public fascination with St Peter's shows no sign of waning.

This coincided with a Vatican Jubilee Year, which is a special period of forgiveness and reconciliation that happens every twenty-five years. Not only does this double the number of tourists in Rome, it is also accompanied by city-wide renovation to many historic buildings.

Given that Rome is a city built on layer upon layer of history, it is not inconceivable that during the restoration work, a builder might pull up some floorboards to reveal an old cellar which has been sealed up and forgotten … and in the corner of that cellar is a damp niche … where they might stumble across a wooden trunk filled with leather portfolios … which contain bundles of paper on which are written the original *Basilica Diaries* … finally found after five hundred years!

Thank you for joining me on this, the fifth adventure in *The Basilica Diaries* series; I hope you enjoyed reading it as much as I enjoyed writing it. I am always fascinated to hear feedback from readers, either through **Amazon** or **Goodreads**, or if you'd rather give me feedback through social media, here are the links:

Website: www.RichardKurti.com
Instagram: RichardKurtiWriter
X (Twitter): @Richard_Kurti

If you get the chance to post a rating or review, or drop me a line with your thoughts, that would be great! In the meantime, I'm rolling up my sleeves to start plotting my next book!

SAPERE
BOOKS

www.ingramcontent.com/pod-product-compliance
Lightning Source LLC
LaVergne TN
LVHW091121080826
845145LV00008B/2008
* 9 7 8 0 8 5 4 9 5 8 4 4 3 *